Rudyard Kipling (1865–1936) was born in India, and lived there till he was sent to England for schooling at the age of five. He returned after completing his studies and worked as a journalist and writer for several years. Kipling made his name as a novelist, poet and short-story writer, through iconic works like *The Jungle Book, Kim,* 'If' and *Plain Tales from the Hills.* He is the youngest person to win the Nobel Prize for Literature, which he did in 1907. He was also awarded the Gold Medal of the Royal Society of Literature in 1926.

I0649537

LESSONS
FOR
MRS HAUKSBEE

Tales of Passion, Intrigue and Scandal

Rudyard Kipling

SPEAKING
TIGER

SPEAKING TIGER PUBLISHING PVT. LTD
4381/4, Ansari Road, Daryaganj
New Delhi 110002

ISBN: 978-93-86702-22-7
eISBN: 978-93-86702-21-0

Typeset in Arno Pro by SÜRYA, New Delhi
Printed at Sanat Printers, Kundli

CONTENTS

GEORGIE PORGIE

Georgie Porgie, pudding and pie,
Kissed the girls and made them cry.
When the girls came out to play
Georgie Porgie ran away.

—Nursery rhyme

If you will admit that a man has no right to enter his drawing-room early in the morning, when the housemaid is setting things right and clearing away the dust, you will concede that civilized people who eat out of china and own card-cases have no right to apply their standard of right and wrong to an unsettled land. When the place is made fit for their reception by those men who are told off to the work, they can come up, bringing in their trunks their own society and the Decalogue, and all the other apparatus. Where the Queen's Law does not carry, it is irrational to expect an observance of other and weaker rules. The men who run ahead of the cars of Decency and Propriety, and make the jungle ways straight, cannot be judged in the same manner as the stay-at-home folk of the ranks of the regular Tchin.

Not many months ago the Queen's Law stopped a few miles north of Thayetmyo on the Irrawaddy. There was no very strong Public Opinion up to that limit, but it existed to keep men in order. When the Government said that the Queen's Law must carry up to Bhamo and the Chinese border the order was given, and some men whose desire was to be ever a little in advance of the rush of Respectability flocked forward with the troops. These were the men who could never pass examinations, and would have been too pronounced in their ideas for the administration of bureau-worked Provinces. The Supreme Government stepped in as soon as might be, with codes and regulations, and all but reduced New Burma to the dead Indian level; but there was a short time during which strong men were necessary and ploughed a field for themselves.

Among the fore-runners of Civilization was Georgie Porgie, reckoned by all who knew him a strong man. He held an appointment in Lower Burma when the order came to break the Frontier, and his friends called him Georgie Porgie because of the singularly Burmese-like manner in which he sang a song whose first line is something like the words 'Georgie Porgie.' Most men who have been in Burma will know the song. It means: 'Puff, puff, puff, puff, great steamboat!' Georgie sang it to his banjo, and his friends shouted with delight, so that you could hear them far away in the teak-forest.

When he went to Upper Burma he had no special regard for God or Man, but he knew how to make himself respected, and to carry out the mixed Military–Civil duties that fell to most men's share in those months. He did his office work and entertained, now and again, the detachments of fever-shaken soldiers who blundered through his part of the world in search of a flying party of dacoits. Sometimes he turned out and dressed down dacoits on his own account; for the country was still smouldering and would blaze when least expected. He enjoyed these charivaris, but the dacoits were not so amused. All the officials who came in contact with him departed with the idea that Georgie Porgie was a valuable person, well able to take care of himself, and, on that belief, he was left to his own devices.

At the end of a few months he wearied of his solitude, and cast about for company and refinement. The Queen's Law had hardly begun to be felt in the country, and Public Opinion, which is more powerful than the Queen's Law, had yet to come. Also, there was a custom in the country which allowed a white man to take to himself a wife of the Daughters of Heth upon due payment. The marriage was not quite so binding as is the nikkah ceremony among Mahomedans, but the wife was very pleasant.

When all our troops are back from Burma there will be a proverb in their mouths, 'As thrifty as a Burmese wife,' and pretty English ladies will wonder what in the world it means.

The headman of the village next to Georgie Porgie's post had a fair daughter who had seen Georgie Porgie and loved him from afar. When news went abroad that the Englishman with the heavy hand who lived in the stockade was looking for a housekeeper, the headman came in and explained that, for five hundred rupees down, he would entrust his daughter to Georgie Porgie's keeping, to be maintained in all honour, respect and comfort, with pretty dresses, according to the custom of the country. This thing was done, and Georgie Porgie never repented it.

He found his rough-and-tumble house put straight and made comfortable, his hitherto unchecked expenses cut down by one half, and himself petted and made much of by his new acquisition, who sat at the head of his table and sang songs to him and ordered his Madrassee servants about, and was in every way as sweet and merry and honest and winning a little woman as the most exacting of bachelors could have desired. No race, men say who know, produces such good wives and heads of households as the Burmese. When the next detachment tramped by on the war-path, the Subaltern in Command found at Georgie Porgie's table a hostess to be deferential to, a woman to be treated in every way as one occupying an assured position. When he gathered his men together next dawn and replunged into the jungle he thought regretfully of the nice little dinner and the pretty face, and envied Georgie Porgie from the bottom of his heart. Yet HE was engaged to a girl at Home, and that is how some men are constructed.

The Burmese girl's name was not a pretty one; but as she was promptly christened Georgina by Georgie Porgie, the blemish did not matter. Georgie Porgie thought well of the petting and the general comfort, and vowed that he had never spent five hundred rupees to a better end.

After three months of domestic life, a great idea struck him. Matrimony—English matrimony—could not be such a bad thing after all. If he were so thoroughly comfortable at the Back of Beyond with this Burmese girl who smoked cheroots, how much more comfortable would he be with a sweet English maiden who would not smoke cheroots, and would play upon a piano instead of a banjo? Also he had a desire to return to his kind, to hear a Band once more, and to feel how it felt to wear a dress-suit again. Decidedly, Matrimony would be a very good thing. He thought the matter out at length of evenings, while Georgina sang to him, or asked him why he was so silent, and whether she had done anything to offend him. As he thought, he smoked, and as he smoked he looked at Georgina, and in his fancy turned her into a fair, thrifty, amusing, merry, little English girl, with hair coming low down on her forehead, and perhaps a cigarette between her lips. Certainly not a big, thick, Burma cheroot, of the brand that Georgina smoked. He would wed a girl with Georgina's eyes and most of her ways. But not all. She could be improved upon. Then he blew thick smoke-wreaths through his nostrils and stretched himself. He would taste marriage. Georgina had helped him to save money, and there were six months' leave due to him.

'See here, little woman,' he said, 'we must put by more money for these next three months. I want it.' That was a direct slur on Georgina's housekeeping; for she prided herself on her thrift; but since her God wanted money she would do her best.

'You want money?' she said with a little laugh. 'I HAVE money. Look!' She ran to her own room and fetched out a small bag of rupees. 'Of all that you give me, I keep back some. See! One hundred and seven rupees. Can you want more money than that? Take it. It is my pleasure if you use it.' She spread out the money on the table and pushed it towards him, with her quick, little, pale yellow fingers.

Georgie Porgie never referred to economy in the household again.

Three months later, after the dispatch and receipt of several mysterious letters which Georgina could not understand, and hated for that reason, Georgie Porgie said that he was going away and she must return to her father's house and stay there.

Georgina wept. She would go with her God from the world's end to the world's end. Why should she leave him? She loved him.

'I am only going to Rangoon,' said Georgie Porgie. 'I shall be back in a month, but it is safer to stay with your father. I will leave you two hundred rupees.'

'If you go for a month, what need of two hundred? Fifty are more than enough. There is some evil here. Do not go, or at least let me go with you.'

Georgie Porgie does not like to remember that scene even at this date. In the end he got rid of Georgina by a compromise of seventy-five rupees. She would not take more. Then he went by steamer and rail to Rangoon.

The mysterious letters had granted him six months' leave. The actual flight and an idea that he might have been treacherous hurt severely at the time, but as soon as the big steamer was well out into the blue, things were easier, and Georgina's face, and the queer little stockaded house, and the memory of the rushes of shouting dacoits by night, the cry and struggle of the first man that he had ever killed with his own hand, and a hundred other more intimate things, faded and faded out of Georgie Porgie's heart, and the vision of approaching England took its place. The steamer was full of men on leave, all rampantly jovial souls who had shaken off the dust and sweat of Upper Burma and were as merry as schoolboys. They helped Georgie Porgie to forget.

Then came England with its luxuries and decencies and comforts, and Georgie Porgie walked in a pleasant dream upon pavements of which he had nearly forgotten the ring, wondering why men in their senses ever left Town. He accepted his keen delight in his furlough as the reward of his services. Providence further arranged for him another and greater delight—all the pleasures of a quiet English wooing, quite different from the brazen businesses of the East, when half the community stand back and bet on the result, and the other half wonder what Mrs So-and-So will say to it.

It was a pleasant girl and a perfect summer, and a big country-house near Petworth where there are acres and acres of purple heather and high-grassed water-meadows to wander through. Georgie Porgie felt that he had at last found something worth the living for, and naturally assumed that the next thing to do was to ask the girl to share his life in India. She, in her ignorance, was willing to go. On this occasion there was no bartering with a village headman. There was a fine middle-class wedding in the country, with a stout Papa and a weeping Mamma, and a best-man in purple and fine linen, and six snub-nosed girls from the Sunday School to throw roses on the path between the tombstones up to the Church door. The local paper described the affair at great length, even down to giving the hymns in full. But that was because the Direction were starving for want of material.

Then came a honeymoon at Arundel, and the Mamma wept copiously before she allowed her one daughter to sail away to India under the care of Georgie Porgie the Bridegroom. Beyond any question, Georgie Porgie was immensely fond of his wife, and she was devoted to him as the best and greatest man in the world. When he reported himself at Bombay he felt justified in demanding a good station for his wife's sake; and, because he had made a little mark in Burma and was beginning to be appreciated, they allowed him nearly all that he asked for, and posted him to a station which we will call Sutrain. It stood upon several hills, and was styled officially a 'Sanitarium,' for the good reason that the drainage was utterly neglected. Here Georgie Porgie settled down, and found married life come very naturally to him. He did not rave, as do many bridegrooms, over the strangeness and delight of seeing his own true love sitting down to breakfast with him every morning 'as though it were the most natural thing in the world.'

'He had been there before,' as the Americans say, and, checking the merits of his own present Grace by those of Georgina, he was more and more inclined to think that he had done well.

But there was no peace or comfort across the Bay of Bengal, under the teak-trees where Georgina lived with her father, waiting for Georgie Porgie to return. The headman was old, and remembered the war of '51. He had been to Rangoon, and knew something of the ways of the Kullahs. Sitting in front of his door in the evenings, he taught Georgina a dry philosophy which did not console her in the least.

The trouble was that she loved Georgie Porgie just as much as the French girl in the English History books loved the priest whose head was broken by the king's bullies. One day she disappeared from the village with all the rupees that Georgie Porgie had given her, and a very small smattering of English— also gained from Georgie Porgie.

The headman was angry at first, but lit a fresh cheroot and said something uncomplimentary about the sex in general. Georgina had started on a search for Georgie Porgie, who might be in Rangoon, or across the Black Water, or dead, for aught that she knew. Chance favoured her. An old Sikh policeman told her that Georgie Porgie had crossed the Black Water. She took a steerage-passage from Rangoon and went to Calcutta, keeping the secret of her search to herself.

In India every trace of her was lost for six weeks, and no one knows what trouble of heart she must have undergone.

She reappeared, four hundred miles north of Calcutta, steadily heading northwards, very worn and haggard, but very fixed in her determination to find Georgie Porgie. She could not understand the language of the people; but India is infinitely charitable, and the women-folk along the Grand Trunk gave her food. Something made her believe that Georgie Porgie was to be found at the end of that pitiless road. She may have seen a sepoy who knew him in Burma, but of this no one can be certain. At last, she found a regiment on the line of march, and met there one of the many subalterns whom Georgie Porgie had invited to dinner in the far-off, old days of the dacoit-hunting. There was a certain amount of amusement among the tents when Georgina threw herself at the man's feet and began to cry. There was no amusement when her story was told; but a collection was made, and that was more to the point. One of the subalterns knew of Georgie Porgie's whereabouts, but not of his marriage. So he told Georgina and she went her way joyfully to the north, in a railway carriage where there was rest for tired feet and shade for a dusty little head. The marches from the train through the hills into Sutrain were trying, but Georgina had money, and families journeying in bullock-carts gave her help. It was an almost miraculous journey, and Georgina felt sure that the good spirits of Burma were looking after her. The hill-road to Sutrain is a chilly stretch, and Georgina caught a bad cold. Still there was Georgie Porgie at the end of all the trouble to take her up in his arms and pet her, as he used to do in the old days when the stockade was shut for the night and he had approved of the evening meal. Georgina went forward as fast as she could; and her good spirits did her one last favour.

An Englishman stopped her, in the twilight, just at the turn of the road into Sutrain, saying, 'Good Heavens! What are you doing here?'

He was Gillis, the man who had been Georgie Porgie's assistant in Upper Burma, and who occupied the next post to Georgie Porgie's in the jungle. Georgie Porgie had applied to have him to work with at Sutrain because he liked him.

'I have come,' said Georgina simply. 'It was such a long way, and I have been months in coming. Where is his house?'

Gillis gasped. He had seen enough of Georgina in the old times to know that explanations would be useless. You cannot explain things to the Oriental. You must show.

'I'll take you there,' said Gillis, and he led Georgina off the road, up the cliff, by a little pathway, to the back of a house set on a platform cut into the hillside.

The lamps were just lit, but the curtains were not drawn. 'Now look,' said Gillis, stopping in front of the drawing-room window. Georgina looked and saw Georgie Porgie and the Bride.

She put her hand up to her hair, which had come out of its top-knot and was straggling about her face. She tried to set her ragged dress in order, but the dress was past pulling straight, and she coughed a queer little cough, for she really had taken a very bad cold. Gillis looked, too, but while Georgina only looked at the Bride once, turning her eyes always on Georgie Porgie, Gillis looked at the Bride all the time.

'What are you going to do?' said Gillis, who held Georgina by the wrist, in case of any unexpected rush into the lamplight. 'Will you go in and tell that English woman that you lived with her husband?'

'No,' said Georgina faintly. 'Let me go. I am going away. I swear that I am going away.' She twisted herself free and ran off into the dark.

'Poor little beast!' said Gillis, dropping on to the main road. 'I'd ha' given her something to get back to Burma with. What a narrow shave though! And that angel would never have forgiven it.'

This seems to prove that the devotion of Gillis was not entirely due to his affection for Georgie Porgie.

The Bride and the Bridegroom came out into the verandah after dinner, in order that the smoke of Georgie Porgie's cheroots might not hang in the new drawing-room curtains.

'What is that noise down there?' said the Bride. Both listened.

'Oh,' said Georgie Porgie, 'I suppose some brute of a hillman has been beating his wife.'

'Beating—his—wife! How ghastly!' said the Bride. 'Fancy YOUR beating ME!' She slipped an arm round her husband's waist, and, leaning her head against his shoulder, looked out across the cloud-filled valley in deep content and security.

But it was Georgina crying, all by herself, down the hillside, among the stones of the water-course where the washermen wash the clothes.

WITHOUT BENEFIT OF CLERGY

Before my Spring I garnered Autumn's gain,
Out of her time my field was white with grain,
The year gave up her secrets to my woe.
Forced and deflowered each sick season lay,
In mystery of increase and decay;
I saw the sunset ere men saw the day,
Who am too wise in that I should not know.

—'Bitter Waters'

I

'But if it be a girl?'

'Lord of my life, it cannot be. I have prayed for so many nights, and sent gifts to Sheikh Badl's shrine so often, that I know God will give us a son—a man-child that shall grow into a man. Think of this and be glad. My mother shall be his mother till I can take him again, and the mullah of the Pattan mosque shall cast his nativity—God send he be born in an auspicious hour!—and then, and then thou wilt never weary of me, thy slave.'

'Since when hast thou been a slave, my queen?'

'Since the beginning—till this mercy came to me. How could I be sure of thy love when I knew that I had been bought with silver?'

'Nay, that was the dowry. I paid it to thy mother.'

'And she has buried it, and sits upon it all day long like a hen. What talk is yours of dower! I was bought as though I had been a Lucknow dancing-girl instead of a child.'

'Art thou sorry for the sale?'

'I have sorrowed; but today I am glad. Thou wilt never cease to love me now?—answer, my king.'

'Never—never. No.'

'Not even though the mem-log—the white women of thy own blood—love thee? And remember, I have watched them driving in the evening; they are very fair.'

'I have seen fire-balloons by the hundred. I have seen the moon, and—then I saw no more fire-balloons.'

Ameera clapped her hands and laughed. 'Very good talk,' she said. Then with an assumption of great stateliness, 'It is enough. Thou hast my permission to depart—if thou wilt.'

The man did not move. He was sitting on a low red-lacquered couch in a room furnished only with a blue and white floor-cloth, some rugs, and a very complete collection of native cushions. At his feet sat a woman of sixteen, and she was all but all the world in his eyes. By every rule and law she should have been otherwise, for he was an Englishman, and she a Mussulman's daughter bought two years before from her mother, who, being left without money, would have sold Ameera shrieking to the Prince of Darkness if the price had been sufficient.

It was a contract entered into with a light heart; but even before the girl had reached her bloom, she came to fill the greater portion of John Holden's life. For her, and the withered hag her mother, he had taken a little house overlooking the great red-walled city, and found—when the marigolds had sprung up by the well in the courtyard and Ameera had established herself according to her own ideas of comfort, and her mother had ceased grumbling at the inadequacy of the cooking-places, the distance from the daily market, and at matters of house-keeping in general—that the house was to him his home. Any one could enter his bachelor's bungalow by day or night, and the life that he led there was an unlovely one. In the house in the city his feet only could pass beyond the outer courtyard to the women's rooms; and when the big wooden gate was bolted behind him he was king in his own territory, with Ameera for queen. And there was going to be added to this kingdom a third person whose arrival Holden felt inclined to resent. It interfered with his perfect happiness. It disarranged the orderly peace of the house that was his own. But Ameera was wild with delight at the thought of it, and her mother not less so. The love of a man, and particularly a white man, was at the best an inconstant affair, but it might, both women argued, be held fast by a baby's hands. 'And then,' Ameera would always say, 'then he will never care for the white mem-log. I hate them all—I hate them all.'

'He will go back to his own people in time,' said the mother; 'but by the blessing of God that time is yet afar off.'

Holden sat silent on the couch thinking of the future, and his thoughts were not pleasant. The drawbacks of a double life are manifold. The Government, with singular care, had ordered him out of the station for a fortnight on special duty in the place of a man who was watching by the bedside of a sick wife. The verbal notification of the transfer had been edged by a cheerful remark that Holden ought to think himself lucky in being a bachelor and a free man. He came to break the news to Ameera.

'It is not good,' she said slowly, 'but it is not all bad. There is my mother here, and no harm will come to me—unless indeed I die of pure joy. Go thou to thy work and think no troublesome thoughts. When the days are done I believe … nay, I am sure. And—and then I shall lay HIM in thy arms, and thou wilt love me for ever. The train goes to-night, at midnight is it not? Go now, and do not let thy heart be heavy by cause of me. But thou wilt not delay in returning? Thou wilt not stay on the road to talk to the bold white mem-log? Come back to me swiftly, my life.'

As he left the courtyard to reach his horse that was tethered to the gate-post, Holden spoke to the white-haired old watchman who guarded the house, and bade him under certain contingencies to despatch the filled-up telegraph-form that Holden gave him. It was all that could be done, and with the sensations of a man who has attended his own funeral, Holden went away by the night mail to his exile. Every hour of the day he dreaded the arrival of the telegram, and every hour of the night he pictured to himself the death of Ameera. In consequence his work for the State was not of first-rate quality, nor was his temper towards his colleagues of the most amiable. The fortnight ended without a sign from his home, and, torn to pieces by his anxieties, Holden returned to be swallowed up for two precious hours by a dinner at the club, wherein he heard, as a man hears in a swoon, voices telling him how execrably he had performed the other man's duties, and how he had endeared himself to all his associates. Then he fled on horseback through the night with his heart in his mouth. There was no answer at first to his blows on the gate, and he had just wheeled his horse round to kick it in when Pir Khan appeared with a lantern and held his stirrup.

'Has aught occurred?' said Holden.

'The news does not come from my mouth, Protector of the Poor, but—' He held out his shaking hand as befitted the bearer of good news who is entitled to a reward.

Holden hurried through the courtyard. A light burned in the upper room. His horse neighed in the gateway, and he heard a shrill little wail that sent all the blood into the apple of his throat. It was a new voice, but it did not prove that Ameera was alive.

'Who is there?' he called up the narrow brick staircase.

There was a cry of delight from Ameera, and then the voice

of the mother, tremulous with old age and pride—'We be two women and—the—man—thy—son.'

On the threshold of the room Holden stepped on a naked dagger, that was laid there to avert ill-luck, and it broke at the hilt under his impatient heel.

'God is great!' cooed Ameera in the half-light. 'Thou hast taken his misfortunes on thy head.'

'Ay, but how is it with thee, life of my life? Old woman, how is it with her?'

'She has forgotten her sufferings for joy that the child is born. There is no harm; but speak softly,' said the mother.

'It only needed thy presence to make me all well,' said Ameera. 'My king, thou hast been very long away. What gifts hast thou for me? Ah, ah! It is I that bring gifts this time. Look, my life, look. Was there ever such a babe? Nay, I am too weak even to clear my arm from him.'

'Rest then, and do not talk. I am here, bachari (little woman).'

'Well said, for there is a bond and a heel-rope (peecharee) between us now that nothing can break. Look—canst thou see in this light? He is without spot or blemish. Never was such a man-child. Ya illah! he shall be a pundit—no, a trooper of the Queen. And, my life, dost thou love me as well as ever, though I am faint and sick and worn? Answer truly.'

'Yea. I love as I have loved, with all my soul. Lie still, pearl, and rest.'

'Then do not go. Sit by my side here—so. Mother, the lord of this house needs a cushion. Bring it.' There was an almost imperceptible movement on the part of the new life that lay in the hollow of Ameera's arm. 'Aho!' she said, her voice breaking with love. 'The babe is a champion from his birth. He is kicking me in the side with mighty kicks. Was there ever such a babe!

And he is ours to us—thine and mine. Put thy hand on his head, but carefully, for he is very young, and men are unskilled in such matters.'

Very cautiously Holden touched with the tips of his fingers the downy head.

'He is of the faith,' said Ameera; 'for lying here in the night-watches I whispered the call to prayer and the profession of faith into his ears. And it is most marvellous that he was born upon a Friday, as I was born. Be careful of him, my life; but he can almost grip with his hands.'

Holden found one helpless little hand that closed feebly on his finger. And the clutch ran through his body till it settled about his heart. Till then his sole thought had been for Ameera. He began to realize that there was some one else in the world, but he could not feel that it was a veritable son with a soul. He sat down to think, and Ameera dozed lightly.

'Get hence, sahib,' said her mother under her breath. 'It is not good that she should find you here on waking. She must be still.'

'I go,' said Holden submissively. 'Here be rupees. See that my baba gets fat and finds all that he needs.'

The chink of the silver roused Ameera. 'I am his mother, and no hireling,' she said weakly. 'Shall I look to him more or less for the sake of money? Mother, give it back. I have born my lord a son.'

The deep sleep of weakness came upon her almost before the sentence was completed. Holden went down to the courtyard very softly with his heart at ease. Pir Khan, the old watchman, was chuckling with delight. 'This house is now complete,' he said, and without further comment thrust into Holden's hands the hilt of a sabre worn many years ago when he, Pir Khan, served the Queen in the police. The bleat of a tethered goat came from the well-kerb.

'There be two,' said Pir Khan, 'two goats of the best. I bought them, and they cost much money; and since there is no birth-party assembled their flesh will be all mine. Strike craftily, sahib! 'Tis an ill-balanced sabre at the best. Wait till they raise their heads from cropping the marigolds.'

'And why?' said Holden, bewildered.

'For the birth-sacrifice. What else? Otherwise the child being unguarded from fate may die. The Protector of the Poor knows the fitting words to be said.'

Holden had learned them once with little thought that he would ever speak them in earnest. The touch of the cold sabre-hilt in his palm turned suddenly to the clinging grip of the child upstairs—the child that was his own son—and a dread of loss filled him.

'Strike!' said Pir Khan. 'Never life came into the world but life was paid for it. See, the goats have raised their heads. Now! With a drawing cut!'

Hardly knowing what he did, Holden cut twice as he muttered the Mahomedan prayer that runs: 'Almighty! In place of this my son I offer life for life, blood for blood, head for head, bone for bone, hair for hair, skin for skin.' The waiting horse snorted and bounded in his pickets at the smell of the raw blood that spirted over Holden's riding-boots.

'Well smitten!' said Pir Khan, wiping the sabre. 'A swordsman was lost in thee. Go with a light heart, Heaven-born. I am thy servant, and the servant of thy son. May the Presence live a thousand years and … the flesh of the goats is all mine?' Pir Khan drew back richer by a month's pay. Holden swung himself into the saddle and rode off through the low-hanging wood-smoke of the evening. He was full of riotous exultation, alternating with a vast vague tenderness directed towards no particular object, that made him choke as he bent over the neck of his uneasy horse. 'I never felt like this in my life,' he thought. 'I'll go to the club and pull myself together.'

A game of pool was beginning, and the room was full of men. Holden entered, eager to get to the light and the company of his fellows, singing at the top of his voice—

In Baltimore a-walking, a lady I did meet!

'Did you?' said the club-secretary from his corner. 'Did she happen to tell you that your boots were wringing wet? Great goodness, man, it's blood!'

'Bosh!' said Holden, picking his cue from the rack. 'May I cut in? It's dew. I've been riding through high crops. My faith! my boots are in a mess though!

And if it be a girl she shall wear a wedding-ring,
And if it be a boy he shall fight for his king,
With his dirk, and his cap, and his little jacket blue,
He shall walk the quarter-deck—

'Yellow on blue—green next player,' said the marker monotonously.

'*He shall walk the quarter-deck*—Am I green, marker? *He shall walk the quarter-deck*—eh! that's a bad shot—*As his daddy used to do!*'

'I don't see that you have anything to crow about,' said a zealous junior civilian acidly. 'The Government is not exactly pleased with your work when you relieved Sanders.'

'Does that mean a wigging from headquarters?' said Holden with an abstracted smile. 'I think I can stand it.'

The talk beat up round the ever-fresh subject of each man's work, and steadied Holden till it was time to go to his dark empty bungalow, where his butler received him as one who knew all his affairs. Holden remained awake for the greater part of the night, and his dreams were pleasant ones.

II

'How old is he now?'

'Ya illah! What a man's question! He is all but six weeks old; and on this night I go up to the housetop with thee, my life, to count the stars. For that is auspicious. And he was born on a Friday under the sign of the Sun, and it has been told to me that he will outlive us both and get wealth. Can we wish for aught better, beloved?'

'There is nothing better. Let us go up to the roof, and thou shalt count the stars—but a few only, for the sky is heavy with cloud.'

'The winter rains are late, and maybe they come out of season. Come, before all the stars are hid. I have put on my richest jewels.'

'Thou hast forgotten the best of all.'

'Ai! Ours. He comes also. He has never yet seen the skies.'

Ameera climbed the narrow staircase that led to the flat roof. The child, placid and unwinking, lay in the hollow of her right arm, gorgeous in silver-fringed muslin with a small skull-cap on his head. Ameera wore all that she valued most. The diamond nose-stud that takes the place of the Western patch in drawing attention to the curve of the nostril, the gold ornament in the centre of the forehead studded with tallow-drop emeralds and flawed rubies, the heavy circlet of beaten gold that was fastened round her neck by the softness of the pure metal, and the chinking curb-patterned silver anklets hanging low over the rosy ankle-bone. She was dressed in jade-green muslin as befitted a daughter of the Faith, and from shoulder to elbow and elbow to wrist ran bracelets of silver tied with floss silk, frail glass bangles slipped over the wrist in proof of the slenderness of the hand, and certain heavy gold bracelets that had no part in her country's ornaments but, since they were Holden's gift and fastened with a cunning European snap, delighted her immensely.

They sat down by the low white parapet of the roof, overlooking the city and its lights.

'They are happy down there,' said Ameera. 'But I do not think that they are as happy as we. Nor do I think the white mem-log are as happy. And thou?'

'I know they are not.'

'How dost thou know?'

'They give their children over to the nurses.'

'I have never seen that,' said Ameera with a sigh, 'nor do I wish to see. Ahi!'—she dropped her head on Holden's shoulder—'I have counted forty stars, and I am tired. Look at the child, love of my life, he is counting too.'

The baby was staring with round eyes at the dark of the heavens. Ameera placed him in Holden's arms, and he lay there without a cry.

'What shall we call him among ourselves?' she said. 'Look! Art thou ever tired of looking? He carries thy very eyes. But the mouth—'

'Is thine, most dear. Who should know better than I?'

''Tis such a feeble mouth. Oh, so small! And yet it holds my heart between its lips. Give him to me now. He has been too long away.'

'Nay, let him lie; he has not yet begun to cry.'

'When he cries thou wilt give him back—eh? What a man of mankind thou art! If he cried he were only the dearer to me. But, my life, what little name shall we give him?'

The small body lay close to Holden's heart. It was utterly helpless and very soft. He scarcely dared to breathe for fear of crushing it. The caged green parrot that is regarded as a sort of guardian-spirit in most native households moved on its perch and fluttered a drowsy wing.

'There is the answer,' said Holden. 'Mian Mittu has spoken. He shall be the parrot. When he is ready he will talk mightily and run about. Mian Mittu is the parrot in thy—in the Mussulman tongue, is it not?'

'Why put me so far off?' said Ameera fretfully. 'Let it be like unto some English name—but not wholly. For he is mine.'

'Then call him Tota, for that is likest English.'

'Ay, Tota, and that is still the parrot. Forgive me, my lord, for a minute ago, but in truth he is too little to wear all the weight of Mian Mittu for name. He shall be Tota—our Tota to us. Hearest thou, O small one? Littlest, thou art Tota.' She touched the child's cheek, and he, waking, wailed, and it was necessary to return him to his mother, who soothed him with the wonderful rhyme of 'A re koko, Ja re koko!' which says:

Oh crow! Go crow! Baby's sleeping sound,
And the wild plums grow in the jungle, only a penny a pound.
Only a penny a pound, baba, only a penny a pound.

Reassured many times as to the price of those plums, Tota cuddled himself down to sleep. The two sleek, white well-bullocks in the courtyard were steadily chewing the cud of their evening meal; old Pir Khan squatted at the head of Holden's horse, his police sabre across his knees, pulling drowsily at a big water-pipe that croaked like a bull-frog in a pond. Ameera's mother sat spinning in the lower verandah, and the wooden gate was shut and barred. The music of a marriage-procession came to the roof above the gentle hum of the city, and a string of flying-foxes crossed the face of the low moon.

'I have prayed,' said Ameera after a long pause, 'I have prayed for two things. First, that I may die in thy stead if thy death is demanded, and in the second that I may die in the place of the child. I have prayed to the Prophet and to Beebee Miriam (the Virgin Mary). Thinkest thou either will hear?'

'From thy lips who would not hear the lightest word?'

'I asked for straight talk, and thou hast given me sweet talk. Will my prayers be heard?'

'How can I say? God is very good.'

'Of that I am not sure. Listen now. When I die, or the child dies, what is thy fate? Living, thou wilt return to the bold white mem-log, for kind calls to kind.'

'Not always.'

'With a woman, no; with a man it is otherwise. Thou wilt in this life, later on, go back to thine own folk. That I could almost endure, for I should be dead. But in thy very death thou wilt be taken away to a strange place and a paradise that I do not know.'

'Will it be paradise?'

'Surely, for who would harm thee? But we two—I and the child—shall be elsewhere, and we cannot come to thee, nor canst thou come to us. In the old days, before the child was born, I did not think of these things; but now I think of them always. It is very hard talk.'

'It will fall as it will fall. To-morrow we do not know, but today and love we know well. Surely we are happy now.'

'So happy that it were well to make our happiness assured. And thy Beebee Miriam should listen to me; for she is also a woman. But then she would envy me! It is not seemly for men to worship a woman.'

Holden laughed aloud at Ameera's little spasm of jealousy.

'Is it not seemly? Why didst thou not turn me from worship of thee, then?'

'Thou a worshipper! And of me? My king, for all thy sweet words, well I know that I am thy servant and thy slave, and the dust under thy feet. And I would not have it otherwise. See!'

Before Holden could prevent her she stooped forward and touched his feet; recovering herself with a little laugh she hugged Tota closer to her bosom. Then, almost savagely—

'Is it true that the bold white mem-log live for three times the length of my life? Is it true that they make their marriages not before they are old women?'

'They marry as do others—when they are women.'

'That I know, but they wed when they are twenty-five. Is that true?'

'That is true.'

'Ya illah! At twenty-five! Who would of his own will take a wife even of eighteen? She is a woman—aging every hour. Twenty-five! I shall be an old woman at that age, and—Those mem-log remain young for ever. How I hate them!'

'What have they to do with us?'

'I cannot tell. I know only that there may now be alive on this earth a woman ten years older than I who may come to thee and take thy love ten years after I am an old woman, gray-headed, and the nurse of Tota's son. That is unjust and evil. They should die too.'

'Now, for all thy years thou art a child, and shalt be picked up and carried down the staircase.'

'Tota! Have a care for Tota, my lord! Thou at least art as foolish as any babe!' Ameera tucked Tota out of harm's way in the hollow of her neck, and was carried downstairs laughing in Holden's arms, while Tota opened his eyes and smiled after the manner of the lesser angels.

He was a silent infant, and, almost before Holden could realize that he was in the world, developed into a small gold-coloured little god and unquestioned despot of the house overlooking the city. Those were months of absolute happiness to Holden and Ameera—happiness withdrawn from the world, shut in behind the wooden gate that Pir Khan guarded. By day Holden did his work with an immense pity for such as were not so fortunate as himself, and a sympathy for small children that amazed and amused many mothers at the little station-gatherings. At nightfall he returned to Ameera—Ameera, full of the wondrous doings of Tota; how he had been seen to clap his hands together and move his fingers with intention and purpose—which was manifestly a miracle—how later, he had of his own initiative crawled out of his low bedstead on to the floor and swayed on both feet for the space of three breaths.

'And they were long breaths, for my heart stood still with delight,' said Ameera.

Then Tota took the beasts into his councils—the well-bullocks, the little gray squirrels, the mongoose that lived in a hole near the well, and especially Mian Mittu, the parrot, whose tail he grievously pulled, and Mian Mittu screamed till Ameera and Holden arrived.

'O villain! Child of strength! This to thy brother on the house-top! Tobah, tobah! Fie! Fie! But I know a charm to make him wise as Suleiman and Aflatoun (Solomon and Plato). Now look,' said Ameera. She drew from an embroidered bag a handful of almonds. 'See! we count seven. In the name of God!'

She placed Mian Mittu, very angry and rumpled, on the top of his cage, and seating herself between the babe and the bird she cracked and peeled an almond less white than her teeth. 'This is a true charm, my life, and do not laugh. See! I give the parrot one half and Tota the other.' Mian Mittu with careful beak took his share from between Ameera's lips, and she kissed the other half into the mouth of the child, who ate it slowly with wondering eyes. 'This I will do each day of seven, and without doubt he who is ours will be a bold speaker and wise. Eh, Tota, what wilt thou be when thou art a man and I am gray-headed?' Tota tucked his fat legs into adorable creases. He could crawl, but he was not going to waste the spring of his youth in idle speech. He wanted Mian Mittu's tail to tweak.

When he was advanced to the dignity of a silver belt—which, with a magic square engraved on silver and hung round his neck, made up the greater part of his clothing—he staggered on a perilous journey down the garden to Pir Khan and proffered him all his jewels in exchange for one little ride on Holden's horse, having seen his mother's mother chaffering with pedlars in the verandah. Pir Khan wept and set the untried feet on his own gray head in sign of fealty, and brought the bold adventurer to his mother's arms, vowing that Tota would be a leader of men ere his beard was grown.

One hot evening, while he sat on the roof between his father and mother watching the never-ending warfare of the kites that the city boys flew, he demanded a kite of his own with Pir Khan to fly it, because he had a fear of dealing with anything larger than himself, and when Holden called him a 'spark,' he rose to his feet and answered slowly in defence of his new-found individuality, 'Hum'park nahin hai. Hum admi hai (I am no spark, but a man).'

The protest made Holden choke and devote himself very seriously to a consideration of Tota's future. He need hardly have taken the trouble. The delight of that life was too perfect to endure. Therefore it was taken away as many things are taken away in India—suddenly and without warning. The little lord of the house, as Pir Khan called him, grew sorrowful and complained of pains, who had never known the meaning of pain. Ameera, wild with terror, watched him through the night, and in the dawning of the second day the life was shaken out of him by fever—the seasonal autumn fever. It seemed altogether impossible that he could die, and neither Ameera nor Holden at first believed the evidence of the little body on the bedstead. Then Ameera beat her head against the wall and would have flung herself down the well in the garden had Holden not restrained her by main force.

One mercy only was granted to Holden. He rode to his office in broad daylight and found waiting him an unusually heavy mail that demanded concentrated attention and hard work. He was not, however, alive to this kindness of the gods.

III

The first shock of a bullet is no more than a brisk pinch. The wrecked body does not send in its protest to the soul till ten or fifteen seconds later. Holden realized his pain slowly, exactly as he had realized his happiness, and with the same imperious necessity for hiding all trace of it. In the beginning he only felt that there had been a loss, and that Ameera needed comforting, where she sat with her head on her knees shivering as Mian Mittu from the housetop called, 'Tota! Tota! Tota!' Later all his world and the daily life of it rose up to hurt him. It was an outrage that any one of the children at the band-stand in the evening should be alive and clamorous, when his own child lay dead. It was more than mere pain when one of them touched him, and stories told by over-fond fathers of their children's latest performances cut him to the quick. He could not declare his pain. He had neither help, comfort, nor sympathy; and Ameera at the end of each weary day would lead him through the hell of self-questioning reproach which is reserved for those who have lost a child, and believe that with a little—just a little—more care it might have been saved.

'Perhaps,' Ameera would say, 'I did not take sufficient heed. Did I, or did I not? The sun on the roof that day when he played so long alone and I was—ahi! braiding my hair—it may be that the sun then bred the fever. If I had warned him from the sun he might have lived. But, oh my life, say that I am guiltless! Thou knowest that I loved him as I love thee. Say that there is no blame on me, or I shall die—I shall die!'

'There is no blame—before God, none. It was written and how could we do aught to save? What has been, has been. Let it go, beloved.'

'He was all my heart to me. How can I let the thought go when my arm tells me every night that he is not here? Ahi! Ahi! O Tota, come back to me—come back again, and let us be all together as it was before!'

'Peace, peace! For thine own sake, and for mine also, if thou lovest me—rest.'

'By this I know thou dost not care; and how shouldst thou? The white men have hearts of stone and souls of iron. Oh, that I had married a man of mine own people—though he beat me—and had never eaten the bread of an alien!'

'Am I an alien—mother of my son?'

'What else—Sahib? ... Oh, forgive me—forgive! The death has driven me mad. Thou art the life of my heart, and the light of my eyes, and the breath of my life, and—and I have put thee from me, though it was but for a moment. If thou goest away, to whom shall I look for help? Do not be angry. Indeed, it was the pain that spoke and not thy slave.'

'I know, I know. We be two who were three. The greater need therefore that we should be one.'

They were sitting on the roof as of custom. The night was a warm one in early spring, and sheet-lightning was dancing on the horizon to a broken tune played by far-off thunder. Ameera settled herself in Holden's arms.

'The dry earth is lowing like a cow for the rain, and I—I am afraid. It was not like this when we counted the stars. But thou lovest me as much as before, though a bond is taken away? Answer!'

'I love more because a new bond has come out of the sorrow that we have eaten together, and that thou knowest.'

'Yea, I knew,' said Ameera in a very small whisper. 'But it is good to hear thee say so, my life, who art so strong to help. I will be a child no more, but a woman and an aid to thee. Listen! Give me my sitar and I will sing bravely.'

She took the light silver-studded sitar and began a song of the great hero Rajah Rasalu. The hand failed on the strings, the tune halted, checked, and at a low note turned off to the poor little nursery-rhyme about the wicked crow—

And the wild plums grow in the jungle, only a penny a pound.
Only a penny a pound, baba—only...

Then came the tears, and the piteous rebellion against fate till she slept, moaning a little in her sleep, with the right arm thrown clear of the body as though it protected something that was not there. It was after this night that life became a little easier for Holden. The ever-present pain of loss drove him into his work, and the work repaid him by filling up his mind for nine or ten hours a day. Ameera sat alone in the house and brooded, but grew happier when she understood that Holden was more at ease, according to the custom of women. They touched happiness again, but this time with caution.

'It was because we loved Tota that he died. The jealousy of God was upon us,' said Ameera. 'I have hung up a large black jar before our window to turn the evil eye from us, and we must make no protestations of delight, but go softly underneath the stars, lest God find us out. Is that not good talk, worthless one?'

She had shifted the accent on the word that means 'beloved,' in proof of the sincerity of her purpose. But the kiss that followed the new christening was a thing that any deity might have envied. They went about henceforward saying, 'It is naught, it is naught;' and hoping that all the Powers heard.

The Powers were busy on other things. They had allowed thirty million people four years of plenty wherein men fed well and the crops were certain, and the birth-rate rose year by year; the districts reported a purely agricultural population varying from nine hundred to two thousand to the square mile of the overburdened earth; and the Member for Lower Tooting, wandering about India in pot-hat and frock-coat, talked largely of the benefits of British rule and suggested as the one thing needful, the establishment of a duly qualified electoral system and a general bestowal of the franchise. His long-suffering hosts smiled and made him welcome, and when he paused to admire, with pretty picked words, the blossom of the blood-red dhak-tree that had flowered untimely for a sign of what was coming, they smiled more than ever.

It was the Deputy Commissioner of Kot–Kumharsen, staying at the club for a day, who lightly told a tale that made Holden's blood run cold as he overheard the end.

'He won't bother any one any more. Never saw a man so astonished in my life. By Jove, I thought he meant to ask a question in the House about it. Fellow-passenger in his ship— dined next him—bowled over by cholera and died in eighteen hours. You needn't laugh, you fellows. The Member for Lower Tooting is awfully angry about it; but he's more scared. I think he's going to take his enlightened self out of India.'

'I'd give a good deal if he were knocked over. It might keep a few vestrymen of his kidney to their own parish. But what's this about cholera? It's full early for anything of that kind,' said the warden of an unprofitable salt-lick.

'Don't know,' said the Deputy Commissioner reflectively. 'We've got locusts with us. There's sporadic cholera all along the north—at least we're calling it sporadic for decency's sake. The spring crops are short in five districts, and nobody seems to know where the rains are. It's nearly March now. I don't want to scare anybody, but it seems to me that Nature's going to audit her accounts with a big red pencil this summer.'

'Just when I wanted to take leave, too!' said a voice across the room.

'There won't be much leave this year, but there ought to be a great deal of promotion. I've come in to persuade the Government to put my pet canal on the list of famine-relief works. It's an ill-wind that blows no good. I shall get that canal finished at last.'

'Is it the old programme then,' said Holden; 'famine, fever and cholera?'

'Oh no. Only local scarcity and an unusual prevalence of seasonal sickness. You'll find it all in the reports if you live till next year. You're a lucky chap. YOU haven't got a wife to send out of harm's way. The hill-stations ought to be full of women this year.'

'I think you're inclined to exaggerate the talk in the bazars,' said a young civilian in the Secretariat. 'Now I have observed—'

'I daresay you have,' said the Deputy Commissioner, 'but you've a great deal more to observe, my son. In the meantime, I wish to observe to you—' and he drew him aside to discuss the construction of the canal that was so dear to his heart. Holden went to his bungalow and began to understand that he was not alone in the world, and also that he was afraid for the sake of another—which is the most soul-satisfying fear known to man.

Two months later, as the Deputy had foretold, Nature began to audit her accounts with a red pencil. On the heels of the spring-reapings came a cry for bread, and the Government, which had decreed that no man should die of want, sent wheat.

Then came the cholera from all four quarters of the compass. It struck a pilgrim-gathering of half a million at a sacred shrine. Many died at the feet of their god; the others broke and ran over the face of the land carrying the pestilence with them. It smote a walled city and killed two hundred a day. The people crowded the trains, hanging on to the footboards and squatting on the roofs of the carriages, and the cholera followed them, for at each station they dragged out the dead and the dying. They died by the roadside, and the horses of the Englishmen shied at the corpses in the grass. The rains did not come, and the earth turned to iron lest man should escape death by hiding in her. The English sent their wives away to the hills and went about their work, coming forward as they were bidden to fill the gaps in the fighting-line. Holden, sick with fear of losing his chiefest treasure on earth, had done his best to persuade Ameera to go away with her mother to the Himalayas.

'Why should I go?' said she one evening on the roof.

'There is sickness, and people are dying, and all the white mem-log have gone.'

'All of them?'

'All—unless perhaps there remain some old scald-head who vexes her husband's heart by running risk of death.'

'Nay; who stays is my sister, and thou must not abuse her, for I will be a scald-head too. I am glad all the bold mem-log are gone.'

'Do I speak to a woman or a babe? Go to the hills and I will see to it that thou goest like a queen's daughter. Think, child. In a red-lacquered bullock-cart, veiled and curtained, with brass peacocks upon the pole and red cloth hangings. I will send two orderlies for guard, and—'

'Peace! Thou art the babe in speaking thus. What use are those toys to me? HE would have patted the bullocks and played with the housings. For his sake, perhaps—thou hast made me very English—I might have gone. Now, I will not. Let the mem-log run.'

'Their husbands are sending them, beloved.'

'Very good talk. Since when hast thou been my husband to tell me what to do? I have but borne thee a son. Thou art only all the desire of my soul to me. How shall I depart when I know that if evil befall thee by the breadth of so much as my littlest finger-nail—is that not small?—I should be aware of it though I were in paradise. And here, this summer thou mayest die—ai, janee, die! and in dying they might call to tend thee a white woman, and she would rob me in the last of thy love!'

'But love is not born in a moment or on a death-bed!'

'What dost thou know of love, stoneheart? She would take thy thanks at least and, by God and the Prophet and Beebee Miriam the mother of thy Prophet, that I will never endure. My lord and my love, let there be no more foolish talk of going away. Where thou art, I am. It is enough.' She put an arm round his neck and a hand on his mouth.

There are not many happinesses so complete as those that are snatched under the shadow of the sword. They sat together and laughed, calling each other openly by every pet name that could move the wrath of the gods. The city below them was locked up in its own torments. Sulphur fires blazed in the streets; the conches in the Hindu temples screamed and bellowed, for the gods were inattentive in those days. There was a service in the great Mahomedan shrine, and the call to prayer from the minarets was almost unceasing. They heard the wailing in the houses of the dead, and once the shriek of a mother who had lost a child and was calling for its return. In the gray dawn they saw the dead borne out through the city gates, each litter with its own little knot of mourners. Wherefore they kissed each other and shivered.

It was a red and heavy audit, for the land was very sick and needed a little breathing-space ere the torrent of cheap life should flood it anew. The children of immature fathers and undeveloped mothers made no resistance. They were cowed and sat still, waiting till the sword should be sheathed in November if it were so willed. There were gaps among the English, but the gaps were filled. The work of superintending famine-relief, cholera-sheds, medicine-distribution, and what little sanitation was possible, went forward because it was so ordered.

Holden had been told to keep himself in readiness to move to replace the next man who should fall. There were twelve hours in each day when he could not see Ameera, and she might die in three. He was considering what his pain would be if he could not see her for three months, or if she died out of his sight. He was absolutely certain that her death would be demanded—so certain that when he looked up from the telegram and saw Pir Khan breathless in the doorway, he laughed aloud. 'And?' said he—

'When there is a cry in the night and the spirit flutters into the throat, who has a charm that will restore? Come swiftly, Heaven-born! It is the black cholera.'

Holden galloped to his home. The sky was heavy with clouds, for the long-deferred rains were near and the heat was stifling. Ameera's mother met him in the courtyard, whimpering, 'She is dying. She is nursing herself into death. She is all but dead. What shall I do, Sahib?'

Ameera was lying in the room in which Tota had been born. She made no sign when Holden entered, because the human soul is a very lonely thing and, when it is getting ready to go away, hides itself in a misty borderland where the living may not follow. The black cholera does its work quietly and without explanation. Ameera was being thrust out of life as though the Angel of Death had himself put his hand upon her. The quick breathing seemed to show that she was either afraid or in pain, but neither eyes nor mouth gave any answer to Holden's kisses. There was nothing to be said or done. Holden could only wait and suffer. The first drops of the rain began to fall on the roof, and he could hear shouts of joy in the parched city.

The soul came back a little and the lips moved. Holden bent down to listen. 'Keep nothing of mine,' said Ameera. 'Take no hair from my head. SHE would make thee burn it later on. That flame I should feel. Lower! Stoop lower! Remember only that I was thine and bore thee a son. Though thou wed a white woman tomorrow, the pleasure of receiving in thy arms thy first son is taken from thee for ever. Remember me when thy son is born—the one that shall carry thy name before all men. His misfortunes be on my head. I bear witness—I bear witness'— the lips were forming the words on his ear—'that there is no God but—thee, beloved!'

Then she died. Holden sat still, and all thought was taken from him—till he heard Ameera's mother lift the curtain.

'Is she dead, Sahib?'

'She is dead.'

'Then I will mourn, and afterwards take an inventory of the furniture in this house. For that will be mine. The Sahib does not mean to resume it? It is so little, so very little, Sahib, and I am an old woman. I would like to lie softly.'

'For the mercy of God be silent a while. Go out and mourn where I cannot hear.'

'Sahib, she will be buried in four hours.'

'I know the custom. I shall go ere she is taken away. That matter is in thy hands. Look to it, that the bed on which—on which she lies—'

'Aha! That beautiful red-lacquered bed. I have long desired—'

'That the bed is left here untouched for my disposal. All else in the house is thine. Hire a cart, take everything, go hence, and before sunrise let there be nothing in this house but that which I have ordered thee to respect.'

'I am an old woman. I would stay at least for the days of mourning, and the rains have just broken. Whither shall I go?'

'What is that to me? My order is that there is a going. The house-gear is worth a thousand rupees and my orderly shall bring thee a hundred rupees to-night.'

'That is very little. Think of the cart-hire.'

'It shall be nothing unless thou goest, and with speed. O woman, get hence and leave me with my dead!'

The mother shuffled down the staircase, and in her anxiety to take stock of the house-fittings forgot to mourn. Holden stayed by Ameera's side and the rain roared on the roof. He could not think connectedly by reason of the noise, though he made many attempts to do so. Then four sheeted ghosts glided dripping into the room and stared at him through their veils. They were the washers of the dead. Holden left the room and went out to his horse. He had come in a dead, stifling calm through ankle-deep dust. He found the courtyard a rain-lashed pond alive with frogs; a torrent of yellow water ran under the gate, and a roaring wind drove the bolts of the rain like buckshot against the mud-walls. Pir Khan was shivering in his little hut by the gate, and the horse was stamping uneasily in the water.

'I have been told the Sahib's order,' said Pir Khan. 'It is well. This house is now desolate. I go also, for my monkey-face would be a reminder of that which has been. Concerning the bed, I will bring that to thy house yonder in the morning; but remember, Sahib, it will be to thee a knife turning in a green wound. I go upon a pilgrimage, and I will take no money. I have grown fat in the protection of the Presence whose sorrow is my sorrow. For the last time I hold his stirrup.'

He touched Holden's foot with both hands and the horse sprang out into the road, where the creaking bamboos were whipping the sky and all the frogs were chuckling. Holden could not see for the rain in his face. He put his hands before his eyes and muttered—

'Oh you brute! You utter brute!'

The news of his trouble was already in his bungalow. He read the knowledge in his butler's eyes when Ahmed Khan brought in food, and for the first and last time in his life laid a hand upon his master's shoulder, saying, 'Eat, Sahib, eat. Meat is good against sorrow. I also have known. Moreover the shadows come and go, Sahib; the shadows come and go. These be curried eggs.'

Holden could neither eat nor sleep. The heavens sent down eight inches of rain in that night and washed the earth clean. The waters tore down walls, broke roads, and scoured open the shallow graves on the Mahomedan burying-ground. All next day it rained, and Holden sat still in his house considering his sorrow. On the morning of the third day he received a telegram which said only, 'Ricketts, Myndonie. Dying. Holden relieve. Immediate.' Then he thought that before he departed he would look at the house wherein he had been master and lord. There was a break in the weather, and the rank earth steamed with vapour.

He found that the rains had torn down the mud pillars of the gateway, and the heavy wooden gate that had guarded his life hung lazily from one hinge. There was grass three inches high in the courtyard; Pir Khan's lodge was empty, and the sodden thatch sagged between the beams. A gray squirrel was in possession of the verandah, as if the house had been untenanted for thirty years instead of three days. Ameera's mother had removed everything except some mildewed matting. The tick-tick of the little scorpions as they hurried across the floor was the only sound in the house. Ameera's room and the other one where Tota had lived were heavy with mildew; and the narrow staircase leading to the roof was streaked and stained with rain-borne mud. Holden saw all these things, and came out again to meet in the road Durga Dass, his landlord—portly, affable, clothed in white muslin, and driving a Cee-spring buggy. He was overlooking his property to see how the roofs stood the stress of the first rains.

'I have heard,' said he, 'you will not take this place any more, Sahib?'

'What are you going to do with it?'

'Perhaps I shall let it again.'

'Then I will keep it on while I am away.'

Durga Dass was silent for some time. 'You shall not take it on, Sahib,' he said. 'When I was a young man I also—but today I am a member of the Municipality. Ho! Ho! No. When the birds have gone what need to keep the nest? I will have it pulled down—the timber will sell for something always. It shall be pulled down, and the Municipality shall make a road across, as they desire, from the burning-ghat to the city wall, so that no man may say where this house stood.'

THREE AND—AN EXTRA

'When halter and heel ropes are slipped, do not give chase with sticks but with gram.'

—Punjabi proverb

After marriage arrives a reaction, sometimes a big, sometimes a little one; but it comes sooner or later, and must be tided over by both parties if they desire the rest of their lives to go with the current.

In the case of the Cusack–Bremmils this reaction did not set in till the third year after the wedding. Bremmil was hard to hold at the best of times; but he was a beautiful husband until the baby died and Mrs Bremmil wore black, and grew thin, and mourned as if the bottom of the universe had fallen out. Perhaps Bremmil ought to have comforted her. He tried to do so, I think; but the more he comforted the more Mrs Bremmil grieved, and, consequently, the more uncomfortable Bremmil grew. The fact was that they both needed a tonic. And they got it. Mrs Bremmil can afford to laugh now, but it was no laughing matter to her at the time.

You see, Mrs Hauksbee appeared on the horizon; and where she existed was fair chance of trouble. At Simla her byename was the 'Stormy Petrel'. She had won that title five times to my own certain knowledge. She was a little, brown, thin, almost skinny, woman with big, rolling, violet-blue eyes, and the sweetest manners in the world. You had only to mention her name at afternoon teas for every woman in the room to rise up, and call her—well—NOT blessed. She was clever, witty, brilliant, and sparkling beyond most of her kind; but possessed of many devils of malice and mischievousness. She could be nice, though, even to her own sex. But that is another story.

Bremmil went off at score after the baby's death and the general discomfort that followed, and Mrs Hauksbee annexed him. She took no pleasure in hiding her captives. She annexed him publicly, and saw that the public saw it. He rode with her, and walked with her, and talked with her, and picnicked with her, and tiffined at Peliti's with her, till people put up their eyebrows and said, 'Shocking!' Mrs Bremmil stayed at home turning over the dead baby's frocks and crying into the empty cradle. She did not care to do anything else. But some eight dear, affectionate lady-friends explained the situation at length to her in case she should miss the cream of it. Mrs Bremmil listened quietly, and thanked them for their good offices. She was not as clever as Mrs Hauksbee, but she was no fool. She kept her own counsel, and did not speak to Bremmil of what she had heard. This is worth remembering. Speaking to, or crying over, a husband never did any good yet.

When Bremmil was at home, which was not often, he was more affectionate than usual; and that showed his hand. The affection was forced, partly to soothe his own conscience and partly to soothe Mrs Bremmil. It failed in both regards.

Then 'the A.D.C. in Waiting was commanded by Their Excellencies, Lord and Lady Lytton, to invite Mr and Mrs Cusack–Bremmil to Peterhoff on July 26th at 9.30 P. M.'— 'Dancing' in the bottom-left-hand corner.

'I can't go,' said Mrs Bremmil, 'it is too soon after poor little Florrie…but it need not stop you, Tom.'

She meant what she said then, and Bremmil said that he would go just to put in an appearance. Here he spoke the thing which was not; and Mrs Bremmil knew it. She guessed—a woman's guess is much more accurate than a man's certainty—

that he had meant to go from the first, and with Mrs Hauksbee. She sat down to think, and the outcome of her thoughts was that the memory of a dead child was worth considerably less than the affections of a living husband. She made her plan and staked her all upon it. In that hour she discovered that she knew Tom Bremmil thoroughly, and this knowledge she acted on.

'Tom,' said she, 'I shall be dining out at the Longmores' on the evening of the 26th. You'd better dine at the club.'

This saved Bremmil from making an excuse to get away and dine with Mrs Hauksbee, so he was grateful, and felt small and mean at the same time—which was wholesome. Bremmil left the house at five for a ride. About half-past five in the evening a large leather-covered basket came in from Phelps' for Mrs Bremmil. She was a woman who knew how to dress; and she had not spent a week on designing that dress and having it gored, and hemmed, and herring-boned, and tucked and rucked (or whatever the terms are) for nothing. It was a gorgeous dress—slight mourning. I can't describe it, but it was what *The Queen* calls 'a creation'—a thing that hit you straight between the eyes and made you gasp. She had not much heart for what she was going to do; but as she glanced at the long mirror she had the satisfaction of knowing that she had never looked so well in her life. She was a large blonde and, when she chose, carried herself superbly.

After the dinner at the Longmores, she went on to the dance—a little late—and encountered Bremmil with Mrs Hauksbee on his arm. That made her flush, and as the men crowded round her for dances she looked magnificent. She filled up all her dances except three, and those she left blank. Mrs Hauksbee caught her eye once; and she knew it was war—real war—between them. She started handicapped in the struggle, for she had ordered Bremmil about just the least little bit in the world too much; and he was beginning to resent it. Moreover, he had never seen his wife look so lovely. He stared at her from doorways, and glared at her from passages as she went about with her partners; and the more he stared, the more taken was he. He could scarcely believe that this was the woman with the red eyes and the black stuff gown who used to weep over the eggs at breakfast.

Mrs Hauksbee did her best to hold him in play, but, after two dances, he crossed over to his wife and asked for a dance.

'I'm afraid you've come too late, MISTER Bremmil,' she said, with her eyes twinkling.

Then he begged her to give him a dance, and, as a great favour, she allowed him the fifth waltz. Luckily, 5 stood vacant on his programme. They danced it together, and there was a little flutter round the room. Bremmil had a sort of notion that his wife could dance, but he never knew she danced so divinely. At the end of that waltz he asked for another—as a favour, not as a right; and Mrs Bremmil said, 'Show me your programme, dear!' He showed it as a naughty little schoolboy hands up contraband sweets to a master. There was a fair sprinkling of 'H' on it besides 'H' at supper. Mrs Bremmil said nothing, but she smiled contemptuously, ran her pencil through 7 and 9— two 'H's—and returned the card with her own name written above—a pet name that only she and her husband used. Then she shook her finger at him, and said, laughing, 'Oh, you silly, SILLY boy!'

Mrs Hauksbee heard that, and—she owned as much— felt that she had the worst of it. Bremmil accepted 7 and 9 gratefully. They danced 7, and sat out 9 in one of the little tents. What Bremmil said and what Mrs Bremmil said is no concern of any one's.

When the band struck up 'The Roast Beef of Old England,' the two went out into the verandah, and Bremmil began looking for his wife's dandy (this was before 'rickshaw days) while she went into the cloak-room. Mrs Hauksbee came up and said, 'You take me in to supper, I think, Mr Bremmil.' Bremmil turned red and looked foolish. 'Ah—h'm! I'm going home with my wife, Mrs Hauksbee. I think there has been a little mistake.' Being a man, he spoke as though Mrs Hauksbee were entirely responsible.

Mrs Bremmil came out of the cloak-room in a swansdown cloak with a white 'cloud' round her head. She looked radiant; and she had a right to.

The couple went off in the darkness together, Bremmil riding very close to the dandy.

Then says Mrs Hauksbee to me—she looked a trifle faded and jaded in the lamplight, 'Take my word for it, the silliest woman can manage a clever man; but it needs a very clever woman to manage a fool.'

Then we went in to supper.

A WAYSIDE COMEDY

'Because to every purpose there is time and judgment,
therefore the misery of man is great upon him.'

—Eccles. viii. 6.

Fate and the Government of India have turned the Station of Kashima into a prison; and, because there is no help for the poor souls who are now lying there in torment, I write this story, praying that the Government of India may be moved to scatter the European population to the four winds.

Kashima is bounded on all sides by the rock-tipped circle of the Dosehri hills. In Spring, it is ablaze with roses; in Summer, the roses die and the hot winds blow from the hills; in Autumn, the white mists from the jhils cover the place as with water, and in Winter the frosts nip everything young and tender to earth-level. There is but one view in Kashima—a stretch of perfectly flat pasture and plough-land, running up to the gray-blue scrub of the Dosehri hills.

There are no amusements, except snipe and tiger shooting; but the tigers have been long since hunted from their lairs in the rock-caves, and the snipe only come once a year. Narkarra one hundred and forty-three miles by road is the nearest station to Kashima. But Kashima never goes to Narkarra, where there are at least twelve English people. It stays within the circle of the Dosehri hills.

All Kashima acquits Mrs Vansuythen of any intention to do harm; but all Kashima knows that she, and she alone, brought about their pain.

Boulte, the Engineer, Mrs Boulte, and Captain Kurrell know this. They are the English population of Kashima, if we except

Major Vansuythen, who is of no importance whatever, and Mrs Vansuythen, who is the most important of all.

You must remember, though you will not understand, that all laws weaken in a small and hidden community where there is no public opinion. When a man is absolutely alone in a Station he runs a certain risk of falling into evil ways. This risk is multiplied by every addition to the population up to twelve, the Jury-number. After that, fear and consequent restraint begin, and human action becomes less grotesquely jerky.

There was deep peace in Kashima till Mrs Vansuythen arrived. She was a charming woman; every one said so everywhere; and she charmed every one. In spite of this, or, perhaps, because of this, since Fate is so perverse, she cared only for one man, and he was Major Vansuythen. Had she been plain or stupid, this matter would have been intelligible to Kashima. But she was a fair woman, with very still gray eyes, the colour of a lake just before the light of the sun touches it. No man who had seen those eyes could, later on, explain what fashion of woman she was to look upon. The eyes dazzled him. Her own sex said that she was 'not bad-looking, but spoilt by pretending to be so grave.' And yet her gravity was natural. It was not her habit to smile. She merely went through life, looking at those who passed; and the women objected while the men fell down and worshipped.

She knows and is deeply sorry for the evil she has done to Kashima; but Major Vansuythen cannot understand why Mrs Boulte does not drop in to afternoon tea at least three times a week. 'When there are only two women in one Station, they ought to see a great deal of each other,' says Major Vansuythen.

Long and long before ever Mrs Vansuythen came out of those far-away places where there is society and amusement, Kurrell had discovered that Mrs Boulte was the one woman in the world for him and you dare not blame them. Kashima was as out of the world as Heaven or the Other Place, and the Dosehri hills kept their secret well. Boulte had no concern in the matter. He was in camp for a fortnight at a time. He was a hard, heavy man, and neither Mrs Boulte nor Kurrell pitied him. They had all Kashima and each other for their very, very own; and Kashima was the Garden of Eden in those days. When Boulte returned from his wanderings he would slap Kurrell between the shoulders and call him 'old fellow,' and the three would dine together. Kashima was happy then when the judgment of God seemed almost as distant as Narkarra or the railway that ran down to the sea. But the Government sent Major Vansuythen to Kashima, and with him came his wife.

The etiquette of Kashima is much the same as that of a desert island. When a stranger is cast away there, all hands go down to the shore to make him welcome. Kashima assembled at the masonry platform close to the Narkarra Road, and spread tea for the Vansuythens. That ceremony was reckoned a formal call, and made them free of the Station, its rights and privileges. When the Vansuythens settled down they gave a tiny house-warming to all Kashima; and that made Kashima free of their house, according to the immemorial usage of the Station.

Then the Rains came, when no one could go into camp, and the Narkarra Road was washed away by the Kasun River, and in the cup-like pastures of Kashima the cattle waded knee-deep. The clouds dropped down from the Dosehri hills and covered everything.

At the end of the Rains, Boulte's manner towards his wife changed and became demonstratively affectionate. They had been married twelve years, and the change startled Mrs Boulte, who hated her husband with the hate of a woman who has met with nothing but kindness from her mate, and, in the teeth of this kindness, has done him a great wrong. Moreover, she had her own trouble to fight with, her watch to keep over her own property, Kurrell. For two months the Rains had hidden the Dosehri hills and many other things besides; but, when they lifted, they showed Mrs Boulte that her man among men, her Ted, for she called him Ted in the old days when Boulte was out of earshot, was slipping the links of the allegiance.

'The Vansuythen Woman has taken him,' Mrs Boulte said to herself; and when Boulte was away, wept over her belief, in the face of the over-vehement blandishments of Ted. Sorrow in Kashima is as fortunate as Love because there is nothing to weaken it save the flight of Time. Mrs Boulte had never breathed her suspicion to Kurrell because she was not certain; and her nature led her to be very certain before she took steps in any direction. That is why she behaved as she did.

Boulte came into the house one evening, and leaned against the door-posts of the drawing-room, chewing his moustache. Mrs Boulte was putting some flowers into a vase. There is a pretence of civilisation even in Kashima.

'Little woman,' said Boulte quietly, 'do you care for me?'

'Immensely,' said she, with a laugh. 'Can you ask it?'

'But I'm serious,' said Boulte. 'Do you care for me?'

Mrs Boulte dropped the flowers, and turned round quickly. 'Do you want an honest answer?'

'Ye-es, I've asked for it.'

Mrs Boulte spoke in a low, even voice for five minutes, very distinctly, that there might be no misunderstanding her meaning. When Samson broke the pillars of Gaza, he did a little thing, and one not to be compared to the deliberate pulling down of a woman's homestead about her own ears. There was no wise female friend to advise Mrs Boulte, the singularly cautious wife, to hold her hand. She struck at Boulte's heart, because her own was sick with suspicion of Kurrell, and worn out with the long strain of watching alone through the Rains. There was no plan or purpose in her speaking. The sentences made themselves; and Boulte listened, leaning against the door-post with his hands in his pockets. When all was over, and Mrs Boulte began to breathe through her nose before breaking out into tears, he laughed and stared straight in front of him at the Dosehri hills.

'Is that all?' he said. 'Thanks, I only wanted to know, you know.'

'What are you going to do?' said the woman, between her sobs.

'Do! Nothing. What should I do? Kill Kurrell, or send you Home, or apply for leave to get a divorce? It's two days' trek into Narkarra.' He laughed again and went on, 'I'll tell you what you can do. You can ask Kurrell to dinner tomorrow no, on Thursday, that will allow you time to pack and you can bolt with him. I give you my word I won't follow.'

He took up his helmet and went out of the room, and Mrs Boulte sat till the moonlight streaked the floor, thinking and thinking and thinking. She had done her best upon the spur of the moment to pull the house down; but it would not fall. Moreover, she could not understand her husband, and she was afraid. Then the folly of her useless truthfulness struck her, and she was ashamed to write to Kurrell, saying, 'I have gone mad and told everything. My husband says that I am free to elope with you. Get a dek for Thursday, and we will fly after dinner.' There was a cold-bloodedness about that procedure which did not appeal to her. So she sat still in her own house and thought.

At dinner-time Boulte came back from his walk, white and worn and haggard, and the woman was touched at his distress.

As the evening wore on she muttered some expression of sorrow, something approaching to contrition. Boulte came out of a brown study and said, 'Oh, that! I wasn't thinking about that. By the way, what does Kurrell say to the elopement?'

'I haven't seen him,' said Mrs Boulte. 'Good God, is that all?'

But Boulte was not listening and her sentence ended in a gulp.

The next day brought no comfort to Mrs Boulte, for Kurrell did not appear, and the new life that she, in the five minutes' madness of the previous evening, had hoped to build out of the ruins of the old, seemed to be no nearer.

Boulte ate his breakfast, advised her to see her Arab pony fed in the verandah, and went out. The morning wore through, and at mid-day the tension became unendurable. Mrs Boulte could not cry. She had finished her crying in the night, and now she did not want to be left alone. Perhaps the Vansuythen Woman would talk to her; and, since talking opens the heart, perhaps there might be some comfort to be found in her company. She was the only other woman in the Station.

In Kashima there are no regular calling-hours. Every one can drop in upon every one else at pleasure. Mrs Boulte put on a big terai hat, and walked across to the Vansuythens' house to borrow last week's *Queen*. The two compounds touched, and instead of going up the drive, she crossed through the gap in the cactus-hedge, entering the house from the back. As she passed through the dining-room, she heard, behind the purdah that cloaked the drawing-room door, her husband's voice, saying,

'But on my Honour! On my Soul and Honour, I tell you she doesn't care for me. She told me so last night. I would have told you then if Vansuythen hadn't been with you. If it is for her sake that you'll have nothing to say to me, you can make your mind easy. It's Kurrell.'

'What?' said Mrs Vansuythen, with a hysterical little laugh. 'Kurrell! Oh, it can't be! You two must have made some horrible mistake. Perhaps you lost your temper, or misunderstood, or something. Things can't be as wrong as you say.'

Mrs Vansuythen had shifted her defence to avoid the man's pleading, and was desperately trying to keep him to a side-issue.

'There must be some mistake,' she insisted, 'and it can be all put right again.'

Boulte laughed grimly.

'It can't be Captain Kurrell! He told me that he had never taken the least interest in your wife, Mr Boulte. Oh, do listen! He said he had not. He swore he had not,' said Mrs Vansuythen.

The purdah rustled, and the speech was cut short by the entry of a little thin woman, with big rings round her eyes. Mrs Vansuythen stood up with a gasp.

'What was that you said?' asked Mrs Boulte. 'Never mind that man. What did Ted say to you? What did he say to you? What did he say to you?'

Mrs Vansuythen sat down helplessly on the sofa, overborne by the trouble of her questioner.

'He said… I can't remember exactly what he said, but I understood him to say…that is… But, really, Mrs Boulte, isn't it rather a strange question?'

'Will you tell me what he said?' repeated Mrs Boulte. Even a tiger will fly before a bear robbed of her whelps, and Mrs Vansuythen was only an ordinarily good woman. She began in a sort of desperation, 'Well, he said that he never cared for you at all, and, of course, there was not the least reason why he should have, and that was all.'

'You said he swore he had not cared for me. Was that true?'

'Yes,' said Mrs Vansuythen very softly.

Mrs Boulte wavered for an instant where she stood, and then fell forward fainting.

'What did I tell you?' said Boulte, as though the conversation had been unbroken. 'You can see for yourself. She cares for him.' The light began to break into his dull mind, and he went on, 'And what was he saying to you?'

But Mrs Vansuythen, with no heart for explanations or impassioned protestations, was kneeling over Mrs Boulte.

'Oh, you brute!' she cried. 'Are all men like this? Help me to get her into my room and her face is cut against the table. Oh, will you be quiet, and help me to carry her? I hate you, and I hate Captain Kurrell. Lift her up carefully, and now go! Go away!'

Boulte carried his wife into Mrs Vansuythen's bedroom, and departed before the storm of that lady's wrath and disgust, impenitent and burning with jealousy. Kurrell had been making love to Mrs Vansuythen, would do Vansuythen as great a wrong as he had done Boulte, who caught himself considering whether Mrs Vansuythen would faint if she discovered that the man she loved had forsworn her.

In the middle of these meditations, Kurrell came cantering along the road and pulled up with a cheery 'Good-mornin'. 'Been mashing Mrs Vansuythen as usual, eh? Bad thing for a sober, married man, that. What will Mrs Boulte say?'

Boulte raised his head and said slowly, 'Oh, you liar!'

Kurrell's face changed. 'What's that?' he asked quickly.

'Nothing much,' said Boulte. 'Has my wife told you that you two are free to go off whenever you please? She has been good enough to explain the situation to me. You've been a true friend to me, Kurrell old man, haven't you?'

Kurrell groaned, and tried to frame some sort of idiotic sentence about being willing to give 'satisfaction.' But his interest in the woman was dead, had died out in the Rains, and, mentally, he was abusing her for her amazing indiscretion. It would have been so easy to have broken off the thing gently and by degrees, and now he was saddled with—Boulte's voice recalled him.

'I don't think I should get any satisfaction from killing you, and I'm pretty sure you'd get none from killing me.'

Then in a querulous tone, ludicrously disproportioned to his wrongs, Boulte added,

'Seems rather a pity that you haven't the decency to keep to the woman, now you've got her. You've been a true friend to her too, haven't you?'

Kurrell stared long and gravely. The situation was getting beyond him.

'What do you mean?' he said.

Boulte answered, more to himself than the questioner: 'My wife came over to Mrs Vansuythen's just now; and it seems you'd been telling Mrs Vansuythen that you'd never cared for Emma. I suppose you lied, as usual. What had Mrs Vansuythen to do with you, or you with her? Try to speak the truth for once in a way.'

Kurrell took the double insult without wincing, and replied by another question, 'Go on. What happened?'

'Emma fainted,' said Boulte simply. 'But, look here, what had you been saying to Mrs Vansuythen?'

Kurrell laughed. Mrs Boulte had, with unbridled tongue, made havoc of his plans; and he could at least retaliate by hurting the man in whose eyes he was humiliated and shown dishonourable.

'Said to her? What does a man tell a lie like that for? I suppose I said pretty much what you've said, unless I'm a good deal mistaken.'

'I spoke the truth,' said Boulte, again more to himself than Kurrell. 'Emma told me she hated me. She has no right in me.'

'No! I suppose not. You're only her husband, y'know. And what did Mrs Vansuythen say after you had laid your disengaged heart at her feet?'

Kurrell felt almost virtuous as he put the question.

'I don't think that matters,' Boulte replied; 'and it doesn't concern you.'

'But it does! I tell you it does,' began Kurrell shamelessly.

The sentence was cut by a roar of laughter from Boulte's lips. Kurrell was silent for an instant, and then he, too, laughed long and loudly, rocking in his saddle. It was an unpleasant sound, the mirthless mirth of these men on the long white line of the Narkarra Road. There were no strangers in Kashima, or they might have thought that captivity within the Dosehri hills had driven half the European population mad. The laughter ended abruptly, and Kurrell was the first to speak.

'Well, what are you going to do?'

Boulte looked up the road, and at the hills. 'Nothing,' said he quietly; 'what's the use? It's too ghastly for anything. We must let the old life go on. I can only call you a hound and a liar, and I can't go on calling you names for ever. Besides which, I don't feel that I'm much better. We can't get out of this place. What is there to do?'

Kurrell looked round the rat-pit of Kashima and made no reply. The injured husband took up the wondrous tale.

'Ride on, and speak to Emma if you want to. God knows I don't care what you do.'

He walked forward, and left Kurrell gazing blankly after him. Kurrell did not ride on either to see Mrs Boulte or Mrs Vansuythen. He sat in his saddle and thought, while his pony grazed by the roadside.

The whir of approaching wheels roused him. Mrs Vansuythen was driving home Mrs Boulte, white and wan, with a cut on her forehead.

'Stop, please,' said Mrs Boulte, 'I want to speak to Ted.'

Mrs Vansuythen obeyed, but as Mrs Boulte leaned forward, putting her hand upon the splashboard of the dog-cart, Kurrell spoke, 'I've seen your husband, Mrs Boulte.'

There was no necessity for any further explanation. The man's eyes were fixed, not upon Mrs Boulte, but her companion. Mrs Boulte saw the look.

'Speak to him!' she pleaded, turning to the woman at her side. 'Oh, speak to him! Tell him what you told me just now. Tell him you hate him. Tell him you hate him!'

She bent forward and wept bitterly, while the sais, impassive, went forward to hold the horse. Mrs Vansuythen turned scarlet and dropped the reins. She wished to be no party to such unholy explanations.

'I've nothing to do with it,' she began coldly; but Mrs Boulte's sobs overcame her, and she addressed herself to the man. 'I don't know what I am to say, Captain Kurrell. I don't know what I can call you. I think you've behaved abominably, and she has cut her forehead terribly against the table.'

'It doesn't hurt. It isn't anything,' said Mrs Boulte feebly. 'That doesn't matter. Tell him what you told me. Say you don't care for him. Oh, Ted, won't you believe her?'

'Mrs Boulte has made me understand that you were fond of her once upon a time,' went on Mrs Vansuythen.

'Well!' said Kurrell brutally. 'It seems to me that Mrs Boulte had better be fond of her own husband first.'

'Stop!' said Mrs Vansuythen. 'Hear me first. I don't care, I don't want to know anything about you and Mrs Boulte; but I want you to know that I hate you, that I think you are a cur, and that I'll never, never speak to you again. Oh, I don't dare to say what I think of you, you man!'

'I want to speak to Ted,' moaned Mrs Boulte, but the dog-cart rattled on, and Kurrell was left on the road, shamed, and boiling with wrath against Mrs Boulte.

He waited till Mrs Vansuythen was driving back to her own house, and she being freed from the embarrassment of Mrs Boulte's presence, learned for the second time her opinion of himself and his actions.

In the evenings it was the wont of all Kashima to meet at the platform on the Narkarra Road, to drink tea and discuss the trivialities of the day. Major Vansuythen and his wife found themselves alone at the gathering-place for almost the first time in their remembrance; and the cheery Major, in the teeth of his wife's remarkably reasonable suggestion that the rest of the Station might be sick, insisted upon driving round to the two bungalows and unearthing the population.

'Sitting in the twilight!' said he, with great indignation, to the Boultes. 'That'll never do! Hang it all, we're one family here! You must come out, and so must Kurrell. I'll make him bring his banjo.'

So great is the power of honest simplicity and a good digestion over guilty consciences that all Kashima did turn out, even down to the banjo; and the Major embraced the company in one expansive grin. As he grinned, Mrs Vansuythen raised her eyes for an instant and looked at all Kashima. Her meaning was clear. Major Vansuythen would never know anything. He was to be the outsider in that happy family whose cage was the Dosehri hills.

'You're singing villainously out of tune, Kurrell,' said the Major truthfully. 'Pass me that banjo.'

And he sang in excruciating-wise till the stars came out and all Kashima went to dinner.

That was the beginning of the New Life of Kashima, the life that Mrs Boulte made when her tongue was loosened in the twilight.

Mrs Vansuythen has never told the Major; and since he insists upon keeping up a burdensome geniality, she has been compelled to break her vow of not speaking to Kurrell. This speech, which must of necessity preserve the semblance of politeness and interest, serves admirably to keep alight the flame of jealousy and dull hatred in Boulte's bosom, as it awakens the same passions in his wife's heart. Mrs Boulte hates Mrs Vansuythen because she has taken Ted from her, and, in some curious fashion, hates her because Mrs Vansuythen, and here the wife's eyes see far more clearly than the husband's, detests Ted. And Ted, that gallant captain and honourable man, knows now that it is possible to hate a woman once loved, to the verge of wishing to silence her for ever with blows. Above all, is he shocked that Mrs Boulte cannot see the error of her ways.

Boulte and he go out tiger-shooting together in all friendship. Boulte has put their relationship on a most satisfactory footing.

'You're a blackguard,' he says to Kurrell, 'and I've lost any self-respect I may ever have had; but when you're with me, I can feel certain that you are not with Mrs Vansuythen, or making Emma miserable.'

Kurrell endures anything that Boulte may say to him. Sometimes they are away for three days together, and then the Major insists upon his wife going over to sit with Mrs Boulte; although Mrs Vansuythen has repeatedly declared that she prefers her husband's company to any in the world. From the way in which she clings to him, she would certainly seem to be speaking the truth.

But of course, as the Major says, 'in a little Station we must all be friendly.'

AT THE PIT'S MOUTH

Men say it was a stolen tide—
The Lord that sent it, He knows all,
But in mine ear will aye abide
The message that the bells let fall—
And awesome bells they were to me,
That in the dark rang, 'Enderby.'

—'The High Tide on the Coast of Lincolnshire' by
Jean Ingelow

Once upon a time there was a Man and his Wife and a Tertium Quid.

All three were unwise, but the Wife was the unwisest. The Man should have looked after his Wife, who should have avoided the Tertium Quid, who, again, should have married a wife of his own, after clean and open flirtations, to which nobody can possibly object, round Jakko or Observatory Hill. When you see a young man with his pony in a white lather and his hat on the back of his head, flying downhill at fifteen miles an hour to meet a girl who will be properly surprised to meet him, you naturally approve of that young man, and wish him Staff appointments, and take an interest in his welfare, and, as the proper time comes, give them sugar-tongs or side-saddles according to your means and generosity.

The Tertium Quid flew downhill on horseback, but it was to meet the Man's Wife; and when he flew uphill it was for the same end. The Man was in the Plains, earning money for his Wife to spend on dresses and four-hundred-rupee bracelets, and inexpensive luxuries of that kind. He worked very hard, and sent her a letter or a post-card daily. She also wrote to him daily, and said that she was longing for him to come up to Simla. The Tertium Quid used to lean over her shoulder and laugh as she wrote the notes. Then the two would ride to the Post Office together.

Now, Simla is a strange place and its customs are peculiar; nor is any man who has not spent at least ten seasons there qualified to pass judgment on circumstantial evidence, which is the most untrustworthy in the Courts. For these reasons, and for others which need not appear, I decline to state positively whether there was anything irretrievably wrong in the relations between the Man's Wife and the Tertium Quid. If there was, and hereon you must form your own opinion, it was the Man's Wife's fault. She was kittenish in her manners, wearing generally an air of soft and fluffy innocence. But she was deadlily learned and evil-instructed; and, now and again, when the mask dropped, men saw this, shuddered and—almost drew back. Men are occasionally particular, and the least particular men are always the most exacting.

Simla is eccentric in its fashion of treating friendships. Certain attachments which have set and crystallized through half-a-dozen seasons acquire almost the sanctity of the marriage bond, and are revered as such. Again, certain attachments equally old, and, to all appearance, equally venerable, never seem to win any recognized official status; while a chance-sprung acquaintance, not two months born, steps into the place which by right belongs to the senior. There is no law reducible to print which regulates these affairs.

Some people have a gift which secures them infinite toleration, and others have not. The Man's Wife had not. If she looked over the garden wall, for instance, women taxed her with stealing their husbands. She complained pathetically that she was not allowed to choose her own friends. When she put up her big white muff to her lips, and gazed over it and under her eyebrows at you as she said this thing, you felt that she had been infamously misjudged, and that all the other women's instincts were all wrong; which was absurd. She was not allowed to own the Tertium Quid in peace; and was so strangely constructed that she would not have enjoyed peace had she been so permitted. She preferred some semblance of intrigue to cloak even her most commonplace actions.

After two months of riding, first round Jakko, then Elysium, then Summer Hill, then Observatory Hill, then under Jutogh, and lastly up and down the Cart Road as far as the Tara Devi gap in the dusk, she said to the Tertium Quid, 'Frank, people say we are too much together, and people are so horrid.'

The Tertium Quid pulled his moustache, and replied that horrid people were unworthy of the consideration of nice people.

'But they have done more than talk—they have written— written to my hubby—I'm sure of it,' said the Man's Wife, and she pulled a letter from her husband out of her saddle-pocket and gave it to the Tertium Quid.

It was an honest letter, written by an honest man, then stewing in the Plains on two hundred rupees a month (for he allowed his wife eight hundred and fifty), and in a silk banian and cotton trousers. It said that, perhaps, she had not thought of the unwisdom of allowing her name to be so generally coupled with the Tertium Quid's; that she was too much of a child to understand the dangers of that sort of thing; that he, her husband, was the last man in the world to interfere jealously with her little amusements and interests, but that it would be better were she to drop the Tertium Quid quietly and for her husband's sake. The letter was sweetened with many pretty little pet names, and it amused the Tertium Quid considerably. He and She laughed over it, so that you, fifty yards away, could see their shoulders shaking while the horses slouched along side by side.

Their conversation was not worth reporting. The upshot of it was that, next day, no one saw the Man's Wife and the Tertium Quid together. They had both gone down to the Cemetery, which, as a rule, is only visited officially by the inhabitants of Simla.

A Simla funeral with the clergyman riding, the mourners riding, and the coffin creaking as it swings between the bearers, is one of the most depressing things on this earth, particularly when the procession passes under the wet, dank dip beneath the Rockcliffe Hotel, where the sun is shut out, and all the hill streams are wailing and weeping together as they go down the valleys.

Occasionally folk tend the graves, but we in India shift and are transferred so often that, at the end of the second year, the Dead have no friends—only acquaintances who are far too busy amusing themselves up the hill to attend to old partners. The idea of using a Cemetery as a rendezvous is distinctly a feminine one. A man would have said simply, 'Let people talk. We'll go down the Mall.' A woman is made differently, especially if she be such a woman as the Man's Wife. She and the Tertium Quid enjoyed each other's society among the graves of men and women whom they had known and danced with aforetime.

They used to take a big horse-blanket and sit on the grass a little to the left of the lower end, where there is a dip in the ground, and where the occupied graves stop short and the ready-made ones are not ready. Each well-regulated Indian Cemetery keeps half-a-dozen graves permanently open for contingencies and incidental wear and tear. In the Hills these are more usually baby's size, because children who come up weakened and sick from the Plains often succumb to the effects of the Rains in the

Hills or get pneumonia from their ayahs taking them through damp pine-woods after the sun has set. In Cantonments, of course, the man's size is more in request; these arrangements varying with the climate and population.

One day when the Man's Wife and the Tertium Quid had just arrived in the Cemetery, they saw some coolies breaking ground. They had marked out a full-size grave, and the Tertium Quid asked them whether any Sahib was sick. They said that they did not know; but it was an order that they should dig a Sahib's grave.

'Work away,' said the Tertium Quid, 'and let's see how it's done.'

The coolies worked away, and the Man's Wife and the Tertium Quid watched and talked for a couple of hours while the grave was being deepened. Then a coolie, taking the earth in baskets as it was thrown up, jumped over the grave.

'That's queer,' said the Tertium Quid. 'Where's my ulster?'

'What's queer?' said the Man's Wife.

'I have got a chill down my back—just as if a goose had walked over my grave.'

'Why do you look at the thing, then?' said the Man's Wife. 'Let us go.'

The Tertium Quid stood at the head of the grave, and stared without answering for a space. Then he said, dropping a pebble down, 'It is nasty—and cold: horribly cold. I don't think I shall come to the Cemetery any more. I don't think grave-digging is cheerful.'

The two talked and agreed that the Cemetery was depressing. They also arranged for a ride next day out from the Cemetery through the Mashobra Tunnel up to Fagoo and back, because all the world was going to a garden-party at Viceregal Lodge, and all the people of Mashobra would go too.

Coming up the Cemetery road, the Tertium Quid's horse tried to bolt uphill, being tired with standing so long, and managed to strain a back sinew.

'I shall have to take the mare to-morrow,' said the Tertium Quid, 'and she will stand nothing heavier than a snaffle.'

They made their arrangements to meet in the Cemetery, after allowing all the Mashobra people time to pass into Simla. That night it rained heavily, and, next day, when the Tertium Quid came to the trysting-place, he saw that the new grave had a foot of water in it, the ground being a tough and sour clay.

''Jove! That looks beastly,' said the Tertium Quid. 'Fancy being boarded up and dropped into that well!'

They then started off to Fagoo, the mare playing with the snaffle and picking her way as though she were shod with satin, and the sun shining divinely. The road below Mashobra to Fagoo is officially styled the Himalayan-Thibet Road; but in spite of its name it is not much more than six feet wide in most places, and the drop into the valley below may be anything between one and two thousand feet.

'Now we're going to Thibet,' said the Man's Wife merrily, as the horses drew near to Fagoo. She was riding on the cliff-side.

'Into Thibet,' said the Tertium Quid, 'ever so far from people who say horrid things, and hubbies who write stupid letters. With you to the end of the world!'

A coolie carrying a log of wood came round a corner, and the mare went wide to avoid him—forefeet in and haunches out, as a sensible mare should go.

'To the world's end,' said the Man's Wife, and looked unspeakable things over her near shoulder at the Tertium Quid.

He was smiling, but, while she looked, the smile froze stiff as it were on his face, and changed to a nervous grin—the sort of grin men wear when they are not quite easy in their saddles.

The mare seemed to be sinking by the stern, and her nostrils cracked while she was trying to realize what was happening. The rain of the night before had rotted the drop-side of the Himalayan-Thibet Road, and it was giving way under her. 'What are you doing?' said the Man's Wife. The Tertium Quid gave no answer. He grinned nervously and set his spurs into the mare, who rapped with her forefeet on the road, and the struggle began. The Man's Wife screamed, 'Oh, Frank, get off!'

But the Tertium Quid was glued to the saddle—his face blue and white—and he looked into the Man's Wife's eyes. Then the Man's Wife clutched at the mare's head and caught her by the nose instead of the bridle. The brute threw up her head and went down with a scream, the Tertium Quid upon her, and the nervous grin still set on his face.

The Man's Wife heard the tinkle-tinkle of little stones and loose earth falling off the roadway, and the sliding roar of the man and horse going down. Then everything was quiet, and she called on Frank to leave his mare and walk up. But Frank did not answer. He was underneath the mare, nine hundred feet below, spoiling a patch of Indian corn.

As the revellers came back from Viceregal Lodge in the mists of the evening, they met a temporarily insane woman, on a temporarily mad horse, swinging round the corners, with her eyes and her mouth open, and her head like the head of a Medusa. She was stopped by a man at the risk of his life, and taken out of the saddle, a limp heap, and put on the bank to explain herself. This wasted twenty minutes, and then she was sent home in a lady's 'rickshaw, still with her mouth open and her hands picking at her riding-gloves.

She was in bed through the following three days, which were rainy; so she missed attending the funeral of the Tertium Quid, who was lowered into eighteen inches of water, instead of the twelve to which he had first objected.

THE HILL OF ILLUSION

What rendered vain their deep desire?
A God, a God their severance ruled,
And bade between their shores to be
The unplumbed, salt, estranging sea.

—'To Marguerite: Continued' by Matthew Arnold

HE. Tell your jhampanies not to hurry so, dear. They forget I'm fresh from the Plains.

SHE. Sure proof that I have not been going out with any one. Yes, they are an untrained crew. Where do we go?

HE. As usual—to the world's end. No, Jakko.

SHE. Have your pony led after you, then. It's a long round.

HE. And for the last time, thank Heaven!

SHE. Do you mean that still? I didn't dare to write to you about it—all these months.

HE. Mean it! I've been shaping my affairs to that end since Autumn. What makes you speak as though it had occurred to you for the first time?

SHE. I? Oh! I don't know. I've had long enough to think, too.

HE. And you've changed your mind?

SHE. No. You ought to know that I am a miracle of constancy. What are your—arrangements?

HE. Ours, Sweetheart, please.

SHE. Ours, be it then. My poor boy, how the prickly heat has marked your forehead! Have you ever tried sulphate of copper in water?

HE. It'll go away in a day or two up here. The arrangements are simple enough. Tonga in the early morning—reach Kalka at twelve—Umballa at seven—down, straight by night train, to Bombay, and then the steamer of the 21st for Rome. That's my idea. The Continent and Sweden—a ten-week honeymoon.

SHE. Ssh! Don't talk of it in that way. It makes me afraid. Guy, how long have we two been insane?

HE. Seven months and fourteen days, I forget the odd hours exactly, but I'll think.

SHE. I only wanted to see if you remembered. Who are those two on the Blessington Road?

HE. Eabrey and the Penner Woman. What do they matter to us? Tell me everything that you've been doing and saying and thinking.

SHE. Doing little, saying less, and thinking a great deal. I've hardly been out at all.

HE. That was wrong of you. You haven't been moping?

SHE. Not very much. Can you wonder that I'm disinclined for amusement?

HE. Frankly, I do. Where was the difficulty?

SHE. In this only. The more people I know and the more I'm known here, the wider spread will be the news of the crash when it comes. I don't like that.

HE. Nonsense. We shall be out of it.

SHE. You think so?

HE. I'm sure of it, if there is any power in steam or horse-flesh to carry us away. Ha! ha!

SHE. And the fun of the situation comes in—where, my Lancelot?

HE. Nowhere, Guinevere. I was only thinking of something.

SHE. They say men have a keener sense of humour than women. Now I was thinking of the scandal.

HE. Don't think of anything so ugly. We shall be beyond it.

SHE. It will be there all the same—in the mouths of Simla—telegraphed over India, and talked of at the dinners—and when He goes out they will stare at Him to see how he takes it. And we shall be dead, Guy dear—dead and cast into the outer darkness where there is—

HE. Love at least. Isn't that enough?

SHE. I have said so.

HE. And you think so still?

SHE. What do you think?

HE. What have I done? It means equal ruin to me, as the world reckons it—outcasting, the loss of my appointment, the breaking off my life's work. I pay my price.

SHE. And are you so much above the world that you can afford to pay it. Am I?

HE. My Divinity—what else?

SHE. A very ordinary woman, I'm afraid, but so far, respectable. How d'you do, Mrs Middleditch? Your husband? I think he's riding down to Annandale with Colonel Statters. Yes, isn't it divine after the rain?—Guy, how long am I to be allowed to bow to Mrs Middleditch? Till the 17th?

HE. Frowsy Scotchwoman! What is the use of bringing her into the discussion? You were saying?

SHE. Nothing. Have you ever seen a man hanged?

HE. Yes. Once.

SHE. What was it for?

HE. Murder, of course.

SHE. Murder. Is that so great a sin after all? I wonder how he felt before the drop fell.

HE. I don't think he felt much. What a gruesome little woman it is this evening! You're shivering. Put on your cape, dear.

SHE. I think I will. Oh! Look at the mist coming over Sanjaoli; and I thought we should have sunshine on the Ladies' Mile! Let's turn back.

HE. What's the good? There's a cloud on Elysium Hill, and that means it's foggy all down the Mall. We'll go on. It'll blow away before we get to the Convent, perhaps. 'Jove! It is chilly.

SHE. You feel it, fresh from below. Put on your ulster. What do you think of my cape?

HE. Never ask a man his opinion of a woman's dress when he is desperately and abjectly in love with the wearer. Let me look. Like everything else of yours it's perfect. Where did you get it from?

SHE. He gave it me, on Wednesday—our wedding-day, you know.

HE. The Deuce He did! He's growing generous in his old age. D'you like all that frilly, bunchy stuff at the throat? I don't.

SHE. Don't you?

> *Kind Sir, o' your courtesy,*
> *As you go by the town, Sir,*
> *Pray you o' your love for me,*
> *Buy me a russet gown, Sir.*

HE. I won't say: *'Keek into the draw-well, Janet, Janet.'* Only wait a little, darling, and you shall be stocked with russet gowns and everything else.

SHE. And when the frocks wear out you'll get me new ones—and everything else?

HE. Assuredly.

SHE. I wonder!

HE. Look here, Sweetheart, I didn't spend two days and two nights in the train to hear you wonder. I thought we'd settled all that at Shaifazehat.

SHE. (*dreamily*). At Shaifazehat? Does the Station go on still? That was ages and ages ago. It must be crumbling to pieces. All except the Amirtollah kutcha road. I don't believe that could crumble till the Day of Judgment.

HE. You think so? What is the mood now?

SHE. I can't tell. How cold it is! Let us get on quickly.

HE. Better walk a little. Stop your jhampanies and get out. What's the matter with you this evening, dear?

SHE. Nothing. You must grow accustomed to my ways. If I'm boring you I can go home. Here's Captain Congleton coming, I daresay he'll be willing to escort me.

HE. Goose! Between us, too! Damn Captain Congleton.

SHE. Chivalrous Knight. Is it your habit to swear much in talking? It jars a little, and you might swear at me.

HE. My angel! I didn't know what I was saying; and you changed so quickly that I couldn't follow. I'll apologize in dust and ashes.

SHE. There'll be enough of those later on—Good-night, Captain Congleton. Going to the singing—quadrilles already? What dances am I giving you next week? No! You must have written them down wrong. Five and Seven, I said. If you've made a mistake, I certainly don't intend to suffer for it. You must alter your programme.

HE. I thought you told me that you had not been going out much this season?

SHE. Quite true, but when I do I dance with Captain Congleton. He dances very nicely.

HE. And sit out with him, I suppose?

SHE. Yes. Have you any objection? Shall I stand under the chandelier in future?

HE. What does he talk to you about?

SHE. What do men talk about when they sit out?

HE. Ugh! Don't! Well, now I'm up, you must dispense with the fascinating Congleton for a while. I don't like him.

SHE. (after a pause). Do you know what you have said?

HE. Can't say that I do exactly. I'm not in the best of tempers.

SHE. So I see—and feel. My true and faithful lover, where is your 'eternal constancy,' 'unalterable trust,' and 'reverent devotion'? I remember those phrases; you seem to have forgotten them. I mention a man's name—

HE. A good deal more than that.

SHE. Well, speak to him about a dance—perhaps the last dance that I shall ever dance in my life before I—before I go away; and you at once distrust and insult me.

HE. I never said a word.

SHE. How much did you imply? Guy, is this amount of confidence to be our stock to start the new life on?

HE. No, of course not. I didn't mean that. On my word and honour, I didn't. Let it pass, dear. Please let it pass.

SHE. This once—yes—and a second time, and again and again, all through the years when I shall be unable to resent it. You want too much, my Lancelot, and—you know too much.

HE. How do you mean?

SHE. That is a part of the punishment. There cannot be perfect trust between us.

HE. In Heaven's name, why not?

SHE. Hush! The Other Place is quite enough. Ask yourself.

HE. I don't follow.

SHE. You trust me so implicitly that when I look at another man—Never mind. Guy, have you ever made love to a girl—a good girl?

HE. Something of the sort. Centuries ago—in the Dark Ages, before I ever met you, dear.

SHE. Tell me what you said to her.

HE. What does a man say to a girl? I've forgotten.

SHE. I remember. He tells her that he trusts her and worships the ground she walks on, and that he'll love and honour and protect her till her dying day; and so she marries in that belief. At least, I speak of one girl who was not protected.

HE. Well, and then?

SHE. And then, Guy, and then, that girl needs ten times the love and trust and honour—yes, honour—that was enough when she was only a mere wife if—if—the other life she chooses to lead is to be made even bearable. Do you understand?

HE. Even bearable! It'll be Paradise.

SHE. Ah! Can you give me all I've asked for—not now, nor a few months later—but when you begin to think of what you might have done if you had kept your own appointment and your caste here—when you begin to look upon me as a drag and a burden? I shall want it most then, Guy, for there will be no one in the wide world but you.

HE. You're a little over-tired to-night, Sweetheart, and you're taking a stage view of the situation. After the necessary business in the Courts, the road is clear to—

SHE. 'The holy state of matrimony!' Ha! ha! ha!

HE. Ssh! Don't laugh in that horrible way!

SHE. I—I—c-c-c-can't help it! Isn't it too absurd! Ah! Ha! ha! ha! Guy, stop me quick or I shall—l-l-laugh till we get to the Church.

HE. For goodness sake, stop! Don't make an exhibition of yourself. What is the matter with you?

SHE. N-nothing. I'm better now.

HE. That's all right. One moment, dear. There's a little wisp of hair got loose from behind your right ear and it's straggling over your cheek. So!

SHE. Thank'oo. I'm 'fraid my hat's on one side, too.

HE. What do you wear these huge dagger bonnet-skewers for? They're big enough to kill a man with.

SHE. Oh! don't kill me, though. You're sticking it into my head! Let me do it. You men are so clumsy.

HE. Have you had many opportunities of comparing us—in this sort of work?

SHE. Guy, what is my name?

HE. Eh! I don't follow.

SHE. Here's my card-case. Can you read?

HE. Yes. Well?

SHE. Well, that answers your question. You know the other's man's name. Am I sufficiently humbled, or would you like to ask me if there is any one else?

HE. I see now. My darling, I never meant that for an instant. I was only joking. There!—Lucky there's no one on the road. They'd be scandalized.

SHE. They'll be more scandalized before the end.

HE. Do-on't! I don't like you to talk in that way.

SHE. Unreasonable man! Who asked me to face the situation and accept it?—Tell me, do I look like Mrs Penner? Do I look like a naughty woman! Swear I don't! Give me your word of honour, my honourable friend, that I'm not like Mrs Buzgago. That's the way she stands, with her hands clasped at the back of her head. D'you like that?

HE. Don't be affected.

SHE. I'm not. I'm Mrs Buzgago. Listen!

> *Pendant une anné' toute entiere,*
> *Le régiment na Pas r'paru.*
> *Au Ministère de la Guerre*
> *On le r'porta comme perdu.*
>
> *On se r'nonçait à r'trouver sa trace,*
> *Quand un matin subitement,*
> *On le vit r'paraître sur la place,*
> *L'Colonel toujours en avant.*

That's the way she rolls her r's. *Am* I like her?

HE. No, but I object when you go on like an actress and sing stuff of that kind. Where in the world did you pick up the Chanson du Colonel? It isn't a drawing-room song. It isn't proper.

SHE. Mrs Buzgago taught it me. She is both drawing-room and proper, and in another month she'll shut her drawing-room to me, and thank God she isn't as improper as I am. Oh, Guy, Guy! I wish I was like some women and had no scruples about—What is it Keene says?—'Wearing a corpse's hair and being false to the bread they eat.'

HE. I am only a man of limited intelligence, and, just now, very bewildered. When you have quite finished flashing through all your moods tell me, and I'll try to understand the last one.

SHE. Moods, Guy! I haven't any. I'm sixteen years old and you're just twenty, and you've been waiting for two hours outside the school in the cold. And now I've met you, and now we're walking home together. Does that suit you, My Imperial Majesty?

HE. No. We aren't children. Why can't you be rational?

SHE. He asks me that when I'm going to commit suicide for his sake, and, and—I don't want to be French and rave about my mother, but have I ever told you that I have a mother, and a brother who was my pet before I married? He's married now. Can't you imagine the pleasure that the news of the elopement will give him? Have you any people at Home, Guy, to be pleased with your performances?

HE. One or two. One can't make omelets without breaking eggs.

SHE. (slowly). I don't see the necessity—

HE. Hah! What do you mean?

SHE. Shall I speak the truth?

HE. Under the circumstances, perhaps it would be as well.

SHE. Guy, I'm afraid.

HE. I thought we'd settled all that. What of?

SHE. Of you.

HE. Oh, damn it all! The old business! This is too bad!

SHE. Of you.

HE. And what now?

SHE. What do you think of me?

HE. Beside the question altogether. What do you intend to do?

SHE. I daren't risk it. I'm afraid. If I could only cheat—

HE. À la Buzgago? No, thanks. That's the one point on which I have any notion of Honour. I won't eat his salt and steal too. I'll loot openly or not at all.

SHE. I never meant anything else.

HE. Then, why in the world do you pretend not to be willing to come?

SHE. It's not pretence, Guy. I am afraid.

HE. Please explain.

SHE. It can't last, Guy. It can't last. You'll get angry, and then you'll swear, and then you'll get jealous, and then you'll mistrust me—you do now—and you yourself will be the best reason for doubting. And I—what shall I do? I shall be no better than Mrs Buzgago found out—no better than any one. And you'll know that. Oh, Guy, can't you see?

HE. I see that you are desperately unreasonable, little woman.

SHE. There! The moment I begin to object, you get angry. What will you do when I am only your property—stolen property? It can't be, Guy. It can't be! I thought it could, but it can't. You'll get tired of me.

HE. I tell you I shall not. Won't anything make you understand that?

SHE. There, can't you see? If you speak to me like that now, you'll call me horrible names later, if I don't do everything as you like. And if you were cruel to me, Guy, where should I go?—where should I go? I can't trust you. Oh! I can't trust you!

HE. I suppose I ought to say that I can trust you. I've ample reason.

SHE. Please don't, dear. It hurts as much as if you hit me.

HE. It isn't exactly pleasant for me.

SHE. I can't help it. I wish I were dead! I can't trust you, and I don't trust myself. Oh, Guy, let it die away and be forgotten!

HE. Too late now. I don't understand you—I won't—and I can't trust myself to talk this evening. May I call to-morrow?

SHE. Yes. No! Oh, give me time! The day after. I get into my 'rickshaw here and meet Him at Peliti's. You ride.

HE. I'll go on to Peliti's too. I think I want a drink. My world's knocked about my ears and the stars are falling. Who are those brutes howling in the Old Library?

SHE. They're rehearsing the singing-quadrilles for the Fancy Ball. Can't you hear Mrs Buzgago's voice? She has a solo. It's quite a new idea. Listen!

Mrs Buzgago (in the Old Library, con molt. exp.).

> See-saw! Margery Daw!
> Sold her bed to lie upon straw.
> Wasn't she a silly slut
> To sell her bed and lie upon dirt?

Captain Congleton, I'm going to alter that to 'flirt.' It sounds better.

HE. No, I've changed my mind about the drink. Good-night, little lady. I shall see you to-morrow?

SHE. Ye—es. Good-night, Guy. Don't be angry with me.

HE. Angry! You know I trust you absolutely. Goodnight and—God bless you!

(Three seconds later. Alone.) Hmm! I'd give something to discover whether there's another man at the back of all this.

THE RESCUE OF PLUFFLES

Thus, for a season, they fought it fair—
She and his cousin May—
Tactful, talented, debonnaire,
Decorous foes were they;
But never can battle of man compare
With merciless feminine fray.

—'Two and One'

Mrs Hauksbee was sometimes nice to her own sex. Here is a story to prove this; and you can believe just as much as ever you please.

Pluffles was a subaltern in the 'Unmentionables'. He was callow, even for a subaltern. He was callow all over—like a canary that had not finished fledging itself. The worst of it was he had three times as much money as was good for him; Pluffles' Papa being a rich man and Pluffles being the only son. Pluffles' Mamma adored him. She was only a little less callow than Pluffles and she believed everything he said.

Pluffles' weakness was not believing what people said. He preferred what he called 'trusting to his own judgment.' He had as much judgment as he had seat or hands; and this preference tumbled him into trouble once or twice. But the biggest trouble Pluffles ever manufactured came about at Simla—some years ago, when he was four-and-twenty.

He began by trusting to his own judgment, as usual, and the result was that, after a time, he was bound hand and foot to Mrs Reiver's 'rickshaw wheels.

There was nothing good about Mrs Reiver, unless it was her dress. She was bad from her hair—which started life on a

Brittany's girl's head—to her boot-heels, which were two and three-eighth inches high. She was not honestly mischievous like Mrs Hauksbee; she was wicked in a business-like way.

There was never any scandal—she had not generous impulses enough for that. She was the exception which proved the rule that Anglo–Indian ladies are in every way as nice as their sisters at Home. She spent her life in proving that rule.

Mrs Hauksbee and she hated each other fervently. They heard far too much to clash; but the things they said of each other were startling—not to say original. Mrs Hauksbee was honest—honest as her own front teeth—and, but for her love of mischief, would have been a woman's woman. There was no honesty about Mrs Reiver; nothing but selfishness. And at the beginning of the season, poor little Pluffles fell a prey to her. She laid herself out to that end, and who was Pluffles, to resist? He went on trusting to his judgment, and he got judged.

I have seen Hayes argue with a tough horse—I have seen a tonga-driver coerce a stubborn pony—I have seen a riotous setter broken to gun by a hard keeper—but the breaking-in of Pluffles of the 'Unmentionables' was beyond all these. He learned to fetch and carry like a dog, and to wait like one, too, for a word from Mrs Reiver. He learned to keep appointments which Mrs Reiver had no intention of keeping. He learned to take thankfully dances which Mrs Reiver had no intention of giving him. He learned to shiver for an hour and a quarter on the windward side of Elysium while Mrs Reiver was making up her mind to come for a ride. He learned to hunt for a 'rickshaw, in a light dress-suit under a pelting rain, and to walk by the side of that 'rickshaw when he had found it. He learned what it was to be spoken to like a coolie and ordered about like a cook. He learned all this and many other things besides. And he paid for his schooling.

Perhaps, in some hazy way, he fancied that it was fine and impressive, that it gave him a status among men, and was altogether the thing to do. It was nobody's business to warn Pluffles that he was unwise. The pace that season was too good to inquire; and meddling with another man's folly is always thankless work. Pluffles' Colonel should have ordered him back to his regiment when he heard how things were going. But Pluffles had got himself engaged to a girl in England the last time he went home; and if there was one thing more than another which the Colonel detested, it was a married subaltern. He chuckled when he heard of the education of Pluffles, and said it was 'good training for the boy.' But it was not good training in the least. It led him into spending money beyond his means, which were good: above that, the education spoilt an average boy and made it a tenth-rate man of an objectionable kind. He wandered into a bad set, and his little bill at Hamilton's was a thing to wonder at.

Then Mrs Hauksbee rose to the occasion. She played her game alone, knowing what people would say of her; and she played it for the sake of a girl she had never seen. Pluffles' fiancée was to come out, under the chaperonage of an aunt, in October, to be married to Pluffles.

At the beginning of August, Mrs Hauksbee discovered that it was time to interfere. A man who rides much knows exactly what a horse is going to do next before he does it. In the same way, a woman of Mrs Hauksbee's experience knows accurately how a boy will behave under certain circumstances—notably when he is infatuated with one of Mrs Reiver's stamp. She said that, sooner or later, little Pluffles would break off that engagement for nothing at all—simply to gratify Mrs Reiver, who, in return, would keep him at her feet and in her service just so long as she found it worth her while. She said she knew the signs of these things. If she did not, no one else could.

Then she went forth to capture Pluffles under the guns of
the enemy; just as Mrs Cusack–Bremmil carried away Bremmil
under Mrs Hauksbee's eyes.

This particular engagement lasted seven weeks—we called
it the Seven Weeks' War—and was fought out inch by inch on
both sides. A detailed account would fill a book, and would be
incomplete then. Any one who knows about these things can
fit in the details for himself. It was a superb fight—there will
never be another like it as long as Jakko stands—and Pluffles
was the prize of victory. People said shameful things about
Mrs Hauksbee. They did not know what she was playing for.
Mrs Reiver fought, partly because Pluffles was useful to her, but
mainly because she hated Mrs Hauksbee, and the matter was
a trial of strength between them. No one knows what Pluffles
thought. He had not many ideas at the best of times, and the
few he possessed made him conceited. Mrs Hauksbee said,
'The boy must be caught; and the only way of catching him is
by treating him well.'

So she treated him as a man of the world and of experience
so long as the issue was doubtful. Little by little, Pluffles fell
away from his old allegiance and came over to the enemy, by
whom he was made much of. He was never sent on out-post
duty after 'rickshaws any more, nor was he given dances which
never came off, nor were the drains on his purse continued.
Mrs Hauksbee held him on the snaffle; and after his treatment
at Mrs Reiver's hands, he appreciated the change.

Mrs Reiver had broken him of talking about himself, and
made him talk about her own merits. Mrs Hauksbee acted
otherwise, and won his confidence, till he mentioned his
engagement to the girl at Home, speaking of it in a high and
mighty way as a 'piece of boyish folly.' This was when he was
taking tea with her one afternoon, and discoursing in what he

considered a gay and fascinating style. Mrs Hauksbee had seen an earlier generation of his stamp bud and blossom, and decay into fat Captains and tubby Majors.

At a moderate estimate there were about three-and-twenty sides to that lady's character. Some men say more. She began to talk to Pluffles after the manner of a mother, and as if there had been three hundred years, instead of fifteen, between them. She spoke with a sort of throaty quaver in her voice which had a soothing effect, though what she said was anything but soothing. She pointed out the exceeding folly, not to say meanness, of Pluffles' conduct, and the smallness of his views. Then he stammered something about 'trusting to his own judgment as a man of the world;' and this paved the way for what she wanted to say next. It would have withered up Pluffles had it come from any other woman; but in the soft cooing style in which Mrs Hauksbee put it, it only made him feel limp and repentant—as if he had been in some superior kind of church. Little by little, very softly and pleasantly, she began taking the conceit out of Pluffles, as you take the ribs out of an umbrella before re-covering it. She told him what she thought of him and his judgment and his knowledge of the world; and how his performances had made him ridiculous to other people; and how it was his intention to make love to herself if she gave him the chance. Then she said that marriage would be the making of him; and drew a pretty little picture—all rose and opal—of the Mrs Pluffles of the future going through life relying on the 'judgment' and 'knowledge of the world' of a husband who had nothing to reproach himself with. How she reconciled these two statements she alone knew. But they did not strike Pluffles as conflicting.

Hers was a perfect little homily—much better than any clergyman could have given—and it ended with touching allusions to Pluffles' Mamma and Papa, and the wisdom of taking his bride Home.

Then she sent Pluffles out for a walk, to think over what she had said. Pluffles left, blowing his nose very hard and holding himself very straight. Mrs Hauksbee laughed.

What Pluffles had intended to do in the matter of the engagement only Mrs Reiver knew, and she kept her own counsel to her death. She would have liked it spoiled as a compliment, I fancy.

Pluffles enjoyed many talks with Mrs Hauksbee during the next few days. They were all to the same end, and they helped Pluffles in the path of Virtue.

Mrs Hauksbee wanted to keep him under her wing to the last. Therefore she discountenanced his going down to Bombay to get married. 'Goodness only knows what might happen by the way!' she said. 'Pluffles is cursed with the curse of Reuben, and India is no fit place for him!'

In the end, the fiancée arrived with her aunt; and Pluffles, having reduced his affairs to some sort of order—here again Mrs Hauksbee helped him—was married.

Mrs Hauksbee gave a sigh of relief when both the 'I wills' had been said, and went her way.

Pluffies took her advice about going Home. He left the Service, and is now raising speckled cattle inside green-painted fences somewhere at Home. I believe he does this very judiciously. He would have come to extreme grief out here.

For these reasons if any one says anything more than usually nasty about Mrs Hauksbee, tell him the story of the Rescue of Pluffles.

ON THE STRENGTH OF A LIKENESS

'If your mirror be broken, look into still water;
but have a care that you do not fall in.'

—Hindu proverb

Next to a requited attachment, one of the most convenient things that a young man can carry about with him at the beginning of his career, is an unrequited attachment. It makes him feel important and business-like, and blasé, and cynical; and whenever he has a touch of liver, or suffers from want of exercise, he can mourn over his lost love, and be very happy in a tender, twilight fashion.

Hannasyde's affair of the heart had been a Godsend to him. It was four years old, and the girl had long since given up thinking of it. She had married and had many cares of her own. In the beginning, she had told Hannasyde that, 'while she could never be anything more than a sister to him, she would always take the deepest interest in his welfare.' This startlingly new and original remark gave Hannasyde something to think over for two years; and his own vanity filled in the other twenty-four months. Hannasyde was quite different from Phil Garron, but, none the less, had several points in common with that far too lucky man.

He kept his unrequited attachment by him as men keep a well-smoked pipe—for comfort's sake, and because it had grown dear in the using. It brought him happily through the Simla season. Hannasyde was not lovely. There was a crudity in his manners, and a roughness in the way in which he helped a lady on to her horse, that did not attract the other sex to him.

Even if he had cast about for their favour, which he did not. He kept his wounded heart all to himself for a while.

Then trouble came to him. All who go to Simla, know the slope from the Telegraph to the Public Works Office. Hannasyde was loafing up the hill, one September morning between calling hours, when a 'rickshaw came down in a hurry, and in the 'rickshaw sat the living, breathing image of the girl who had made him so happily unhappy. Hannasyde leaned against the railing and gasped. He wanted to run downhill after the 'rickshaw, but that was impossible; so he went forward with most of his blood in his temples. It was impossible, for many reasons, that the woman in the 'rickshaw could be the girl he had known. She was, he discovered later, the wife of a man from Dindigul, or Coimbatore, or some out-of-the-way place, and she had come up to Simla early in the season for the good of her health. She was going back to Dindigul, or wherever it was, at the end of the season; and in all likelihood would never return to Simla again, her proper Hill-station being Ootacamund. That night, Hannasyde, raw and savage from the raking up of all old feelings, took counsel with himself for one measured hour. What he decided upon was this; and you must decide for yourself how much genuine affection for the old love, and how much a very natural inclination to go abroad and enjoy himself, affected the decision. Mrs Landys–Haggert would never in all human likelihood cross his path again. So whatever he did didn't much matter. She was marvellously like the girl who 'took a deep interest' and the rest of the formula. All things considered, it would be pleasant to make the acquaintance of Mrs Landys–Haggert, and for a little time—only a very little time—to make believe that he was with Alice Chisane again. Every one is more or less mad on one point. Hannasyde's particular monomania was his old love, Alice Chisane.

He made it his business to get introduced to Mrs Haggert, and the introduction prospered. He also made it his business to see as much as he could of that lady. When a man is in earnest as to interviews, the facilities which Simla offers are startling. There are garden-parties, and tennis-parties, and picnics, and luncheons at Annandale, and rifle-matches, and dinners and balls; besides rides and walks, which are matters of private arrangement. Hannasyde had started with the intention of seeing a likeness, and he ended by doing much more. He wanted to be deceived, he meant to be deceived, and he deceived himself very thoroughly. Not only were the face and figure, the face and figure of Alice Chisane, but the voice and lower tones were exactly the same, and so were the turns of speech; and the little mannerisms, that every woman has, of gait and gesticulation, were absolutely and identically the same. The turn of the head was the same; the tired look in the eyes at the end of a long walk was the same; the stoop and wrench over the saddle to hold in a pulling horse was the same; and once, most marvellous of all, Mrs Landys–Haggert singing to herself in the next room, while Hannasyde was waiting to take her for a ride, hummed, note for note, with a throaty quiver of the voice in the second line: 'Poor Wandering One!' exactly as Alice Chisane had hummed it for Hannasyde in the dusk of an English drawing-room. In the actual woman herself—in the soul of her—there was not the least likeness; she and Alice Chisane being cast in different moulds. But all that Hannasyde wanted to know and see and think about, was this maddening and perplexing likeness of face and voice and manner. He was bent on making a fool of himself that way; and he was in no sort disappointed.

Open and obvious devotion from any sort of man is always pleasant to any sort of woman; but Mrs Landys–Haggert, being a woman of the world, could make nothing of Hannasyde's admiration.

He would take any amount of trouble—he was a selfish man habitually—to meet and forestall, if possible, her wishes. Anything she told him to do was law; and he was, there could be no doubting it, fond of her company so long as she talked to him, and kept on talking about trivialities. But when she launched into expression of her personal views and her wrongs, those small social differences that make the spice of Simla life, Hannasyde was neither pleased nor interested. He didn't want to know anything about Mrs Landys–Haggert, or her experiences in the past—she had travelled nearly all over the world, and could talk cleverly—he wanted the likeness of Alice Chisane before his eyes and her voice in his ears. Anything outside that, reminding him of another personality, jarred, and he showed that it did.

Under the new Post Office, one evening, Mrs Landys–Haggert turned on him, and spoke her mind shortly and without warning. 'Mr Hannasyde,' said she, 'will you be good enough to explain why you have appointed yourself my special cavalier servente? I don't understand it. But I am perfectly certain, somehow or other, that you don't care the least little bit in the world for ME.' This seems to support, by the way, the theory that no man can act or tell lies to a woman without being found out. Hannasyde was taken off his guard. His defence never was a strong one, because he was always thinking of himself, and he blurted out, before he knew what he was saying, this inexpedient answer: 'No more I do.'

The queerness of the situation and the reply, made Mrs Landys–Haggert laugh. Then it all came out; and at the end of Hannasyde's lucid explanation, Mrs Haggert said, with the least little touch of scorn in her voice: 'So I'm to act as the lay-figure for you to hang the rags of your tattered affections on, am I?'

Hannasyde didn't see what answer was required, and he devoted himself generally and vaguely to the praise of Alice Chisane, which was unsatisfactory. Now it is to be thoroughly made clear that Mrs Haggert had not the shadow of a ghost of an interest in Hannasyde. Only... only no woman likes being made love through instead of to—specially on behalf of a musty divinity of four years' standing.

Hannasyde did not see that he had made any very particular exhibition of himself. He was glad to find a sympathetic soul in the arid wastes of Simla.

When the season ended, Hannasyde went down to his own place and Mrs Haggert to hers. 'It was like making love to a ghost,' said Hannasyde to himself, 'and it doesn't matter; and now I'll get to my work.' But he found himself thinking steadily of the Haggert–Chisane ghost; and he could not be certain whether it was Haggert or Chisane that made up the greater part of the pretty phantom.

~

He got understanding a month later.

A peculiar point of this peculiar country is the way in which a heartless Government transfers men from one end of the Empire to the other. You can never be sure of getting rid of a friend or an enemy till he or she dies. There was a case once— but that's another story.

Haggert's Department ordered him up from Dindigul to the Frontier at two days' notice, and he went through, losing money at every step, from Dindigul to his station. He dropped Mrs Haggert at Lucknow, to stay with some friends there, to take part in a big ball at the Chutter Munzil, and to come on when he had made the new home a little comfortable. Lucknow was Hannasyde's station, and Mrs Haggert stayed a week there. Hannasyde went to meet her. As the train came in, he discovered which he had been thinking of for the past month. The unwisdom of his conduct also struck him. The Lucknow week, with two dances, and an unlimited quantity of rides together, clinched matters; and Hannasyde found himself pacing this circle of thought: He adored Alice Chisane—at least he HAD adored her. AND he admired Mrs Landys–Haggert because she was like Alice Chisane. BUT Mrs Landys–Haggert was not in the least like Alice Chisane, being a thousand times more adorable. NOW Alice Chisane was 'the bride of another,' and so was Mrs Landys–Haggert, and a good and honest wife too. THEREFORE, he, Hannasyde, was…here he called himself several hard names, and wished that he had been wise in the beginning.

Whether Mrs Landys–Haggert saw what was going on in his mind, she alone knows. He seemed to take an unqualified interest in everything connected with herself, as distinguished from the Alice–Chisane likeness, and he said one or two things which, if Alice Chisane had been still betrothed to him, could scarcely have been excused, even on the grounds of the likeness. But Mrs Haggert turned the remarks aside, and spent a long time in making Hannasyde see what a comfort and a pleasure she had been to him because of her strange resemblance to his old love. Hannasyde groaned in his saddle and said, 'Yes, indeed,' and busied himself with preparations for her departure to the Frontier, feeling very small and miserable.

The last day of her stay at Lucknow came, and Hannasyde saw her off at the Railway Station. She was very grateful for his kindness and the trouble he had taken, and smiled pleasantly and sympathetically as one who knew the Alice-Chisane reason of that kindness. And Hannasyde abused the coolies with the luggage, and hustled the people on the platform, and prayed that the roof might fall in and slay him.

As the train went out slowly, Mrs Landys–Haggert leaned out of the window to say goodbye: 'On second thoughts au revoir, Mr Hannasyde. I go Home in the Spring, and perhaps I may meet you in Town.'

Hannasyde shook hands, and said very earnestly and adoringly: 'I hope to Heaven I shall never see your face again!'

And Mrs Haggert understood.

VENUS ANNODOMINI

And the years went on as the years must do;
But our great Diana was always new—
Fresh, and blooming, and blonde, and fair,
With azure eyes and with aureate hair;
And all the folk, as they came or went,
Offered her praise to her heart's content.

—'Diana of Ephesus'

She had nothing to do with Number Eighteen in the Braccio Nuovo of the Vatican, between Visconti's Ceres and the God of the Nile. She was purely an Indian deity—an Anglo–Indian deity, that is to say—and we called her THE Venus Annodomini, to distinguish her from other Annodominis of the same everlasting order. There was a legend among the Hills that she had once been young; but no living man was prepared to come forward and say boldly that the legend was true. Men rode up to Simla, and stayed, and went away and made their name and did their life's work, and returned again to find the Venus Annodomini exactly as they had left her. She was as immutable as the Hills. But not quite so green. All that a girl of eighteen could do in the way of riding, walking, dancing, picnicking and over-exertion generally, the Venus Annodomini did, and showed no sign of fatigue or trace of weariness. Besides perpetual youth, she had discovered, men said, the secret of perpetual health; and her fame spread about the land. From a mere woman, she grew to be an Institution, insomuch that no young man could be said to be properly formed, who had not, at some time or another, worshipped at the shrine of the

Venus Annodomini. There was no one like her, though there were many imitations. Six years in her eyes were no more than six months to ordinary women; and ten made less visible impression on her than does a week's fever on an ordinary woman. Every one adored her, and in return she was pleasant and courteous to nearly every one. Youth had been a habit of hers for so long, that she could not part with it—never realized, in fact, the necessity of parting with it—and took for her more chosen associates young people.

Among the worshippers of the Venus Annodomini was young Gayerson. 'Very Young' Gayerson, he was called to distinguish him from his father 'Young' Gayerson, a Bengal Civilian, who affected the customs—as he had the heart—of youth. 'Very Young' Gayerson was not content to worship placidly and for form's sake, as the other young men did, or to accept a ride or a dance, or a talk from the Venus Annodomini in a properly humble and thankful spirit. He was exacting, and, therefore, the Venus Annodomini repressed him. He worried himself nearly sick in a futile sort of way over her; and his devotion and earnestness made him appear either shy or boisterous or rude, as his mood might vary, by the side of the older men who, with him, bowed before the Venus Annodomini. She was sorry for him. He reminded her of a lad who, three-and-twenty years ago, had professed a boundless devotion for her, and for whom in return she had felt something more than a week's weakness. But that lad had fallen away and married another woman less than a year after he had worshipped her; and the Venus Annodomini had almost—not quite—forgotten his name. 'Very Young' Gayerson had the same big blue eyes and the same way of pouting his underlip when he was excited or troubled. But the Venus Annodomini checked him sternly none the less. Too much zeal was a thing that she did not approve of; preferring instead, a tempered and sober tenderness.

'Very Young' Gayerson was miserable, and took no trouble to conceal his wretchedness. He was in the Army—a Line regiment I think, but am not certain—and, since his face was a looking-glass and his forehead an open book, by reason of his innocence, his brothers in arms made his life a burden to him and embittered his naturally sweet disposition. No one except 'Very Young' Gayerson, and he never told his views, knew how old 'Very Young' Gayerson believed the Venus Annodomini to be. Perhaps he thought her five and twenty, or perhaps she told him that she was this age. 'Very Young' Gayerson would have forded the Gugger in flood to carry her lightest word, and had implicit faith in her. Every one liked him, and every one was sorry when they saw him so bound a slave of the Venus Annodomini. Every one, too, admitted that it was not her fault; for the Venus Annodomini differed from Mrs Hauksbee and Mrs Reiver in this particular—she never moved a finger to attract any one; but, like Ninon de l'Enclos, all men were attracted to her. One could admire and respect Mrs Hauksbee, despise and avoid Mrs Reiver, but one was forced to adore the Venus Annodomini.

'Very Young' Gayerson's papa held a Division or a Collectorate or something administrative in a particularly unpleasant part of Bengal—full of Babus who edited newspapers proving that 'Young' Gayerson was a 'Nero' and a 'Scylla' and a 'Charybdis'; and, in addition to the Babus, there was a good deal of dysentery and cholera abroad for nine months of the year. 'Young' Gayerson—he was about five and forty—rather liked Babus; they amused him, but he objected to dysentery, and when he could get away, went to Darjiling for the most part. This particular season he fancied that he would come up to Simla, and see his boy. The boy was not altogether pleased. He told the Venus Annodomini that his father was coming up, and she flushed a little and said that she should be delighted to make his acquaintance. Then she looked long and thoughtfully at 'Very Young' Gayerson; because she was very, very sorry for him, and he was a very, very big idiot.

'My daughter is coming out in a fortnight, Mr Gayerson,' she said.

'Your WHAT?' said he.

'Daughter,' said the Venus Annodomini. 'She's been out for a year at Home already, and I want her to see a little of India. She is nineteen and a very sensible, nice girl I believe.'

'Very Young' Gayerson, who was a short twenty-two years old, nearly fell out of his chair with astonishment; for he had persisted in believing, against all belief, in the youth of the Venus Annodomini. She, with her back to the curtained window, watched the effect of her sentences and smiled.

'Very Young' Gayerson's papa came up twelve days later, and had not been in Simla four-and-twenty hours, before two men, old acquaintances of his, had told him how 'Very Young' Gayerson had been conducting himself.

'Young' Gayerson laughed a good deal, and inquired who the Venus Annodomini might be. Which proves that he had been living in Bengal where nobody knows anything except the rate of Exchange. Then he said, 'Boys will be boys,' and spoke to his son about the matter. 'Very Young' Gayerson said that he felt wretched and unhappy; and 'Young' Gayerson said that he repented of having helped to bring a fool into the world. He suggested that his son had better cut his leave short and go down to his duties. This led to an unfilial answer, and relations were strained, until 'Young' Gayerson demanded that they should call on the Venus Annodomini. 'Very Young' Gayerson went with his papa, feeling, somehow, uncomfortable and small.

The Venus Annodomini received them graciously and 'Young' Gayerson said, 'By Jove! It's Kitty!' 'Very Young'

Gayerson would have listened for an explanation, if his time had not been taken up with trying to talk to a large, handsome, quiet, well-dressed girl—introduced to him by the Venus Annodomini as her daughter. She was far older in manners, style and repose than 'Very Young' Gayerson; and, as he realized this thing, he felt sick.

Presently, he heard the Venus Annodomini saying, 'Do you know that your son is one of my most devoted admirers?'

'I don't wonder,' said 'Young' Gayerson. Here he raised his voice, 'He follows his father's footsteps. Didn't I worship the ground you trod on, ever so long ago, Kitty—and you haven't changed since then. How strange it all seems!'

'Very Young' Gayerson said nothing. His conversation with the daughter of the Venus Annodomini was, through the rest of the call, fragmentary and disjointed.

~

'At five, tomorrow then,' said the Venus Annodomini. 'And mind you are punctual.'

'At five punctual,' said 'Young' Gayerson. 'You can lend your old father a horse I dare say, youngster, can't you? I'm going for a ride tomorrow afternoon.'

'Certainly,' said 'Very Young' Gayerson. 'I am going down tomorrow morning. My ponies are at your service, Sir.'

The Venus Annodomini looked at him across the half-light of the room, and her big gray eyes filled with moisture. She rose and shook hands with him.

'Good-bye, Tom,' whispered the Venus Annodomini.

TO BE FILED FOR REFERENCE

By the hoof of the Wild Goat up-tossed
From the Cliff where She lay in the Sun,
    Fell the Stone
To the Tarn where the daylight is lost;
So She fell from the light of the Sun,
And alone.

Now the fall was ordained from the first,
With the Goat and the Cliff and the Tarn,
    But the Stone
Knows only Her life is accursed,
As She sinks in the depths of the Tarn,
And alone.

Oh, Thou who hast builded the world!
Oh, Thou who hast lighted the Sun!
Oh, Thou who hast darkened the Tarn!
    Judge Thou
The sin of the Stone that was hurled
By the Goat from the light of the Sun,
As She sinks in the mire of the Tarn,
      Even now—even now—even now!
        —From the unpublished papers of McIntosh Jellaludin

'SAY is it dawn, is it dusk in thy Bower,
Thou whom I long for, who longest for me?
Oh, be it night—be it—'

    Here he fell over a little camel-colt that was sleeping in the Serai where the horse-traders and the best of the blackguards from Central Asia live; and, because he was very drunk indeed and the night was dark, he could not rise again till I helped him. That was the beginning of my acquaintance with McIntosh Jellaludin. When a loafer, and drunk, sings 'The Song of the Bower,' he must be worth cultivating. He got off the camel's back and said, rather thickly, 'I—I—I'm a bit screwed, but a dip in Loggerhead will put me right again; and, I say, have you spoken to Symonds about the mare's knees?'

Now Loggerhead was six thousand weary miles away from us, close to Mesopotamia, where you mustn't fish and poaching is impossible, and Charley Symonds' stable a half mile farther across the paddocks. It was strange to hear all the old names, on a May night, among the horses and camels of the Sultan Caravanserai. Then the man seemed to remember himself and sober down at the same time. He leaned against the camel and pointed to a corner of the Serai where a lamp was burning.

'I live there,' said he, 'and I should be extremely obliged if you would be good enough to help my mutinous feet thither; for I am more than usually drunk—most—most phenomenally tight. But not in respect to my head. "My brain cries out against"—how does it go? But my head rides on the—rolls on the dunghill I should have said, and controls the qualm—'

I helped him through the gangs of tethered horses, and he collapsed on the edge of the verandah in front of the line of native quarters.

'Thanks—a thousand thanks! O Moon and little, little Stars! To think that a man should so shamelessly... Infamous liquor too. Ovid in exile drank no worse. Better. It was frozen. Alas! I had no ice. Good-night. I would introduce you to my wife were I sober—or she civilized.'

A native woman came out of the darkness of the room and began calling the man names, so I went away. He was the most interesting loafer that I had had the pleasure of knowing for a long time; and later on, he became a friend of mine. He was a tall, well-built, fair man, fearfully shaken with drink, and he looked nearer fifty than the thirty-five which, he said, was his real age. When a man begins to sink in India, and is not sent Home by his friends as soon as may be, he falls very low from a respectable point of view. By the time that he changes his creed, as did McIntosh, he is past redemption.

In most big cities natives will tell you of two or three sahibs, generally low-caste, who have turned Hindu or Mussulman, and who live more or less as such. But it is not often that you can get to know them. As McIntosh himself used to say, 'If I change my religion for my stomach's sake, I do not seek to become a martyr to missionaries, nor am I anxious for notoriety.'

At the outset of acquaintance McIntosh warned me. 'Remember this. I am not an object for charity. I require neither your money, your food, nor your cast-off raiment. I am that rare animal, a self-supporting drunkard. If you choose, I will smoke with you, for the tobacco of the bazars does not, I admit, suit my palate; and I will borrow any books which you may not specially value. It is more than likely that I shall sell them for bottles of excessively filthy country-liquors. In return, you shall share such hospitality as my house affords. Here is a charpoy on which two can sit, and it is possible that there may, from time to time, be food in that platter. Drink, unfortunately, you will find on the premises at any hour; and thus I make you welcome to all my poor establishment.'

I was admitted to the McIntosh household—I and my good tobacco. But nothing else. Unluckily, one cannot visit a loafer in the Serai by day. Friends buying horses would not understand it. Consequently, I was obliged to see McIntosh after dark. He laughed at this, and said simply, 'You are perfectly right. When

I enjoyed a position in society, rather higher than yours, I should have done exactly the same thing. Good Heavens! I was once'—he spoke as though he had fallen from the Command of a Regiment—'an Oxford Man!' This accounted for the reference to Charley Symonds' stable.

'You,' said McIntosh slowly, 'have not had that advantage; but, to outward appearance, you do not seem possessed of a craving for strong drinks. On the whole, I fancy that you are the luckier of the two. Yet I am not certain. You are—forgive my saying so even while I am smoking your excellent tobacco— painfully ignorant of many things.'

We were sitting together on the edge of his bedstead, for he owned no chairs, watching the horses being watered for the night, while the native woman was preparing dinner. I did not like being patronized by a loafer, but I was his guest for the time being, though he owned only one very torn alpaca coat and a pair of trousers made out of gunny-bags. He took the pipe out of his mouth, and went on judicially, 'All things considered, I doubt whether you are the luckier. I do not refer to your extremely limited classical attainments, or your excruciating quantities, but to your gross ignorance of matters more immediately under your notice. That, for instance;' he pointed to a woman cleaning a samovar near the well in the centre of the Serai. She was flicking the water out of the spout in regular cadenced jerks.

'There are ways and ways of cleaning samovars. If you knew why she was doing her work in that particular fashion, you would know what the Spanish Monk meant when he said—

> *I the Trinity illustrate,*
> *Drinking watered orange-pulp—*
> *In three sips the Arian frustrate,*
> *While he drains his at one gulp—*

—and many other things which now are hidden from your eyes. However, Mrs McIntosh has prepared dinner. Let us come and eat after the fashion of the people of the country—of whom, by the way, you know nothing.'

The native woman dipped her hand in the dish with us. This was wrong. The wife should always wait until the husband has eaten. McIntosh Jellaludin apologized, saying,

'It is an English prejudice which I have not been able to overcome; and she loves me. Why, I have never been able to understand. I forgathered with her at Jullundur, three years ago, and she has remained with me ever since. I believe her to be moral, and know her to be skilled in cookery.'

He patted the woman's head as he spoke, and she cooed softly. She was not pretty to look at.

McIntosh never told me what position he had held before his fall. He was, when sober, a scholar and a gentleman. When drunk, he was rather more of the first than the second. He used to get drunk about once a week for two days. On those occasions the native woman tended him while he raved in all tongues except his own. One day, indeed, he began reciting 'Atalanta in Calydon', and went through it to the end, beating time to the swing of the verse with a bedstead-leg. But he did most of his ravings in Greek or German. The man's mind was a perfect rag-bag of useless things. Once, when he was beginning to get sober, he told me that I was the only rational being in the Inferno into which he had descended—a Virgil in the Shades, he said—and that, in return for my tobacco, he would, before he died, give me the materials of a new Inferno that should make me greater than Dante. Then he fell asleep on a horse-blanket and woke up quite calm.

'Man,' said he, 'when you have reached the utter-most depths of degradation, little incidents which would vex a higher life are to you of no consequence. Last night my soul was among the Gods; but I make no doubt that my bestial body was writhing down here in the garbage.'

'You were abominably drunk, if that's what you mean,' I said.

'I *was* drunk—filthily drunk. I who am the son of a man with whom you have no concern—I who was once Fellow of a College whose buttery-hatch you have not seen—I was loathsomely drunk. But consider how lightly I am touched. It is nothing to me—less than nothing; for I do not even feel the headache which should be my portion. Now, in a higher life, how ghastly would have been my punishment, how bitter my repentance! Believe me, my friend with the neglected education, the highest is as the lowest—always supposing each degree extreme.'

He turned round on the blanket, put his head between his fists and continued,

'On the Soul which I have lost and on the Conscience which I have killed, I tell you that I cannot feel! I am as the Gods, knowing good and evil, but untouched by either. Is this enviable or is it not?'

When a man has lost the warning of 'next morning's head' he must be in a bad state. I answered, looking at McIntosh on the blanket, with his hair over his eyes and his lips blue-white, that I did not think the insensibility good enough.

'For pity's sake, don't say that! I tell you it *is* good and most enviable. Think of my consolations!'

'Have you so many, then, McIntosh?'

'Certainly; your attempts at sarcasm, which is essentially the weapon of a cultured man, are crude. First, my attainments, my classical and literary knowledge, blurred, perhaps, by immoderate drinking—which reminds me that before my soul went to the Gods last night I sold the Dickering Horace you so kindly lent me. Ditta Mull the clothesman has it. It fetched ten annas, and may be redeemed for a rupee—but still infinitely superior to yours. Secondly, the abiding affection of Mrs McIntosh, best of wives. Thirdly, a monument, more enduring than brass, which I have built up in the seven years of my degradation.'

He stopped here, and crawled across the room for a drink of water. He was very shaky and sick.

He referred several times to his 'treasure'—some great possession that he owned—but I held this to be the raving of drink. He was as poor and as proud as he could be. His manner was not pleasant, but he knew enough about the natives, among whom seven years of his life had been spent, to make his acquaintance worth having. He used actually to laugh at Strickland as an ignorant man—'ignorant West and East'—he said. His boast was, first, that he was an Oxford Man of rare and shining parts, which may or may not have been true—I did not know enough to check his statements; and, secondly, that he 'had his hand on the pulse of native life'—which was a fact. As an Oxford man, he struck me as a prig: he was always throwing his education about. As a Mahommedan faquir—as McIntosh Jellaludin—he was all that I wanted for my own ends. He smoked several pounds of my tobacco, and taught me several ounces of things worth knowing; but he would never accept any gifts, not even when the cold weather came, and gripped the poor thin chest under the poor thin alpaca coat. He grew very angry, and said that I had insulted him, and that he was not going into hospital. He had lived like a beast and he would die rationally, like a man.

As a matter of fact, he died of pneumonia; and on the night of his death sent over a grubby note asking me to come and help him to die.

The native woman was weeping by the side of the bed. McIntosh, wrapped in a cotton cloth, was too weak to resent a fur coat being thrown over him. He was very active as far as his mind was concerned, and his eyes were blazing. When he had abused the Doctor who came with me so foully that the indignant old fellow left, he cursed me for a few minutes and calmed down.

Then he told his wife to fetch out 'The Book' from a hole in the wall. She brought out a big bundle, wrapped in the tail of a petticoat, of old sheets of miscellaneous notepaper, all numbered and covered with fine cramped writing. McIntosh ploughed his hand through the rubbish and stirred it up lovingly.

'This,' he said, 'is my work—the Book of McIntosh Jellaludin, showing what he saw and how he lived, and what befell him and others; being also an account of the life and sins and death of Mother Maturin. What Mirza Murad Ali Beg's book is to all other books on native life, will my work be to Mirza Murad Ali Beg's!'

This, as will be conceded by any one who knows Mirza Murad Ali Beg's book, was a sweeping statement. The papers did not look specially valuable; but McIntosh handled them as if they were currency-notes. Then said he slowly,

'In despite the many weaknesses of your education, you have been good to me. I will speak of your tobacco when I reach the Gods. I owe you much thanks for many kindnesses. But I abominate indebtedness. For this reason I bequeath to you now the monument more enduring than brass—my one book—rude and imperfect in parts, but oh, how rare in others! I wonder if you will understand it. It is a gift more honourable than ... Bah! where is my brain rambling to? You will mutilate it horribly. You will knock out the gems you call Latin quotations, you Philistine, and you will butcher the style to carve into your own jerky jargon; but you cannot destroy the whole of it. I bequeath it to you. Ethel… My brain again! …Mrs McIntosh, bear witness that I give the Sahib all these papers. They would be of no use to you, Heart of my Heart; and I lay it upon you,' he turned to me here, 'that you do not let my book die in its present form. It is yours unconditionally—the story of McIntosh Jellaludin, which is not the story of McIntosh Jellaludin, but of a greater man than he, and of a far greater woman. Listen now! I am neither mad nor drunk! That book will make you famous.'

I said, 'Thank you,' as the native woman put the bundle into my arms.

'My only baby!' said McIntosh, with a smile. He was sinking fast, but he continued to talk as long as breath remained. I waited for the end; knowing that, in six cases out of ten, a dying man calls for his mother. He turned on his side and said,

'Say how it came into your possession. No one will believe you, but my name, at least, will live. You will treat it brutally, I know you will. Some of it must go; the public are fools and prudish fools. I was their servant once. But do your mangling gently—very gently. It is a great work, and I have paid for it in seven years' damnation.'

His voice stopped for ten or twelve breaths, and then he began mumbling a prayer of some kind in Greek. The native woman cried very bitterly. Lastly, he rose in bed and said, as loudly as slowly, 'Not guilty, my Lord!'

Then he fell back, and the stupor held him till he died. The native woman ran into the Serai among the horses, and screamed and beat her breasts; for she had loved him.

Perhaps his last sentence in life told what McIntosh had once gone through; but, saving the big bundle of old sheets in the cloth, there was nothing in his room to say who or what he had been.

The papers were in a hopeless muddle.

Strickland helped me to sort them, and he said that the writer was either an extreme liar or a most wonderful person. He thought the former. One of these days you may be able to judge for yourselves. The bundle needed much expurgation, and was full of Greek nonsense at the head of the chapters, which has all been cut out.

If the thing is ever published, some one may perhaps remember this story, now printed as a safeguard to prove that McIntosh Jellaludin and not I myself wrote the *Book of Mother Maturin*.

I don't want the *Giant's Robe* to come true in my case.

CONSEQUENCES

Rosicrucian subtleties
In the Orient had rise;
Ye may find their teachers still
Under Jacatala's Hill.
Seek ye Bombast Paracelsus,
Read what Flood the Seeker tells us
Of the Dominant that runs
Through the cycles of the Suns—
Read my story last and see
Luna at her apogee.

There are yearly appointments, and two-yearly appointments, and five-yearly appointments at Simla, and there are, or used to be, permanent appointments, whereon you stayed up for the term of your natural life and secured red cheeks and a nice income. Of course, you could descend in the cold weather; for Simla is rather dull then.

Tarrion came from goodness knows where—all away and away in some forsaken part of Central India, where they call Pachmari a 'Sanitarium,' and drive behind trotting bullocks, I believe. He belonged to a regiment; but what he really wanted to do was to escape from his regiment and live in Simla forever and ever. He had no preference for anything in particular, beyond a good horse and a nice partner. He thought he could do everything well; which is a beautiful belief when you hold it with all your heart. He was clever in many ways, and good to look at, and always made people round him comfortable—even in Central India.

So he went up to Simla, and, because he was clever and amusing, he gravitated naturally to Mrs Hauksbee, who could forgive everything but stupidity. Once he did her great service by changing the date on an invitation-card for a big dance which Mrs Hauksbee wished to attend, but couldn't because she had quarrelled with the A.D.C., who took care, being a mean man, to invite her to a small dance on the 6th instead of the big Ball of the 26th. It was a very clever piece of forgery; and when Mrs Hauksbee showed the A.D.C. her invitation-card, and chaffed him mildly for not better managing his vendettas, he really thought he had made a mistake; and—which was wise—realized that it was no use to fight with Mrs Hauksbee. She was grateful to Tarrion and asked what she could do for him. He said simply, 'I'm a Freelance up here on leave, and on the lookout for what I can loot. I haven't a square inch of interest in all Simla. My name isn't known to any man with an appointment in his gift, and I want an appointment—a good, sound, pukka one. I believe you can do anything you turn yourself to do. Will you help me?' Mrs Hauksbee thought for a minute, and passed the lash of her riding-whip through her lips, as was her custom when thinking. Then her eyes sparkled, and she said, 'I will;' and she shook hands on it. Tarrion, having perfect confidence in this great woman, took no further thought of the business at all. Except to wonder what sort of an appointment he would win.

Mrs Hauksbee began calculating the prices of all the Heads of Departments and Members of Council she knew, and the more she thought the more she laughed, because her heart was in the game and it amused her. Then she took a Civil List and ran over a few of the appointments. There are some beautiful appointments in the Civil List. Eventually, she decided that, though Tarrion was too good for the Political Department, she had better begin by trying to get him in there. What were her own plans to this end, does not matter in the least, for Luck or Fate played into her hands, and she had nothing to do but to watch the course of events and take the credit of them.

All Viceroys, when they first come out, pass through the 'Diplomatic Secrecy' craze. It wears off in time; but they all catch it in the beginning, because they are new to the country. The particular Viceroy who was suffering from the complaint just then—this was a long time ago, before Lord Dufferin ever came from Canada, or Lord Ripon from the bosom of the English Church—had it very badly; and the result was that men who were new to keeping official secrets went about looking unhappy; and the Viceroy plumed himself on the way in which he had instilled notions of reticence into his Staff.

Now, the Supreme Government have a careless custom of committing what they do to printed papers. These papers deal with all sorts of things—from the payment of Rs 200 to a 'secret service' native, up to rebukes administered to Vakils and Motamids of Native States, and rather brusque letters to Native Princes, telling them to put their houses in order, to refrain from kidnapping women, or filling offenders with pounded red pepper, and eccentricities of that kind. Of course, these things could never be made public, because Native Princes never err officially, and their States are, officially, as well administered as Our territories. Also, the private allowances to various queer people are not exactly matters to put into newspapers, though they give quaint reading sometimes. When the Supreme Government is at Simla, these papers are prepared there, and go round to the people who ought to see them in office-boxes or by post. The principle of secrecy was to that Viceroy quite as important as the practice, and he held that a benevolent despotism like Ours should never allow even little things, such as appointments of subordinate clerks, to leak out till the proper time. He was always remarkable for his principles.

There was a very important batch of papers in preparation at that time. It had to travel from one end of Simla to the other by hand. It was not put into an official envelope, but a large, square, pale-pink one; the matter being in MS. on soft crinkley paper. It was addressed to 'The Head Clerk, etc., etc.' Now, between 'The Head Clerk, etc., etc.,' and 'Mrs Hauksbee' and a flourish, is no very great difference if the address be written in a very bad hand, as this was. The chaprassi who took the envelope was not more of an idiot than most chaprassis. He merely forgot where this most unofficial cover was to be delivered, and so asked the first Englishman he met, who happened to be a man riding down to Annandale in a great hurry. The Englishman hardly looked, said, 'Hauksbee Sahib ki Mem,' and went on. So did the chaprassi, because that letter was the last in stock and he wanted to get his work over. There was no book to sign; he thrust the letter into Mrs Hauksbee's bearer's hands and went off to smoke with a friend. Mrs Hauksbee was expecting some cut-out pattern things in flimsy paper from a friend. As soon as she got the big square packet, therefore, she said, 'Oh, the DEAR creature!' and tore it open with a paper-knife, and all the MS. enclosures tumbled out on the floor.

Mrs Hauksbee began reading. I have said the batch was rather important. That is quite enough for you to know. It referred to some correspondence, two measures, a peremptory order to a native chief and two dozen other things. Mrs Hauksbee gasped as she read, for the first glimpse of the naked machinery of the Great Indian Government, stripped of its casings and lacquer and paint and guard-rails, impresses even the most stupid man. And Mrs Hauksbee was a clever woman. She was a little afraid at first, and felt as if she had laid hold of a lightning-flash by the tail, and did not quite know what to do with it. There were remarks and initials at the side of the papers; and some of the remarks were rather more severe than the papers. The initials belonged to men who are all dead or gone now; but they were great in their day. Mrs Hauksbee read on and thought calmly as she read. Then the value of her trove struck her, and she cast about for the best method of using it. Then Tarrion dropped in, and they read through all the papers together, and Tarrion, not knowing how she had come by them, vowed that Mrs Hauksbee was the greatest woman on earth. Which I believe was true, or nearly so.

'The honest course is always the best,' said Tarrion after an hour-and-a-half of study and conversation. 'All things considered, the Intelligence Branch is about my form. Either that or the Foreign Office. I go to lay siege to the High Gods in their Temples.'

He did not seek a little man, or a little big man, or a weak Head of a strong Department, but he called on the biggest and strongest man that the Government owned, and explained that he wanted an appointment at Simla on a good salary. The compound insolence of this amused the Strong Man, and, as he had nothing to do for the moment, he listened to the proposals of the audacious Tarrion. 'You have, I presume, some special qualifications, besides the gift of self-assertion, for the claims you put forwards?' said the Strong Man. 'That, Sir,' said Tarrion, 'is for you to judge.' Then he began, for he had a good memory, quoting a few of the more important notes in the papers—slowly and one by one as a man drops chlorodyne into a glass. When he had reached the peremptory order—and it WAS a peremptory order—the Strong Man was troubled.

Tarrion wound up, 'And I fancy that special knowledge of this kind is at least as valuable for, let us say, a berth in the Foreign Office, as the fact of being the nephew of a distinguished officer's wife.' That hit the Strong Man hard, for the last appointment to the Foreign Office had been by black favour, and he knew it. 'I'll see what I can do for you,' said the Strong Man. 'Many thanks,' said Tarrion. Then he left, and the Strong Man departed to see how the appointment was to be blocked.

~

Followed a pause of eleven days; with thunders and lightnings and much telegraphing. The appointment was not a very important one, carrying only between Rs 500 and Rs 700 a month; but, as the Viceroy said, it was the principle of diplomatic secrecy that had to be maintained, and it was more than likely that a boy so well supplied with special information would be worth translating. So they translated him. They must have suspected him, though he protested that his information was due to singular talents of his own. Now, much of this story, including the after-history of the missing envelope, you must fill in for yourself, because there are reasons why it cannot be written. If you do not know about things Up Above, you won't understand how to fill it in and you will say it is impossible.

What the Viceroy said when Tarrion was introduced to him was, 'So, this is the boy who "rusked" the Government of India, is it? Recollect, Sir, that is not done TWICE.' So he must have known something.

What Tarrion said when he saw his appointment gazetted was, 'If Mrs Hauksbee were twenty years younger, and I her husband, I should be Viceroy of India in twenty years.'

What Mrs Hauksbee said, when Tarrion thanked her, almost with tears in his eyes, was first, 'I told you so!' and next, to herself, 'What fools men are!'

KIDNAPPED

There is a tide in the affairs of men,
Which, taken any way you please, is bad,
And strands them in forsaken guts and creeks
No decent soul would think of visiting.
You cannot stop the tide; but now and then,
You may arrest some rash adventurer
Who—h'm—will hardly thank you for your pains.

—'Vibart's *Moralities*'

We are a high-caste and enlightened race, and infant-marriage is very shocking and the consequences are sometimes peculiar; but, nevertheless, the Hindu notion—which is the Continental notion—which is the aboriginal notion—of arranging marriages irrespective of the personal inclinations of the married, is sound. Think for a minute, and you will see that it must be so; unless, of course, you believe in 'affinities.' In which case you had better not read this tale. How can a man who has never married; who cannot be trusted to pick up at sight a moderately sound horse; whose head is hot and upset with visions of domestic felicity, go about the choosing of a wife? He cannot see straight or think straight if he tries; and the same disadvantages exist in the case of a girl's fancies. But when mature, married and discreet people arrange a match between a boy and a girl, they do it sensibly, with a view to the future, and the young couple live happily ever afterwards. As everybody knows.

Properly speaking, Government should establish a Matrimonial Department, efficiently officered, with a Jury of

Matrons, a Judge of the Chief Court, a Senior Chaplain, and an Awful Warning, in the shape of a love-match that has gone wrong, chained to the trees in the courtyard. All marriages should be made through the Department, which might be subordinate to the Educational Department, under the same penalty as that attaching to the transfer of land without a stamped document. But Government won't take suggestions. It pretends that it is too busy. However, I will put my notion on record, and explain the example that illustrates the theory.

Once upon a time there was a good young man—a first-class officer in his own Department—a man with a career before him and, possibly, a K. C. G. E. at the end of it. All his superiors spoke well of him, because he knew how to hold his tongue and his pen at the proper times. There are today only eleven men in India who possess this secret; and they have all, with one exception, attained great honour and enormous incomes.

This good young man was quiet and self-contained—too old for his years by far. Which always carries its own punishment. Had a Subaltern, or a Tea–Planter's Assistant, or anybody who enjoys life and has no care for tomorrow, done what he tried to do not a soul would have cared. But when Peythroppe—the estimable, virtuous, economical, quiet, hard-working, young Peythroppe—fell, there was a flutter through five Departments.

The manner of his fall was in this way. He met a Miss Castries—d'Castries it was originally, but the family dropped the d' for administrative reasons—and he fell in love with her even more energetically than he worked. Understand clearly that there was not a breath of a word to be said against Miss Castries—not a shadow of a breath. She was good and very lovely—possessed what innocent people at home call a 'Spanish' complexion, with thick blue-black hair growing low down on her forehead, into a 'widow's peak,' and big violet eyes under eyebrows as black and as straight as the borders of a Gazette Extraordinary when a big man dies. But—but—but—Well, she was a VERY sweet girl and very pious, but for many reasons she was 'impossible.' Quite so. All good Mammas know what 'impossible' means. It was obviously absurd that Peythroppe should marry her. The little opal-tinted onyx at the base of her finger-nails said this as plainly as print. Further, marriage with Miss Castries meant marriage with several other Castries—Honorary Lieutenant Castries, her Papa, Mrs Eulalie Castries, her Mamma, and all the ramifications of the Castries family, on incomes ranging from Rs 175 to Rs 470 a month, and THEIR wives and connections again.

It would have been cheaper for Peythroppe to have assaulted a Commissioner with a dog-whip, or to have burned the records of a Deputy Commissioner's Office, than to have contracted an alliance with the Castries. It would have weighted his after-career less—even under a Government which never forgets and NEVER forgives. Everybody saw this but Peythroppe. He was going to marry Miss Castries, he was—being of age and drawing a good income—and woe betide the house that would not afterwards receive Mrs Virginie Saulez Peythroppe with the deference due to her husband's rank. That was Peythroppe's ultimatum, and any remonstrance drove him frantic.

These sudden madnesses most afflict the sanest men. There was a case once—but I will tell you of that later on. You cannot account for the mania, except under a theory directly contradicting the one about the Place wherein marriages are made. Peythroppe was burningly anxious to put a millstone round his neck at the outset of his career and argument had not the least effect on him. He was going to marry Miss Castries, and the business was his own business. He would thank you to keep your advice to yourself. With a man in this condition, mere words only fix him in his purpose. Of course he cannot see that marriage out here does not concern the individual but the Government he serves.

Do you remember Mrs Hauksbee—the most wonderful woman in India? She saved Pluffles from Mrs Reiver, won Tarrion his appointment in the Foreign Office, and was defeated in open field by Mrs Cusack–Bremmil. She heard of the lamentable condition of Peythroppe, and her brain struck out the plan that saved him. She had the wisdom of the Serpent, the logical coherence of the Man, the fearlessness of the Child, and the triple intuition of the Woman. Never—no, never—as long as a tonga buckets down the Solon dip, or the couples go a-riding at the back of Summer Hill, will there be such a genius as Mrs Hauksbee. She attended the consultation of Three Men on Peythroppe's case; and she stood up with the lash of her riding-whip between her lips and spake.

~

Three weeks later, Peythroppe dined with the Three Men, and the *Gazette of India* came in. Peythroppe found to his surprise that he had been gazetted a month's leave. Don't ask me how this was managed. I believe firmly that if Mrs Hauksbee gave the order, the whole Great Indian Administration would stand on its head.

The Three Men had also a month's leave each. Peythroppe put the *Gazette* down and said bad words. Then there came from the compound the soft 'pad-pad' of camels—'thieves' camels,' the Bikaneer breed that don't bubble and howl when they sit down and get up.

After that I don't know what happened. This much is certain. Peythroppe disappeared—vanished like smoke—and the long foot-rest chair in the house of the Three Men was broken to splinters. Also a bedstead departed from one of the bedrooms.

Mrs Hauksbee said that Mr Peythroppe was shooting in Rajputana with the Three Men; so we were compelled to believe her.

At the end of the month, Peythroppe was gazetted twenty days' extension of leave; but there was wrath and lamentation in the house of Castries. The marriage-day had been fixed, but the bridegroom never came; and the D'Silvas, Pereiras, and Ducketts lifted their voices and mocked Honorary Lieutenant Castries as one who had been basely imposed upon. Mrs Hauksbee went to the wedding, and was much astonished when Peythroppe did not appear. After seven weeks, Peythroppe and the Three Men returned from Rajputana. Peythroppe was in hard, tough condition, rather white, and more self-contained than ever.

One of the Three Men had a cut on his nose, caused by the kick of a gun. Twelve-bores kick rather curiously.

Then came Honorary Lieutenant Castries, seeking for the blood of his perfidious son-in-law to be. He said things— vulgar and 'impossible' things which showed the raw rough 'ranker' below the 'Honorary,' and I fancy Peythroppe's eyes were opened. Anyhow, he held his peace till the end; when he spoke briefly. Honorary Lieutenant Castries asked for a 'peg' before he went away to die or bring a suit for breach of promise.

Miss Castries was a very good girl. She said that she would have no breach of promise suits. She said that, if she was not a lady, she was refined enough to know that ladies kept their broken hearts to themselves; and, as she ruled her parents, nothing happened. Later on, she married a most respectable and gentlemanly person. He travelled for an enterprising firm in Calcutta, and was all that a good husband should be.

So Peythroppe came to his right mind again, and did much good work, and was honoured by all who knew him. One of these days he will marry; but he will marry a sweet pink-and-white maiden on the Government House List, with a little money and some influential connections, as every wise man should. And he will never, all his life, tell her what happened during the seven weeks of his shooting-tour in Rajputana.

But just think how much trouble and expense—for camel hire is not cheap, and those Bikaneer brutes had to be fed like humans—might have been saved by a properly conducted Matrimonial Department, under the control of the Director General of Education, but corresponding direct with the Viceroy.

WATCHES OF THE NIGHT

*'What is in the Brahmin's books that is in the Brahmin's heart.
Neither you nor I knew there was so much evil in the world.'*

—Hindu proverb

This began in a practical joke; but it has gone far enough now, and is getting serious.

Platte, the Subaltern, being poor, had a Waterbury watch and a plain leather guard.

The Colonel had a Waterbury watch also, and for guard, the lip-strap of a curb-chain. Lip-straps make the best watch guards. They are strong and short. Between a lip-strap and an ordinary leather guard there is no great difference; between one Waterbury watch and another there is none at all. Every one in the station knew the Colonel's lip-strap. He was not a horsey man, but he liked people to believe he had been one once; and he wove fantastic stories of the hunting-bridle to which this particular lip-strap had belonged. Otherwise he was painfully religious.

Platte and the Colonel were dressing at the Club—both late for their engagements, and both in a hurry. That was Kismet. The two watches were on a shelf below the looking-glass— guards hanging down. That was carelessness. Platte changed first, snatched a watch, looked in the glass, settled his tie, and ran. Forty seconds later, the Colonel did exactly the same thing; each man taking the other's watch.

You may have noticed that many religious people are deeply suspicious. They seem—for purely religious purposes, of course—to know more about iniquity than the Unregenerate.

Perhaps they were specially bad before they became converted!
At any rate, in the imputation of things evil, and in putting the
worst construction on things innocent, a certain type of good
people may be trusted to surpass all others. The Colonel and
his Wife were of that type. But the Colonel's Wife was the
worst. She manufactured the Station scandal, and—TALKED
TO HER AYAH! Nothing more need be said. The Colonel's
Wife broke up the Laplaces' home. The Colonel's Wife stopped
the Ferris–Haughtrey engagement. The Colonel's Wife induced
young Buxton to keep his wife down in the Plains through the
first year of the marriage. Whereby little Mrs Buxton died, and
the baby with her. These things will be remembered against the
Colonel's Wife so long as there is a regiment in the country.

But to come back to the Colonel and Platte. They went their
several ways from the dressing-room. The Colonel dined with
two Chaplains, while Platte went to a bachelor-party, and whist
to follow.

Mark how things happen! If Platte's sais had put the new
saddle-pad on the mare, the butts of the territs would not have
worked through the worn leather, and the old pad into the
mare's withers, when she was coming home at two o'clock in
the morning. She would not have reared, bolted, fallen into a
ditch, upset the cart, and sent Platte flying over an aloe-hedge
on to Mrs Larkyn's well-kept lawn; and this tale would never
have been written. But the mare did all these things, and while
Platte was rolling over and over on the turf, like a shot rabbit,
the watch and guard flew from his waistcoat—as an Infantry
Major's sword hops out of the scabbard when they are firing
a feu de joie—and rolled and rolled in the moonlight, till it
stopped under a window.

Platte stuffed his handkerchief under the pad, put the cart
straight, and went home.

Mark again how Kismet works! This would not happen once in a hundred years. Towards the end of his dinner with the two Chaplains, the Colonel let out his waistcoat and leaned over the table to look at some Mission Reports. The bar of the watch-guard worked through the buttonhole, and the watch—Platte's watch—slid quietly on to the carpet. Where the bearer found it next morning and kept it.

Then the Colonel went home to the wife of his bosom; but the driver of the carriage was drunk and lost his way. So the Colonel returned at an unseemly hour and his excuses were not accepted. If the Colonel's Wife had been an ordinary 'vessel of wrath appointed for destruction,' she would have known that when a man stays away on purpose, his excuse is always sound and original. The very baldness of the Colonel's explanation proved its truth.

See once more the workings of Kismet! The Colonel's watch which came with Platte hurriedly on to Mrs Larkyn's lawn, chose to stop just under Mrs Larkyn's window, where she saw it early in the morning, recognized it, and picked it up. She had heard the crash of Platte's cart at two o'clock that morning, and his voice calling the mare names. She knew Platte and liked him. That day she showed him the watch and heard his story. He put his head on one side, winked and said, 'How disgusting! Shocking old man! with his religious training, too! I should send the watch to the Colonel's Wife and ask for explanations.'

Mrs Larkyn thought for a minute of the Laplaces—whom she had known when Laplace and his wife believed in each other—and answered, 'I will send it. I think it will do her good. But remember, we must NEVER tell her the truth.'

Platte guessed that his own watch was in the Colonel's possession, and thought that the return of the lip-strapped Waterbury with a soothing note from Mrs Larkyn, would

merely create a small trouble for a few minutes. Mrs Larkyn
knew better. She knew that any poison dropped would find
good holding-ground in the heart of the Colonel's Wife.

The packet, and a note containing a few remarks on the
Colonel's calling-hours, were sent over to the Colonel's Wife,
who wept in her own room and took counsel with herself.

If there was one woman under Heaven whom the Colonel's
Wife hated with holy fervour, it was Mrs Larkyn. Mrs Larkyn
was a frivolous lady, and called the Colonel's Wife 'old cat.'
The Colonel's Wife said that somebody in Revelations was
remarkably like Mrs Larkyn. She mentioned other Scripture
people as well. From the Old Testament. (But the Colonel's
Wife was the only person who cared or dared to say anything
against Mrs Larkyn. Every one else accepted her as an amusing,
honest little body.) Wherefore, to believe that her husband had
been shedding watches under that 'Thing's' window at ungodly
hours, coupled with the fact of his late arrival on the previous
night, was...

At this point she rose up and sought her husband. He
denied everything except the ownership of the watch. She
besought him, for his Soul's sake, to speak the truth. He denied
afresh, with two bad words. Then a stony silence held the
Colonel's Wife, while a man could draw his breath five times.

The speech that followed is no affair of mine or yours. It
was made up of wifely and womanly jealousy; knowledge of
old age and sunken cheeks; deep mistrust born of the text that
says even little babies' hearts are as bad as they make them;
rancorous hatred of Mrs Larkyn, and the tenets of the creed of
the Colonel's Wife's upbringing.

Over and above all, was the damning lip-strapped
Waterbury, ticking away in the palm of her shaking, withered
hand. At that hour, I think, the Colonel's Wife realized a little of

the restless suspicions she had injected into old Laplace's mind, a little of poor Miss Haughtrey's misery, and some of the canker that ate into Buxton's heart as he watched his wife dying before his eyes. The Colonel stammered and tried to explain. Then he remembered that his watch had disappeared; and the mystery grew greater. The Colonel's Wife talked and prayed by turns till she was tired, and went away to devise means for 'chastening the stubborn heart of her husband.' Which translated, means, in our slang, 'tail-twisting.'

You see, being deeply impressed with the doctrine of Original Sin, she could not believe in the face of appearances. She knew too much, and jumped to the wildest conclusions.

But it was good for her. It spoilt her life, as she had spoilt the life of the Laplaces. She had lost her faith in the Colonel, and— here the creed-suspicion came in—he might, she argued, have erred many times, before a merciful Providence, at the hands of so unworthy an instrument as Mrs Larkyn, had established his guilt. He was a bad, wicked, gray-haired profligate. This may sound too sudden a revulsion for a long-wedded wife; but it is a venerable fact that, if a man or woman makes a practice of, and takes a delight in, believing and spreading evil of people indifferent to him or her, he or she will end in believing evil of folk very near and dear. You may think, also, that the mere incident of the watch was too small and trivial to raise this misunderstanding. It is another aged fact that, in life as well as racing, all the worst accidents happen at little ditches and cut-down fences. In the same way, you sometimes see a woman who would have made a Joan of Arc in another century and climate, threshing herself to pieces over all the mean worry of housekeeping. But that is another story.

Her belief only made the Colonel's Wife more wretched, because it insisted so strongly on the villainy of men.

Remembering what she had done, it was pleasant to watch her unhappiness, and the penny-farthing attempts she made to hide it from the Station. But the Station knew and laughed heartlessly; for they had heard the story of the watch, with much dramatic gesture, from Mrs Larkyn's lips.

Once or twice Platte said to Mrs Larkyn, seeing that the Colonel had not cleared himself, 'This thing has gone far enough. I move we tell the Colonel's Wife how it happened.' Mrs Larkyn shut her lips and shook her head, and vowed that the Colonel's Wife must bear her punishment as best she could. Now Mrs Larkyn was a frivolous woman, in whom none would have suspected deep hate. So Platte took no action, and came to believe gradually, from the Colonel's silence, that the Colonel must have 'run off the line' somewhere that night, and, therefore, preferred to stand sentence on the lesser count of rambling into other people's compounds out of calling hours. Platte forgot about the watch business after a while, and moved down-country with his regiment. Mrs Larkyn went home when her husband's tour of Indian service expired. She never forgot.

But Platte was quite right when he said that the joke had gone too far. The mistrust and the tragedy of it—which we outsiders cannot see and do not believe in—are killing the Colonel's Wife, and are making the Colonel wretched. If either of them read this story, they can depend upon its being a fairly true account of the case, and can 'kiss and make friends.'

Shakespeare alludes to the pleasure of watching an Engineer being shelled by his own Battery. Now this shows that poets should not write about what they do not understand. Any one could have told him that Sappers and Gunners are perfectly different branches of the Service. But, if you correct the sentence, and substitute Gunner for Sapper, the moral comes just the same.

THE GATE OF A HUNDRED SORROWS

'If I can attain Heaven for a pice,
why should you be envious?'

—Opium smoker's proverb

This is no work of mine. My friend, Gabral Misquitta, the half-caste, spoke it all, between moonset and morning, six weeks before he died; and I took it down from his mouth as he answered my questions so:

It lies between the Copper-smith's Gully and the pipe-stem sellers' quarter, within a hundred yards, too, as the crow flies, of the Mosque of Wazir Khan. I don't mind telling any one this much, but I defy him to find the Gate, however well he may think he knows the City. You might even go through the very gully it stands in a hundred times, and be none the wiser. We used to call the gully, 'the Gully of the Black Smoke,' but its native name is altogether different of course. A loaded donkey couldn't pass between the walls; and, at one point, just before you reach the Gate, a bulged house-front makes people go along all sideways.

It isn't really a gate though. It's a house. Old Fung–Tching had it first five years ago. He was a boot-maker in Calcutta. They say that he murdered his wife there when he was drunk. That was why he dropped bazar-rum and took to the Black Smoke instead. Later on, he came up north and opened the Gate as a house where you could get your smoke in peace and quiet. Mind you, it was a pukka, respectable opium-house, and not one of those stifling, sweltering chandoo-khanas, that you can find all over the City. No; the old man knew his business thoroughly, and he was most clean for a Chinaman. He was a one-eyed little chap, not much more than five feet high, and both his middle fingers were gone. All the same, he was the handiest man at rolling black pills I have ever seen. Never seemed to be touched by the Smoke, either; and what he took day and night, night and day, was a caution. I've been at it five years, and I can do my fair share of the Smoke with any one; but I was a child to Fung–Tching that way. All the same, the old man was keen on his money, very keen; and that's what I can't understand. I heard he saved a good deal before he died, but his nephew has got all that now; and the old man's gone back to China to be buried.

He kept the big upper room, where his best customers gathered, as neat as a new pin. In one corner used to stand Fung–Tching's Joss—almost as ugly as Fung–Tching—and there were always sticks burning under his nose; but you never smelt 'em when the pipes were going thick. Opposite the Joss was Fung–Tching's coffin. He had spent a good deal of his savings on that, and whenever a new man came to the Gate he was always introduced to it. It was lacquered black, with red and gold writings on it, and I've heard that Fung–Tching brought it out all the way from China. I don't know whether that's true or not, but I know that, if I came first in the evening, I used to spread my mat just at the foot of it. It was a quiet corner you see, and a sort of breeze from the gully came in at the window now and then. Besides the mats, there was no other furniture in the room—only the coffin, and the old Joss all green and blue and purple with age and polish.

Fung–Tching never told us why he called the place 'The Gate of a Hundred Sorrows.' (He was the only Chinaman I know who used bad-sounding fancy names. Most of them are flowery. As you'll see in Calcutta.) We used to find that out for ourselves. Nothing grows on you so much, if you're white, as the Black Smoke. A yellow man is made different. Opium doesn't tell on him scarcely at all; but white and black suffer a good deal. Of course, there are some people that the Smoke doesn't touch any more than tobacco would at first. They just doze a bit, as one would fall asleep naturally, and next morning they are almost fit for work. Now, I was one of that sort when I began, but I've been at it for five years pretty steadily, and it's different now. There was an old aunt of mine, down Agra way, and she left me a little at her death. About sixty rupees a month secured. Sixty isn't much. I can recollect a time, seems hundreds and hundreds of years ago, that I was getting my three hundred a month, and pickings, when I was working on a big timber contract in Calcutta.

I didn't stick to that work for long. The Black Smoke does not allow of much other business; and even though I am very little affected by it, as men go, I couldn't do a day's work now to save my life. After all, sixty rupees is what I want. When old Fung–Tching was alive he used to draw the money for me, give me about half of it to live on (I eat very little), and the rest he kept himself. I was free of the Gate at any time of the day and night, and could smoke and sleep there when I liked, so I didn't care. I know the old man made a good thing out of it; but that's no matter. Nothing matters, much to me; and, besides, the money always came fresh and fresh each month.

There was ten of us met at the Gate when the place was first opened. Me, and two Babus from a Government Office somewhere in Anarkulli, but they got the sack and couldn't pay (no man who has to work in the daylight can do the Black Smoke for any length of time straight on); a Chinaman that was Fung–Tching's nephew; a bazar-woman that had got a lot of money somehow; an English loafer—Mac–Somebody

I think, but I have forgotten—that smoked heaps, but never seemed to pay anything (they said he had saved Fung–Tching's life at some trial in Calcutta when he was a barrister): another Eurasian, like myself, from Madras; a half-caste woman, and a couple of men who said they had come from the north. I think they must have been Persians or Afghans or something.

There are not more than five of us living now, but we come regular. I don't know what happened to the Babus; but the bazar-woman, she died after six months of the Gate, and I think Fung–Tching took her bangles and nose-ring for himself. But I'm not certain. The Englishman, he drank as well as smoked, and he dropped off. One of the Persians got killed in a row at night by the big well near the mosque a long time ago, and the Police shut up the well, because they said it was full of foul air. They found him dead at the bottom of it. So, you see, there is only me, the Chinaman, the half-caste woman that we call the Memsahib (she used to live with Fung–Tching), the other Eurasian, and one of the Persians. The Memsahib looks very old now. I think she was a young woman when the Gate was opened; but we are all old for the matter of that. Hundreds and hundreds of years old. It is very hard to keep count of time in the Gate, and besides, time doesn't matter to me. I draw my sixty rupees fresh and fresh every month. A very, very long while ago, when I used to be getting three hundred and fifty rupees a month, and pickings, on a big timber-contract at Calcutta, I had a wife of sorts. But she's dead now. People said that I killed her by taking to the Black Smoke. Perhaps I did, but it's so long since it doesn't matter. Sometimes when I first came to the Gate, I used to feel sorry for it; but that's all over and done with long ago, and I draw my sixty rupees fresh and fresh every month, and am quite happy. Not DRUNK happy, you know, but always quiet and soothed and contented.

How did I take to it? It began at Calcutta. I used to try it in my own house, just to see what it was like. I never went very far, but I think my wife must have died then. Anyhow, I found myself here, and got to know Fung–Tching. I don't remember rightly how that came about; but he told me of the Gate and I used to go there, and, somehow, I have never got away from it since. Mind you, though, the Gate was a respectable place in Fung–Tching's time where you could be comfortable, and not at all like the chandoo-khanas where the niggers go. No; it was clean and quiet, and not crowded. Of course, there were others beside us ten and the man; but we always had a mat apiece with a wadded woollen head-piece, all covered with black and red dragons and things; just like a coffin in the corner.

At the end of one's third pipe the dragons used to move about and fight. I've watched 'em, many and many a night through. I used to regulate my Smoke that way, and now it takes a dozen pipes to make 'em stir. Besides, they are all torn and dirty, like the mats, and old Fung–Tching is dead. He died a couple of years ago, and gave me the pipe I always use now—a silver one, with queer beasts crawling up and down the receiver-bottle below the cup. Before that, I think, I used a big bamboo stem with a copper cup, a very small one, and a green jade mouthpiece. It was a little thicker than a walking-stick stem, and smoked sweet, very sweet. The bamboo seemed to suck up the smoke. Silver doesn't, and I've got to clean it out now and then, that's a great deal of trouble, but I smoke it for the old man's sake. He must have made a good thing out of me, but he always gave me clean mats and pillows, and the best stuff you could get anywhere.

When he died, his nephew Tsin-ling took up the Gate, and he called it the 'Temple of the Three Possessions;' but we old ones speak of it as the 'Hundred Sorrows,' all the same. The nephew does things very shabbily, and I think the Memsahib must help him. She lives with him; same as she used to do with the old man. The two let in all sorts of low people, niggers and all, and the Black Smoke isn't as good as it used to be. I've found burnt bran in my pipe over and over again. The old man would have died if that had happened in his time. Besides, the room is never cleaned, and all the mats are torn and cut at the edges. The coffin has gone—gone to China again—with the old man and two ounces of smoke inside it, in case he should want 'em on the way.

The Joss doesn't get so many sticks burnt under his nose as he used to; that's a sign of ill-luck, as sure as Death. He's all brown, too, and no one ever attends to him. That's the Memsahib's work, I know; because, when Tsin-ling tried to burn gilt paper before him, she said it was a waste of money, and, if he kept a stick burning very slowly, the Joss wouldn't know the difference. So now we've got the sticks mixed with a lot of glue, and they take half-an-hour longer to burn, and smell stinky. Let alone the smell of the room by itself. No business can get on if they try that sort of thing. The Joss doesn't like it. I can see that. Late at night, sometimes, he turns all sorts of queer colors—blue and green and red—just as he used to do when old Fung–Tching was alive; and he rolls his eyes and stamps his feet like a devil.

I don't know why I don't leave the place and smoke quietly in a little room of my own in the bazar. Most like, Tsin-ling would kill me if I went away—he draws my sixty rupees now— and besides, it's so much trouble, and I've grown to be very fond of the Gate. It's not much to look at. Not what it was in the old man's time, but I couldn't leave it. I've seen so many come in and out. And I've seen so many die here on the mats that I should be afraid of dying in the open now. I've seen some things that people would call strange enough; but nothing is strange when you're on the Black Smoke, except the Black Smoke. And if it was, it wouldn't matter. Fung–Tching used to be very particular about his people, and never got in any one who'd give trouble by dying messy and such. But the nephew isn't half so careful. He tells everywhere that he keeps a 'first-chop' house. Never tries to get men in quietly, and make them comfortable like Fung–Tching did. That's why the Gate is getting a little bit more known than it used to be. Among the niggers of course. The nephew daren't get a white, or, for matter of that, a mixed skin into the place. He has to keep us three of course—me and the Memsahib and the other Eurasian. We're fixtures. But he wouldn't give us credit for a pipeful—not for anything.

One of these days, I hope, I shall die in the Gate. The Persian and the Madras man are terrible shaky now. They've got a boy to light their pipes for them. I always do that myself. Most like, I shall see them carried out before me. I don't think I shall ever outlive the Memsahib or Tsin-ling. Women last longer than men at the Black Smoke, and Tsin-ling has a deal of the old man's blood in him, though he DOES smoke cheap stuff. The bazar-woman knew when she was going two days before her time; and SHE died on a clean mat with a nicely wadded pillow, and the old man hung up her pipe just above the Joss. He was always fond of her, I fancy. But he took her bangles just the same.

I should like to die like the bazar-woman—on a clean, cool mat with a pipe of good stuff between my lips. When I feel I'm going, I shall ask Tsin-ling for them, and he can draw my sixty rupees a month, fresh and fresh, as long as he pleases, and watch the black and red dragons have their last big fight together; and then…

Well, it doesn't matter. Nothing matters much to me—only I wished Tsin-ling wouldn't put bran into the Black Smoke.

IN ERROR

They burnt a corpse upon the sand—
The light shone out afar;
It guided home the plunging boats
That beat from Zanzibar.
Spirit of Fire, where'er Thy altars rise.
Thou art Light of Guidance to our eyes!

—Salsette boat-song

There is hope for a man who gets publicly and riotously drunk more often that he ought to do; but there is no hope for the man who drinks secretly and alone in his own house—the man who is never seen to drink.

This is a rule; so there must be an exception to prove it. Moriarty's case was that exception.

He was a Civil Engineer, and the Government, very kindly, put him quite by himself in an out-district, with nobody but natives to talk to and a great deal of work to do. He did his work well in the four years he was utterly alone; but he picked up the vice of secret and solitary drinking, and came up out of the wilderness more old and worn and haggard than the dead-alive life had any right to make him. You know the saying that a man who has been alone in the jungle for more than a year is never quite sane all his life after. People credited Moriarty's queerness of manner and moody ways to the solitude, and said it showed how Government spoilt the futures of its best men. Moriarty had built himself the plinth of a very god reputation in the bridge-dam-girder line. But he knew, every night of the week, that he was taking steps to undermine that reputation with L. L. L. and 'Christopher' and little nips of liqueurs and filth of that kind. He had a sound constitution and a great brain, or else he would have broken down and died like a sick camel in the district, as better men have done before him.

Government ordered him to Simla after he had come out of the desert; and he went up meaning to try for a post then vacant. That season, Mrs Reiver—perhaps you will remember her—was in the height of her power, and many men lay under her yoke. Everything bad that could be said has already been said about Mrs Reiver, in another tale. Moriarty was heavily-built and handsome, very quiet and nervously anxious to please his neighbours when he wasn't sunk in a brown study. He started a good deal at sudden noises or if spoken to without warning; and, when you watched him drinking his glass of water at dinner, you could see the hand shake a little. But all this was put down to nervousness, and the quiet, steady, 'sip-sip-sip, fill and sip-sip-sip, again,' that went on in his own room when he was by himself, was never known. Which was miraculous, seeing how everything in a man's private life is public property out here.

Moriarty was drawn, not into Mrs Reiver's set, because they were not his sort, but into the power of Mrs Reiver, and he fell down in front of her and made a goddess of her. This was due to his coming fresh out of the jungle to a big town. He could not scale things properly or see who was what.

Because Mrs Reiver was cold and hard, he said she was stately and dignified. Because she had no brains, and could not talk cleverly, he said she was reserved and shy. Mrs Reiver shy! Because she was unworthy of honour or reverence from any one, he reverenced her from a distance and dowered her with all the virtues in the Bible and most of those in Shakespeare.

This big, dark, abstracted man who was so nervous when

a pony cantered behind him, used to moon in the train of Mrs Reiver, blushing with pleasure when she threw a word or two his way. His admiration was strictly platonic: even other women saw and admitted this. He did not move out in Simla, so he heard nothing against his idol: which was satisfactory. Mrs Reiver took no special notice of him, beyond seeing that he was added to her list of admirers, and going for a walk with him now and then, just to show that he was her property, claimable as such. Moriarty must have done most of the talking, for Mrs Reiver couldn't talk much to a man of his stamp; and the little she said could not have been profitable. What Moriarty believed in, as he had good reason to, was Mrs Reiver's influence over him, and, in that belief, set himself seriously to try to do away with the vice that only he himself knew of.

His experiences while he was fighting with it must have been peculiar, but he never described them. Sometimes he would hold off from everything except water for a week. Then, on a rainy night, when no one had asked him out to dinner, and there was a big fire in his room, and everything comfortable, he would sit down and make a big night of it by adding little nip to little nip, planning big schemes of reformation meanwhile, until he threw himself on his bed hopelessly drunk. He suffered next morning.

One night, the big crash came. He was troubled in his own mind over his attempts to make himself 'worthy of the friendship' of Mrs Reiver. The past ten days had been very bad ones, and the end of it all was that he received the arrears of two-and-three-quarter years of sipping in one attack of delirium tremens of the subdued kind; beginning with suicidal depression, going on to fits and starts and hysteria and ending with downright raving. As he sat in a chair in front of the fire, or walked up and down the room picking a handkerchief to pieces, you heard what poor Moriarty really thought of Mrs Reiver, for he raved about her and his own fall for the most part; though he ravelled some P. W. D. accounts into the same skein of thought. He talked, and talked, and talked in a low dry whisper to himself, and there was no stopping him. He seemed to know that there was something wrong, and twice tried to pull himself together and confer rationally with the Doctor; but his mind ran out of control at once, and he fell back to a whisper and the story of his troubles. It is terrible to hear a big man babbling like a child of all that a man usually locks up, and puts away in the deep of his heart. Moriarty read out his very soul for the benefit of any one who was in the room between ten-thirty that night and two-forty-five next morning.

From what he said, one gathered how immense an influence Mrs Reiver held over him, and how thoroughly he felt for his own lapse. His whisperings cannot, of course, be put down here; but they were very instructive as showing the errors of his estimates.

~

When the trouble was over, and his few acquaintances were pitying him for the bad attack of jungle-fever that had so pulled him down, Moriarty swore a big oath to himself and went abroad again with Mrs Reiver till the end of the season, adoring her in a quiet and deferential way as an angel from heaven. Later on he took to riding—not hacking, but honest riding—which was good proof that he was improving, and you could slam doors behind him without his jumping to his feet with a gasp. That, again, was hopeful.

How he kept his oath, and what it cost him in the beginning, nobody knows. He certainly managed to compass the hardest thing that a man who has drank heavily can do. He took his

peg and wine at dinner, but he never drank alone, and never let
what he drank have the least hold on him.

Once he told a bosom-friend the story of his great trouble,
and how the 'influence of a pure honest woman, and an angel
as well' had saved him. When the man—startled at anything
good being laid to Mrs Reiver's door—laughed, it cost him
Moriarty's friendship. Moriarty, who is married now to a
woman ten thousand times better than Mrs Reiver—a woman
who believes that there is no man on earth as good and clever as
her husband—will go down to his grave vowing and protesting
that Mrs Reiver saved him from ruin in both worlds.

That she knew anything of Moriarty's weakness nobody
believed for a moment. That she would have cut him dead,
thrown him over, and acquainted all her friends with her
discovery, if she had known of it, nobody who knew her
doubted for an instant.

Moriarty thought her something she never was, and in that
belief saved himself. Which was just as good as though she had
been everything that he had imagined.

But the question is, what claim will Mrs Reiver have to
the credit of Moriarty's salvation, when her day of reckoning
comes?

THE EDUCATION OF OTIS YEERE

I

In the pleasant orchard-closes
'God bless all our gains,' say we;
But 'may God bless all our losses,'
Better suits with our degree.

—'The Lost Bower' by E.B. Browning

This is the history of a failure; but the woman who failed said that it might be an instructive tale to put into print for the benefit of the younger generation. The younger generation does not want instruction, being perfectly willing to instruct if any one will listen to it. None the less, here begins the story where every right-minded story should begin, that is to say at Simla, where all things begin and many come to an evil end.

The mistake was due to a very clever woman making a blunder and not retrieving it. Men are licensed to stumble, but a clever woman's mistake is outside the regular course of Nature and Providence; since all good people know that a woman is the only infallible thing in this world, except Government Paper of the '79 issue, bearing interest at four-and-a-half per cent. Yet, we have to remember that six consecutive days of rehearsing the leading part of *The Fallen Angel*, at the New Gaiety Theatre where the plaster is not yet properly dry, might have brought about an unhingement of spirits which, again, might have led to eccentricities.

Mrs Hauksbee came to 'The Foundry' to tiffin with Mrs Mallowe, her one bosom friend, for she was in no sense 'a woman's woman.' And it was a woman's tiffin, the door shut to all the world; and they both talked *chiffons*, which is French for Mysteries.

'I've enjoyed an interval of sanity,' Mrs Hauksbee announced, after tiffin was over and the two were comfortably settled in the little writing-room that opened out of Mrs Mallowe's bedroom.

'My dear girl, what has *he* done?' said Mrs Mallowe, sweetly. It is noticeable that ladies of a certain age call each other 'dear girl,' just as commissioners of twenty-eight years' standing address their equals in the Civil List as 'my boy.'

'There's no *he* in the case. Who am I that an imaginary man should be always credited to me? Am I an Apache?'

'No, dear, but somebody's scalp is generally drying at your wigwam-door. Soaking, rather.'

This was an allusion to the Hawley Boy, who was in the habit of riding all across Simla in the Rains, to call on Mrs Hauksbee. That lady laughed.

'For my sins, the Aide at Tyrconnel last night told me off to The Mussuck. Hsh! Don't laugh. One of my most devoted admirers. When the duff came—some one really ought to teach them to make pudding at Tyrconnel—The Mussuck was at liberty to attend to me.'

'Sweet soul! I know his appetite,' said Mrs Mallowe. 'Did he, oh, *did* he, begin his wooing?'

'By a special mercy of Providence, *no*. He explained his importance as a Pillar of the Empire. I didn't laugh.'

'Lucy, I don't believe you.'

'Ask Captain Sangar; he was on the other side. Well, as I was saying, The Mussuck dilated.'

'I think I can see him doing it,' said Mrs Mallowe, pensively, scratching her fox-terrier's ears.

'I was properly impressed. Most properly. I yawned openly. "Strict supervision, and play them off one against the other," said The Mussuck, shoveling down his ice by *tureenfuls*, I assure you. "*That*, Mrs Hauksbee, is the secret of our Government."'

Mrs Mallowe laughed long and merrily. 'And what did you say?'

'Did you ever know me at loss for an answer yet? I said: "So I have observed in my dealings with you." The Mussuck swelled with pride. He is coming to call on me tomorrow. The Hawley Boy is coming too.'

'"Strict supervision and play them off one against the other." *That*, Mrs Hauksbee, is the secret of *our* Government.' And I dare say if we could get to The Mussuck's heart, we should find that he considers himself a man of the world.'

'As he is of the other two things. I like The Mussuck, and I won't have you call him names. He amuses me.'

'He has reformed you, too, by what appears. Explain the interval of sanity, and hit Tim on the nose with the paper-cutter, please. That dog is too fond of sugar. Do you take milk in yours?'

'No, thanks. Polly, I'm wearied of this life. It's hollow.'

'Turn religious, then. I always said that Rome would be your fate.'

'Only exchanging half a dozen *attachés* in red for one and in black, and if I fasted, the wrinkles would come, and never, *never* go. Has it ever struck you, dear, that I'm getting old?'

'Thanks for your courtesy. I'll return it. Ye-es we are both not exactly—how shall I put it?'

'What we have been. "I feel it in my bones," as Mrs Crossley says. Polly, I've wasted my life.'

'As how?'

'Never mind how. I feel it. I want to be a Power before I die.'

'Be a Power then. You've wits enough for anything— and beauty?'

Mrs Hauksbee pointed a teaspoon straight at her hostess. 'Polly, if you heap compliments on me like this, I shall cease to believe that you're a woman. Tell me how I am to be a Power.'

'Inform The Mussuck that he is the most fascinating and slimmest man in Asia, and he'll tell you anything and everything you please.'

'Bother The Mussuck! I mean an intellectual Power—not a gas-power. Polly, I'm going to start a *salon*.'

Mrs Mallowe turned lazily on the sofa and rested her head on her hand. 'Hear the words of the Preacher, the son of Baruch,' she said.

'Will you talk sensibly?'

'I will, dear, for I see that you are going to make a mistake.'

'I never made a mistake in my life at least, never one that I couldn't explain away afterward.'

'Going to make a mistake,' went on Mrs Mallowe, composedly. 'It is impossible to start a salon in Simla. A bar would be much more to the point.'

'Perhaps, but why? It seems so easy'

'Just what makes it so difficult. How many clever women are there in Simla?'

'Myself and yourself,' said Mrs Hauksbee, without a moment's hesitation.

'Modest woman! Mrs Feardon would thank you for that. And how many clever men?'

'Oh—er—hundreds,' said Mrs Hauksbee, vaguely.

'What a fatal blunder! Not one. They are all bespoke of the Government. Take my husband, for instance. Jack was a clever man, though I say so who shouldn't. Government has eaten him up. All his ideas and powers of conversation—he really used to be a good talker, even to his wife, in the old days—are taken from him by this—this kitchen-sink of a Government.

That's the case with every man up here who is at work. I don't suppose a Russian convict under the knout is able to amuse the rest of his gang; and all our men-folk here are gilded convicts.'

'But there are scores—'

'I know what you're going to say. Scores of idle men up on leave. I admit it, but they are all of two objectionable sets, The Civilian who'd be delightful if he had the military man's knowledge of the world and style, and the military man who'd be adorable if he had the Civilian's culture.'

'Detestable word! Have Civilians culchaw? I never studied the breed deeply.'

'Don't make fun of Jack's Service. Yes. They're like the teapoys in the Lakka Bazar—good material but not polished. They can't help themselves, poor dears. A Civilian only begins to be tolerable after he has knocked about the world for fifteen years.'

'And a military man?'

'When he has had the same amount of service. The young of both species are horrible. You would have scores of them in your salon.'

'I would not!' said Mrs Hauksbee fiercely. 'I would tell the bearer to darwaza band them. I'd put their own colonels and commissioners at the door to turn them away. I'd give them to the Topsham Girl to play with.'

'The Topsham Girl would be grateful for the gift. But to go back to the salon. Allowing that you had gathered all your men and women together, what would you do with them? Make them talk? They would all with one accord begin to flirt. Your salon would become a glorified Peliti's—a "Scandal Point" by lamplight.'

'There's a certain amount of wisdom in that view.'

'There's all the wisdom in the world in it. Surely, twelve Simla seasons ought to have taught you that you can't focus anything in India; and a salon, to be any good at all, must be permanent. In two seasons your roomful would be scattered all over Asia. We are only little bits of dirt on the hillsides—here one day and blown down the khud the next. We have lost the art of talking—at least our men have. We have no cohesion—'

'George Eliot in the flesh,' interpolated Mrs Hauksbee wickedly.

'And collectively, my dear scoffer, we, men and women alike, have no influence. Come into the verandah and look at the Mall!'

The two looked down on the now rapidly filling road, for all Simla was abroad to steal a stroll between a shower and a fog.

'How do you propose to fix that river? Look! There's The Mussuck—head of goodness knows what. He is a power in the land, though he does eat like a costermonger. There's Colonel Blone, and General Grucher, and Sir Dugald Delane, and Sir Henry Haughton, and Mr Jellalatty. All Heads of Departments, and all powerful.'

'And all my fervent admirers,' said Mrs Hauksbee piously. 'Sir Henry Haughton raves about me. But go on.'

'One by one, these men are worth something. Collectively, they're just a mob of Anglo-Indians. Who cares for what Anglo-Indians say? Your salon won't weld the Departments together and make you mistress of India, dear. And these creatures won't talk administrative "shop" in a crowd—at your salon—because they are so afraid of the men in the lower ranks overhearing it. They have forgotten what of Literature and Art they ever knew, and the women—'

'Can't talk about anything except the last Gymkhana, or the sins of their last nurse. I was calling on Mrs Derwills this morning.'

'You admit that? They can talk to the subalterns though, and the subalterns can talk to them. Your salon would suit their views admirably, if you respected the religious prejudices of the country and provided plenty of kala juggahs.'

'Plenty of kala juggahs. Oh my poor little idea! Kala juggahs in a salon! But who made you so awfully clever?'

'Perhaps I've tried myself; or perhaps I know a woman who has. I have preached and expounded the whole matter and the conclusion thereof—'

"You needn't go on. "Is Vanity." Polly, I thank you. These vermin'—Mrs Hauksbee waved her hand from the verandah to two men in the crowd below who had raised their hats to her—'these vermin shall not rejoice in a new Scandal Point or an extra Peliti's. I will abandon the notion of a salon. It did seem so tempting, though. But what shall I do? I must do something.'

'Why? Are not Abana and Pharpar—'

'Jack has made you nearly as bad as himself! I want to, of course. I'm tired of everything and everybody, from a moonlight picnic at Seepee to the blandishments of The Mussuck.'

'Yes—that comes, too, sooner or later. Have you nerve enough to make your bow yet?'

Mrs Hauksbee's mouth shut grimly. Then she laughed. 'I think I see myself doing it. Big pink placards on the Mall: "Mrs Hauksbee! Positively her last appearance on any stage! This is to give notice!" No more dances; no more rides; no more luncheons; no more theatricals with supper to follow; no more sparring with one's dearest, dearest friend; no more fencing with an inconvenient man who hasn't wit enough to clothe what he's pleased to call his sentiments in passable speech; no more parading of The Mussuck while Mrs Tarkass calls all round Simla, spreading horrible stories about me! No more of anything that is thoroughly wearying, abominable and detestable, but, all the same, makes life worth the having. Yes! I see it all! Don't interrupt, Polly, I'm inspired. A mauve and white striped "cloud" round my excellent shoulders, a seat in the fifth row of the Gaiety, and both horses sold. Delightful vision! A comfortable arm-chair, situated in three different draughts, at every ball-room; and nice, large, sensible shoes for all the couples to stumble over as they go into the verandah! Then at supper. Can't you imagine the scene? The greedy mob gone away. Reluctant subaltern, pink all over like a newly-powdered baby—they really ought to tan subalterns before they are exported, Polly—sent back by the hostess to do his duty. Slouches up to me across the room, tugging at a glove two sizes too large for him—I hate a man who wears gloves like overcoats—and trying to look as if he'd thought of it from the first. "May I ah-have the pleasure 'f takin' you 'nt' supper?" Then I get up with a hungry smile. Just like this.'

'Lucy, how can you be so absurd?'

'And sweep out on his arm. So! After supper I shall go away early, you know, because I shall be afraid of catching cold. No one will look for my 'rickshaw. Mine, so please you! I shall stand, always with that mauve and white 'cloud' over my head, while the wet soaks into my dear, old, venerable feet, and Tom swears and shouts for the Memsahib's gharri. Then home to bed at half-past eleven! Truly excellent life— helped out by the visits of the Padri, just fresh from burying somebody down below there.' She pointed through the pines toward the Cemetery, and continued with vigorous dramatic gesture:—

'Listen! I see it all down—down even to the stays! Such stays! Six-eight a pair, Polly, with red flannel—or list—is it? that they put into the tops of those fearful things. I can draw you a picture of them.'

'Lucy, for Heaven's sake, don't go waving your arms about in that idiotic manner! Recollect every one can see you from the Mall.'

'Let them see! They'll think I am rehearsing for *The Fallen Angel*. Look! There's The Mussuck. How badly he rides. There!'

She blew a kiss to the venerable Indian administrator with infinite grace.

'Now,' she continued, 'he'll be chaffed about that at the Club in the delicate manner those brutes of men affect, and the Hawley Boy will tell me all about it—softening the details for fear of shocking me. That boy is too good to live, Polly. I've serious thoughts of recommending him to throw up his commission and go into the Church. In his present frame of mind he would obey me. Happy, happy child!'

'Never again,' said Mrs Mallowe, with an affectation of indignation, 'shall you tiffin here! "Lucindy your behaviour is scand'lus."'

'All your fault,' retorted Mrs Hauksbee, 'for suggesting such a thing as my abdication. No! *Jamais! nevaire!* I will act, dance, ride, frivol, talk scandal, dine out and appropriate the legitimate captives of any woman I choose, until I d-r-r-rop, or a better woman than I puts me to shame before all Simla—and it's dust and ashes in my mouth while I'm doing it!'

She swept into the drawing-room. Mrs Mallowe followed and put an arm round her waist.

'I'm *not*!' said Mrs Hauksbee defiantly, rummaging for her handkerchief. 'I've been dining out the last ten nights, and rehearsing in the afternoon. You'd be tired yourself. It's only because I'm tired.'

Mrs Mallowe did not offer Mrs Hauksbee any pity or ask her to lie down, but gave her another cup of tea, and went on with the talk.

'I've been through that too, dear,' she said.

'I remember,' said Mrs Hauksbee, a gleam of fun on her face. 'In '84, wasn't it? You went out a great deal less next season.'

Mrs Mallowe smiled in a superior and Sphinx-like fashion.

'I became an Influence,' said she.

'Good gracious, child, you didn't join the Theosophists and kiss Buddha's big toe, did you? I tried to get into their set once, but they cast me out for a sceptic without a chance of improving my poor little mind, too.'

'No, I didn't Theosophilander. Jack says—'

'Never mind Jack. What a husband says is known before. What did you do?'

'I made a lasting impression.'

'So have I for four months. But that didn't console me in the least. I hated the man. Will you stop smiling in that inscrutable way and tell me what you mean?'

Mrs Mallowe told.

~

'And—you—mean—to—say that it is absolutely Platonic on both sides?'

'Absolutely, or I should never have taken it up.'

'And his last promotion was due to you?'

Mrs Mallowe nodded.

"And you warned him against the Topsham Girl?'

Another nod.

'And told him of Sir Dugald Delane's private memo about him?'

A third nod.

'Why?'

'What a question to ask a woman! Because it amused me at first. I am proud of my property now. If I live, he shall continue to be successful. Yes, I will put him upon the straight road to Knighthood, and everything else that a man values. The rest depends upon himself.'

'Polly, you are a most extraordinary woman.'

'Not in the least. I'm concentrated, that's all. You diffuse yourself, dear; and though all Simla knows your skill in managing a team—'

'Can't you choose a prettier word?'

'Team, of half-a-dozen, from The Mussuck to the Hawley Boy, you gain nothing by it. Not even amusement.'

'And you?'

'Try my recipe. Take a man, not a boy, mind, but an almost mature, unattached man, and be his guide, philosopher, and friend. You'll find it the most interesting occupation that you ever embarked on. It can be done—you needn't look like that—because I've done it.'

'There's an element of risk about it that makes the notion attractive. I'll get such a man and say to him, "Now, understand that there must be no flirtation. Do exactly what I tell you, profit by my instruction and counsels, and all will yet be well." Is that the idea?'

'More or less,' said Mrs Mallowe, with an unfathomable smile. 'But be sure he understands.'

II

Dribble-dribble—trickle-trickle—
What a lot of raw dust!
My dollie's had an accident
And out came all the sawdust!

—Nursery rhyme

So Mrs Hauksbee, in 'The Foundry' which overlooks Simla Mall, sat at the feet of Mrs Mallowe and gathered wisdom. The end of the Conference was the Great Idea upon which Mrs Hauksbee so plumed herself.

'I warn you,' said Mrs Mallowe, beginning to repent of her suggestion, 'that the matter is not half so easy as it looks. Any woman—even the Topsham Girl—can catch a man, but very, very few know how to manage him when caught.'

'My child,' was the answer, 'I've been a female St. Simon Stylites looking down upon men for these these years past. Ask The Mussuck whether I can manage them.'

Mrs Hauksbee departed humming, *I'll go to him and say to him* in manner most ironical. Mrs Mallowe laughed to herself. Then she grew suddenly sober. 'I wonder whether I've done well in advising that amusement? Lucy's a clever woman, but a thought too careless.'

A week later the two met at a Monday Pop. 'Well?' said Mrs Mallowe.

'I've caught him!' said Mrs Hauksbee: her eyes were dancing with merriment.

'Who is it, mad woman? I'm sorry I ever spoke to you about it.'

'Look between the pillars. In the third row; fourth from the end. You can see his face now. Look!'

'Otis Yeere! Of all the improbable and impossible people! I don't believe you.'

'Hsh! Wait till Mrs Tarkass begins murdering Milton Wellings; and I'll tell you all about it. S-s-ss! That woman's voice always reminds me of an Underground train coming into Earl's Court with the brakes on. Now listen. It is really Otis Yeere.'

'So I see, but does it follow that he is your property!'

'He is! By right of trove. I found him, lonely and unbefriended, the very next night after our talk, at the Dugald Delanes' burra-khana. I liked his eyes, and I talked to him. Next day he called. Next day we went for a ride together, and to-day he's tied to my 'rickshaw-wheels hand and foot. You'll see when the concert's over. He doesn't know I'm here yet.'

'Thank goodness you haven't chosen a boy. What are you going to do with him, assuming that you've got him?'

'Assuming, indeed! Does a woman—do I—ever make a mistake in that sort of thing? First'—Mrs Hauksbee ticked off the items ostentatiously on her little gloved fingers—'First, my dear, I shall dress him properly. At present his raiment is a disgrace, and he wears a dress-shirt like a crumpled sheet of the *Pioneer*. Secondly, after I have made him presentable, I shall form his manners—his morals are above reproach.'

'You seem to have discovered a great deal about him considering the shortness of your acquaintance.'

'Surely you ought to know that the first proof a man gives of his interest in a woman is by talking to her about his own sweet self. If the woman listens without yawning, he begins to like her. If she flatters the animal's vanity, he ends by adoring her.'

'In some cases.'

'Never mind the exceptions. I know which one you are thinking of. Thirdly, and lastly, after he is polished and made pretty, I shall, as you said, be his guide, philosopher, and friend, and he shall become a success—as great a success as your friend. I always wondered how that man got on. Did The Mussuck come to you with the Civil List and, dropping on one knee—no, two knees, à la Gibbon—hand it to you and say, "Adorable angel, choose your friend's appointment"?'

'Lucy, your long experiences of the Military Department have demoralized you. One doesn't do that sort of thing on the Civil Side.'

'No disrespect meant to Jack's Service, my dear. I only asked for information. Give me three months, and see what changes I shall work in my prey.'

'Go your own way since you must. But I'm sorry that I was weak enough to suggest the amusement.'

'"I am all discretion, and may be trusted to an in-fin-ite extent,"' quoted Mrs Hauksbee from *The Fallen Angel*; and the conversation ceased with Mrs Tarkass's last, long-drawn war-whoop.

Her bitterest enemies—and she had many—could hardly accuse Mrs Hauksbee of wasting her time. Otis Yeere was one of those wandering 'dumb' characters, foredoomed through life to be nobody's property. Ten years in Her Majesty's Bengal Civil Service, spent, for the most part, in undesirable Districts, had given him little to be proud of, and nothing to bring confidence. Old enough to have lost the first fine careless rapture that showers on the immature 'Stunt imaginary Commissionerships and Stars, and sends him into the collar with coltish earnestness and abandon; too young to be yet able to look back upon the progress he had made, and thank Providence that under the conditions of the day he had come even so far, he stood upon the dead-centre of his career. And when a man stands still he feels the slightest impulse from without. Fortune had ruled that Otis Yeere should be, for the first part of his service, one of the rank and file who are ground up in the wheels of the Administration; losing heart and soul, and mind and strength, in the process. Until steam replaces manual power in the working of the Empire, there must always be this percentage—must always be the men who are used up, expended, in the mere mechanical routine. For these promotion is far off and the mill-grind of every day very instant. The Secretariats know them only by name; they are not the picked men of the Districts with Divisions and Collectorates awaiting them. They are simply the rank and file—the food for fever—sharing with the ryot and the plough-bullock the honour of being the plinth on which the State rests. The older ones have lost their aspirations; the younger are putting theirs aside with a sigh. Both learn to endure patiently until the end of the day. Twelve years in the rank and file, men say, will sap the hearts of the bravest and dull the wits of the most keen.

Out of this life Otis Yeere had fled for a few months; drifting, in the hope of a little masculine society, into Simla. When his leave was over he would return to his swampy, sour-green, under-manned Bengal district; to the native Assistant, the native Doctor, the native Magistrate, the steaming, sweltering Station, the ill-kempt City, and the undisguised insolence of the Municipality that babbled away the lives of men. Life was cheap, however. The soil spawned humanity, as it bred frogs in the Rains, and the gap of the sickness of one season was filled to overflowing by the fecundity of the next. Otis was unfeignedly thankful to lay down his work for a little while and escape from the seething, whining, weakly hive, impotent to help itself, but strong in its power to cripple, thwart, and annoy the sunken-eyed man who, by official irony, was said to be 'in charge' of it.

~

'I knew there were women-dowdies in Bengal. They come up here sometimes. But I didn't know that there were men-dowds, too.'

Then, for the first time, it occurred to Otis Yeere that his clothes wore rather the mark of the ages. It will be seen that his friendship with Mrs Hauksbee had made great strides.

As that lady truthfully says, a man is never so happy as when he is talking about himself. From Otis Yeere's lips Mrs Hauksbee, before long, learned everything that she wished to know about the subject of her experiment: learned what manner of life he had led in what she vaguely called 'those awful cholera districts'; learned, too, but this knowledge came later, what manner of life he had purposed to lead and what dreams he had dreamed in the year of grace '77, before the reality had knocked the heart out of him. Very pleasant are the shady bridle-paths round Prospect Hill for the telling of such confidences.

'Not yet,' said Mrs Hauksbee to Mrs Maliowe. 'Not yet. I must wait until the man is properly dressed, at least. Great heavens, is it possible that he doesn't know what an honour it is to be taken up by Me!'

Mrs Hauksbee did not reckon false modesty as one of her failings.

'Always with Mrs Hauksbee!' murmured Mrs Mallowe, with her sweetest smile, to Otis. 'Oh you men, you men! Here are our Punjabis growling because you've monopolized the nicest woman in Simla. They'll tear you to pieces on the Mall, some day, Mr Yeere.'

Mrs Mallowe rattled downhill, having satisfied herself, by a glance through the fringe of her sunshade, of the effect of her words.

The shot went home. Of a surety Otis Yeere was somebody in this bewildering whirl of Simla—had monopolized the nicest woman in it, and the Punjabis were growling. The notion justified a mild glow of vanity. He had never looked upon his acquaintance with Mrs Hauksbee as a matter for general interest.

The knowledge of envy was a pleasant feeling to the man of no account. It was intensified later in the day when a luncher at the Club said spitefully, 'Well, for a debilitated Ditcher, Yeere, you are going it. Hasn't any kind friend told you that she's the most dangerous woman in Simla?'

Yeere chuckled and passed out. When, oh, when would his new clothes be ready? He descended into the Mall to inquire; and Mrs Hauksbee, coming over the Church Ridge in her 'rickshaw, looked down upon him approvingly. 'He's learning to carry himself as if he were a man, instead of a piece of furniture, and'—she screwed up her eyes to see the better through the sunlight—'he is a man when he holds himself like that. O blessed Conceit, what should we be without you?'

With the new clothes came a new stock of self-confidence. Otis Yeere discovered that he could enter a room without breaking into a gentle perspiration—could cross one, even to talk to Mrs Hauksbee, as though rooms were meant to be crossed. He was, for the first time in nine years, proud of himself, and contented with his life, satisfied with his new clothes, and rejoicing in the friendship of Mrs Hauksbee.

'Conceit is what the poor fellow wants,' she said in confidence to Mrs Mallowe. 'I believe they must use Civilians to plough the fields with in Lower Bengal. You see I have to begin from the very beginning—haven't I? But you'll admit, won't you, dear, that he is immensely improved since I took him in hand. Only give me a little more time and he won't know himself.'

Indeed, Yeere was rapidly beginning to forget what he had been. One of his own rank and file put the matter brutally when he asked Yeere, in reference to nothing, 'And who has been making you a Member of Council, lately? You carry the side of half-a-dozen of 'em.'

'I—I'm awf'ly sorry. I didn't mean it, you know,' said Yeere apologetically.

'There'll be no holding you,' continued the old stager grimly. 'Climb down, Otis climb down, and get all that beastly affectation knocked out of you with fever! Three thousand a month wouldn't support it.'

Yeere repeated the incident to Mrs Hauksbee. He had come to look upon her as his Mother Confessor.

'And you apologized!' she said. 'Oh, shame! I hate a man who apologizes. Never apologize for what your friend called "side." Never! It's a man's business to be insolent and overbearing until he meets with a stronger. Now, you bad boy, listen to me.'

Simply and straightforwardly, as the 'rickshaw loitered round Jakko, Mrs Hauksbee preached to Otis Yeere the Great Gospel of Conceit, illustrating it with living pictures encountered during their Sunday afternoon stroll.

'Good gracious!'—she ended with the personal argument—'you'll apologise next for being my *attaché*!'

'Never!' said Otis Yeere. 'That's another thing altogether. I shall always be—'

'What's coming?' thought Mrs Hauksbee.

'Proud of that,' said Otis.

'Safe for the present,' she said to herself.

'But I'm afraid I have grown conceited. Like Jeshurun, you know. When he waxed fat, then he kicked. It's the having no worry on one's mind and the Hill air, I suppose.'

'Hill air, indeed!' said Mrs Hauksbee to herself. 'He'd have been hiding in the Club till the last day of his leave, if I hadn't discovered him.' And aloud—

"Why shouldn't you be? You have every right to.'

'I! Why?'

'Oh, hundreds of things. I'm not going to waste this lovely afternoon by explaining; but I know you have. What was that heap of manuscript you showed me about the grammar of the aboriginal—what's their names?'

'Gullals. A piece of nonsense. I've far too much work to do to bother over Gullals now. You should see my District. Come down with your husband some day and I'll show you round. Such a lovely place in the Rains! A sheet of water with the railway-embankment and the snakes sticking out, and, in the summer, green flies and green squash. The people would die of fear if you shook a dogwhip at 'em. But they know you're forbidden to do that, so they conspire to make your life a burden to you. My District's worked by some man at Darjiling, on the strength of a native pleader's false reports. Oh, it's a heavenly place!' Otis Yeere laughed bitterly.

'There's not the least necessity that you should stay in it. Why do you?'

'Because I must. How'm I to get out of it?'

'How! In a hundred and fifty ways. If there weren't so many people on the road I'd like to box your ears. Ask, my dear boy, ask! Look! There is young Hexarly with six years' service and half your talents. He asked for what he wanted, and he got it. See, down by the Convent! There's McArthurson, who has come to his present position by asking—sheer, downright asking—after he had pushed himself out of the rank and file. One man is as good as another in your service—believe me. I've seen Simla for more seasons than I care to think about. Do you suppose men are chosen for appointments because of their special fitness beforehand? You have all passed a high test—what do you call it?—in the beginning, and, except for the few who have gone altogether to the bad, you can all work hard. Asking does the rest. Call it cheek, call it insolence, call it anything you like, but ask! Men argue—yes, I know what men say—that a man, by the mere audacity of his request, must have some good in him. A weak man doesn't say: "Give me this and that." He whines: "Why haven't I been given this and that?" If you were in the Army, I should say learn to spin plates or play a tambourine with your toes. As it is—ask! You belong to a Service that ought to be able to command the Channel Fleet, or set a leg at twenty minutes' notice, and yet you hesitate over asking to escape from a squashy green district where you admit you are not master. Drop the Bengal Government altogether. Even Darjiling is a little out-of-the-way hole. I was there once, and the rents were extortionate. Assert yourself. Get the Government of India to take you over. Try to get on the Frontier, where every man has a grand chance if he can trust himself. Go somewhere! Do something! You have twice the wits and three times the presence of the men up here, and, and'—Mrs Hauksbee paused for breath; then continued—'and in any way you look at it, you ought to. You who could go so far!'

'I don't know,' said Yeere, rather taken aback by the unexpected eloquence. 'I haven't such a good opinion of myself.'

It was not strictly Platonic, but it was Policy. Mrs Hauksbee laid her hand lightly upon the ungloved paw that rested on the turned-back 'rickshaw hood, and, looking the man full in the face, said tenderly, almost too tenderly, 'I believe in you if you mistrust yourself. Is that enough, my friend?'

'It is enough,' answered Otis very solemnly.

He was silent for a long time, redreaming the dreams that he had dreamed eight years ago, but through them all ran, as sheet-lightning through golden cloud, the light of Mrs Hauksbee's violet eyes.

Curious and impenetrable are the mazes of Simla life—
the only existence in this desolate land worth the living.
Gradually it went abroad among men and women, in the
pauses between dance, play and Gymkhana, that Otis Yeere,
the man with the newly-lit light of self-confidence in his eyes,
had 'done something decent' in the wilds whence he came. He
had brought an erring Municipality to reason, appropriated
the funds on his own responsibility, and saved the lives of
hundreds. He knew more about the Gullals than any living man.
Had a vast knowledge of the aboriginal tribes; was, in spite of
his juniority, the greatest authority on the aboriginal Gullals.
No one quite knew who or what the Gullals were till The
Mussuck, who had been calling on Mrs Hauksbee, and prided
himself upon picking people's brains, explained they were a
tribe of ferocious hillmen, somewhere near Sikkim, whose
friendship even the Great Indian Empire would find it worth
her while to secure. Now we know that Otis Yeere had showed
Mrs Hauksbee his MS. notes of six years' standing on these same
Gullals. He had told her, too, how, sick and shaken with the
fever their negligence had bred, crippled by the loss of his pet
clerk, and savagely angry at the desolation in his charge, he had
once damned the collective eyes of his 'intelligent local board'
for a set of haramzadas. Which act of 'brutal and tyrannous
oppression' won him a Reprimand Royal from the Bengal
Government; but in the anecdote as amended for Northern
consumption we find no record of this. Hence we are forced to
conclude that Mrs Hauksbee edited his reminiscences before
sowing them in idle ears, ready, as she well knew, to exaggerate
good or evil. And Otis Yeere bore himself as befitted the hero
of many tales.

'You can talk to me when you don't fall into a brown study.
Talk now, and talk your brightest and best,' said Mrs Hauksbee.

Otis needed no spur. Look to a man who has the counsel of a woman of or above the world to back him. So long as he keeps his head, he can meet both sexes on equal ground—an advantage never intended by Providence, who fashioned Man on one day and Woman on another, in sign that neither should know more than a very little of the other's life. Such a man goes far, or, the counsel being withdrawn, collapses suddenly while his world seeks the reason.

Generalled by Mrs Hauksbee, who, again, had all Mrs Mallowe's wisdom at her disposal, proud of himself and, in the end, believing in himself because he was believed in, Otis Yeere stood ready for any fortune that might befall, certain that it would be good. He would fight for his own hand, and intended that this second struggle should lead to better issue than the first helpless surrender of the bewildered 'Stunt.

What might have happened it is impossible to say. This lamentable thing befell, bred directly by a statement of Mrs Hauksbee that she would spend the next season in Darjiling.

'Are you certain of that?' said Otis Yeere.

'Quite. We're writing about a house now.'

Otis Yeere 'stopped dead,' as Mrs Hauksbee put it in discussing the relapse with Mrs Mallowe.

'He has behaved,' she said angrily, 'just like Captain Kerrington's pony—only Otis is a donkey—at the last Gymkhana. Planted his forefeet and refused to go on another step. Polly, my man's going to disappoint me. What shall I do?'

As a rule, Mrs Mallowe does not approve of staring, but on this occasion she opened her eyes to the utmost. 'You have managed cleverly so far,' she said. 'Speak to him, and ask him what he means.'

'I will—at to-night's dance.'

'No—o, not at a dance,' said Mrs Mallowe cautiously. 'Men are never themselves quite at dances. Better wait till to-morrow morning.'

'Nonsense. If he's going to 'vert in this insane way there isn't a day to lose. Are you going? No? Then sit up for me, there's a dear. I shan't stay longer than supper under any circumstances.'

Mrs Mallowe waited through the evening, looking long and earnestly into the fire, and sometimes smiling to herself.

~

'Oh! oh! oh! The man's an idiot! A raving, positive idiot! I'm sorry I ever saw him!'

Mrs Hauksbee burst into Mrs Mallowe's house, at midnight, almost in tears.

'What in the world has happened?' said Mrs Mallowe, but her eyes showed that she had guessed an answer.

'Happened! Everything has happened! He was there. I went to him and said, "Now, what does this nonsense mean?" Don't laugh, dear, I can't bear it. But you know what I mean I said. Then it was a square, and I sat it out with him and wanted an explanation, and he said—Oh! I haven't patience with such idiots! You know what I said about going to Darjiling next year? It doesn't matter to me where I go. I'd have changed the Station and lost the rent to have saved this. He said, in so many words, that he wasn't going to try to work up any more, because—because he would be shifted into a province away from Darjiling, and his own District, where these creatures are, is within a day's journey—'

'Ah—hh!' said Mrs Mallowe, in a tone of one who has successfully tracked an obscure word through a large dictionary.

'Did you ever hear of anything so mad—so absurd? And he had the ball at his feet. He had only to kick it! I would have made him anything! Anything in the wide world. He could have gone to the world's end. I would have helped him. I made him, didn't I, Polly? Didn't I create that man? Doesn't he owe everything to me? And to reward me, just when everything was nicely arranged, by this lunacy that spoilt everything!'

'Very few men understand your devotion thoroughly.'

'Oh, Polly, don't laugh at me! I give men up from this hour. I could have killed him then and there. What right had this man—this Thing I had picked out of his filthy paddy-fields to make love to me?'

'He did that, did he?'

'He did. I don't remember half he said, I was so angry. Oh, but such a funny thing happened! I can't help laughing at it now, though I felt nearly ready to cry with rage. He raved and I stormed—I'm afraid we must have made an awful noise in our kala juggah. Protect my character, dear, if it's all over Simla by to-morrow—and then he bobbed forward in the middle of this insanity—I firmly believe the man's demented—and kissed me.'

'"Morals above reproach,"' purred Mrs Mallowe.

'So they were—so they are! It was the most absurd kiss. I don't believe he'd ever kissed a woman in his life before. I threw my head back, and it was a sort of slidy, pecking dab, just on the end of the chin—here.' Mrs Hauksbee tapped her masculine little chin with her fan. 'Then, of course, I was furiously angry, and told him that he was no gentleman, and I was sorry I'd ever met him, and so on. He was crushed so easily then I couldn't be very angry. Then I came away straight to you.'

'Was this before or after supper?'

'Oh! before—oceans before. Isn't it perfectly disgusting?'

'Let me think. I withhold judgment till tomorrow. Morning brings counsel.'

But morning brought only a servant with a dainty bouquet of Annandale roses for Mrs Hauksbee to wear at the dance at Viceregal Lodge that night.

'He doesn't seem to be very penitent,' said Mrs Mallowe. 'What's the billet-doux in the centre?'

Mrs Hauksbee opened the neatly-folded note—another accomplishment that she had taught Otis—read it, and groaned tragically.

'Last wreck of a feeble intellect! Poetry! Is it his own, do you think? Oh, that I ever built my hopes on such a maudlin idiot!'

'No. It's a quotation from Mrs Browning, and in view of the facts of the case, as Jack says, uncommonly well chosen. Listen:

> *Sweet, thou hast trod on a heart,*
> *   Pass! There's a world full of men;*
> *And women as fair as thou art*
> *   Must do such things now and then.*
>
> *Thou only hast stepped unaware—*
> *   Malice not one can impute;*
> *And why should a heart have been there,*
> *   In the way of a fair woman's foot?*

'I didn't—I didn't—I didn't!' said Mrs Hauksbee angrily, her eyes filling with tears, 'there was no malice at all. Oh, it's too vexatious!'

'You've misunderstood the compliment,' said Mrs Mallowe. 'He clears you completely and—ahem—I should think by this, that he has cleared completely too. My experience of men is that when they begin to quote poetry they are going to flit. Like swans singing before they die, you know.'

'Polly, you take my sorrows in a most unfeeling way.'

'Do I? Is it so terrible? If he's hurt your vanity, I should say that you've done a certain amount of damage to his heart.'

'Oh, you can never tell about a man!' said Mrs Hauksbee.

YOKED WITH AN UNBELIEVER

'I am dying for you, and you are dying for another.'

—Punjabi proverb

When the Gravesend tender left the P. & O. steamer for Bombay and went back to catch the train to Town, there were many people in it crying. But the one who wept most, and most openly was Miss Agnes Laiter. She had reason to cry, because the only man she ever loved—or ever could love, so she said—was going out to India; and India, as every one knows, is divided equally between jungle, tigers, cobras, cholera, and sepoys.

Phil Garron, leaning over the side of the steamer in the rain, felt very unhappy too; but he did not cry. He was sent out to 'tea.' What 'tea' meant he had not the vaguest idea, but fancied that he would have to ride on a prancing horse over hills covered with tea-vines, and draw a sumptuous salary for doing so; and he was very grateful to his uncle for getting him the berth. He was really going to reform all his slack, shiftless ways, save a large proportion of his magnificent salary yearly, and, in a very short time, return to marry Agnes Laiter. Phil Garron had been lying loose on his friends' hands for three years, and, as he had nothing to do, he naturally fell in love. He was very nice; but he was not strong in his views and opinions and principles, and though he never came to actual grief, his friends were thankful when he said good-bye, and went out to this mysterious 'tea' business near Darjiling. They said, 'God bless you, dear boy! Let us never see your face again,'—or at least that was what Phil was given to understand.

When he sailed, he was very full of a great plan to prove himself several hundred times better than any one had given him credit for—to work like a horse, and triumphantly marry Agnes Laiter. He had many good points besides his good looks; his only fault being that he was weak, the least little bit in the world weak. He had as much notion of economy as the Morning Sun; and yet you could not lay your hand on any one item, and say: 'Herein Phil Garron is extravagant or reckless.' Nor could you point out any particular vice in his character; but he was 'unsatisfactory' and as workable as putty.

Agnes Laiter went about her duties at home—her family objected to the engagement—with red eyes, while Phil was sailing to Darjiling—'a port on the Bengal Ocean,' as his mother used to tell her friends. He was popular enough on board ship, made many acquaintances and a moderately large liquor bill, and sent off huge letters to Agnes Laiter at each port. Then he fell to work on this plantation, somewhere between Darjiling and Kangra, and, though the salary and the horse and the work were not quite all he had fancied, he succeeded fairly well, and gave himself much unnecessary credit for his perseverance.

In the course of time, as he settled more into collar, and his work grew fixed before him, the face of Agnes Laiter went out of his mind and only came when he was at leisure, which was not often. He would forget all about her for a fortnight, and remember her with a start, like a school-boy who has forgotten to learn his lesson. She did not forget Phil, because she was of the kind that never forgets. Only, another man—a really desirable young man—presented himself before Mrs Laiter; and the chance of a marriage with Phil was as far off as ever; and his letters were so unsatisfactory; and there was a certain amount of domestic pressure brought to bear on the girl; and the young man really was an eligible person as incomes go; and the end of all things was that Agnes married him, and wrote a tempestuous whirlwind of a letter to Phil in the wilds of Darjiling, and said she should never know a happy moment all the rest of her life. Which was a true prophecy.

Phil got that letter, and held himself ill-treated. This was two years after he had come out; but by dint of thinking fixedly of Agnes Laiter, and looking at her photograph, and patting himself on the back for being one of the most constant lovers in history, and warming to the work as he went on, he really fancied that he had been very hardly used. He sat down and wrote one final letter—a really pathetic 'world without end, amen,' epistle; explaining how he would be true to Eternity, and that all women were very much alike, and he would hide his broken heart, etc., etc.; but if, at any future time, etc., etc., he could afford to wait, etc., etc., unchanged affections, etc., etc., return to her old love, etc., etc., for eight closely-written pages. From an artistic point of view, it was very neat work, but an ordinary Philistine, who knew the state of Phil's real feelings— not the ones he rose to as he went on writing—would have called it the thoroughly mean and selfish work of a thoroughly mean and selfish, weak man. But this verdict would have been incorrect. Phil paid for the postage, and felt every word he had written for at least two days and a half. It was the last flicker before the light went out.

That letter made Agnes Laiter very unhappy, and she cried and put it away in her desk, and became Mrs Somebody Else for the good of her family. Which is the first duty of every Christian maid.

Phil went his ways, and thought no more of his letter, except as an artist thinks of a neatly touched-in sketch. His ways were not bad, but they were not altogether good until they brought him across Dunmaya, the daughter of a Rajput ex-

Subadar–Major of our Native Army. The girl had a strain of Hill blood in her, and, like the Hill women, was not a purdah nashin. Where Phil met her, or how he heard of her, does not matter. She was a good girl and handsome, and, in her way, very clever and shrewd; though, of course, a little hard. It is to be remembered that Phil was living very comfortably, denying himself no small luxury, never putting by an anna, very satisfied with himself and his good intentions, was dropping all his English correspondents one by one, and beginning more and more to look upon this land as his home. Some men fall this way; and they are of no use afterwards. The climate where he was stationed was good, and it really did not seem to him that there was anything to go Home for.

He did what many planters have done before him—that is to say, he made up his mind to marry a Hill girl and settle down. He was seven-and-twenty then, with a long life before him, but no spirit to go through with it. So he married Dunmaya by the forms of the English Church, and some fellow-planters said he was a fool, and some said he was a wise man. Dunmaya was a thoroughly honest girl, and, in spite of her reverence for an Englishman, had a reasonable estimate of her husband's weaknesses. She managed him tenderly, and became, in less than a year, a very passable imitation of an English lady in dress and carriage. (It is curious to think that a Hill man, after a lifetime's education, is a Hill man still; but a Hill woman can in six months master most of the ways of her English sisters. There was a coolie woman once. But that is another story.) Dunmaya dressed by preference in black and yellow, and looked well.

Meantime the letter lay in Agnes's desk, and now and again she would think of poor resolute hard-working Phil among the cobras and tigers of Darjiling, toiling in the vain hope that she might come back to him. Her husband was worth ten Phils, except that he had rheumatism of the heart. Three years after he was married—and after he had tried Nice and Algeria for his complaint—he went to Bombay, where he died, and set Agnes free. Being a devout woman, she looked on his death and the place of it, as a direct interposition of Providence, and when she had recovered from the shock, she took out and reread Phil's letter with the 'etc., etc.,' and the big dashes, and the little dashes, and kissed it several times. No one knew her in Bombay; she had her husband's income, which was a large one, and Phil was close at hand. It was wrong and improper, of course, but she decided, as heroines do in novels, to find her old lover, to offer him her hand and her gold, and with him spend the rest of her life in some spot far from unsympathetic souls. She sat for two months, alone in Watson's Hotel, elaborating this decision, and the picture was a pretty one. Then she set out in search of Phil Garron, Assistant on a tea plantation with a more than usually unpronounceable name.

~

She found him. She spent a month over it, for his plantation was not in the Darjiling district at all, but nearer Kangra. Phil was very little altered, and Dunmaya was very nice to her.

Now the particular sin and shame of the whole business is that Phil, who really is not worth thinking of twice, was and is loved by Dunmaya, and more than loved by Agnes, the whole of whose life he seems to have spoilt.

Worst of all, Dunmaya is making a decent man of him; and he will be ultimately saved from perdition through her training.

Which is manifestly unfair.

IN FLOOD TIME

Tweed said tae Till:
'What gars ye rin sae still?'
Till said tae Tweed:
'Though ye rin wi' speed
An' I rin slaw—
Yet where ye droon ae man
I droon twa.'

—'Two Rivers', *Anon.*

There is no getting over the river to-night, Sahib. They say that a bullock-cart has been washed down already, and the ekka that went over a half hour before you came has not yet reached the far side. Is the Sahib in haste? I will drive the ford-elephant in to show him. Ohe, mahout there in the shed! Bring out Ram Pershad, and if he will face the current, good. An elephant never lies, Sahib, and Ram Pershad is separated from his friend Kala Nag. He, too, wishes to cross to the far side. Well done! Well done! my King! Go half way across, mahoutji, and see what the river says. Well done, Ram Pershad! Pearl among elephants, go into the river! Hit him on the head, fool! Was the goad made only to scratch thy own fat back with, bastard? Strike! Strike! What are the boulders to thee, Ram Pershad, my Rustum, my mountain of strength? Go in! Go in!

No, Sahib! It is useless. You can hear him trumpet. He is telling Kala Nag that he cannot come over. See! He has swung round and is shaking his head. He is no fool. He knows what the Barhwi means when it is angry. Aha! Indeed, thou art no fool, my child! Salaam, Ram Pershad, Bahadur! Take him

under the trees, mahout, and see that he gets his spices. Well
done, thou chiefest among tuskers. Salaam to the Sirkar and go
to sleep.

What is to be done? The Sahib must wait till the river goes
down. It will shrink tomorrow morning, if God pleases, or the
day after at the latest. Now why does the Sahib get so angry? I
am his servant. Before God, *I* did not create this stream! What
can I do? My hut and all that is therein is at the service of the
Sahib, and it is beginning to rain. Come away, my Lord. How
will the river go down for your throwing abuse at it? In the
old days the English people were not thus. The fire-carriage
has made them soft. In the old days, when they drave behind
horses by day or by night, they said naught if a river barred
the way, or a carriage sat down in the mud. It was the will of
God—not like a fire-carriage which goes and goes and goes,
and would go though all the devils in the land hung on to its
tail. The fire-carriage hath spoiled the English people. After all,
what is a day lost, or, for that matter, what are two days? Is the
Sahib going to his own wedding, that he is so mad with haste?
Ho! Ho! Ho! I am an old man and see few Sahibs. Forgive me
if I have forgotten the respect that is due to them. The Sahib is
not angry?

His own wedding! Ho! Ho! Ho! The mind of an old man is
like the numah-tree. Fruit, bud, blossom and the dead leaves
of all the years of the past flourish together. Old and new and
that which is gone out of remembrance, all three are there!
Sit on the bedstead, Sahib, and drink milk. Or—would the
Sahib in truth care to drink my tobacco? It is good. It is the
tobacco of Nuklao. My son, who is in service there, sent it to
me. Drink, then, Sahib, if you know how to handle the tube.
The Sahib takes it like a Mussulman. Wah! Wah! Where did
he learn that? His own wedding! Ho! Ho! Ho! The Sahib says

that there is no wedding in the matter at all? Now *is* it likely
that the Sahib would speak true talk to me who am only a black
man? Small wonder, then, that he is in haste. Thirty years have
I beaten the gong at this ford, but never have I seen a Sahib in
such haste. Thirty years, Sahib! That is a very long time. Thirty
years ago this ford was on the track of the bunjaras, and I
have seen two thousand pack-bullocks cross in one night. Now
the rail has come, and the fire-carriage says *buz-buz-buz,* and
a hundred lakhs of maunds slide across that big bridge. It
is very wonderful; but the ford is lonely now that there are
no bunjaras to camp under the trees.

Nay, do not trouble to look at the sky without. It will rain till
the dawn. Listen! The boulders are talking tonight in the bed
of the river. Hear them! They would be husking your bones,
Sahib, had you tried to cross. See, I will shut the door and no
rain can enter. Wahi! Ahi! Ugh! Thirty years on the banks of
the ford! An old man am I and—where is the oil for the lamp?

Your pardon, but, because of my years, I sleep no sounder
than a dog; and you moved to the door. Look, then, Sahib.
Look and listen. A full half kos from bank to bank is the stream
now—you can see it under the stars—and there are ten feet of
water therein. It will not shrink because of the anger in your
eyes, and it will not be quiet on account of your curses. Which
is louder, Sahib—your voice or the voice of the river? Call to
it—perhaps it will be ashamed. Lie down and sleep afresh,
Sahib. I know the anger of the Barhwi when there has fallen
rain in the foot-hills. I swam the flood, once, on a night ten-fold
worse than this, and by the Favour of God I was released from
Death when I had come to the very gates thereof.

May I tell the tale? Very good talk. I will fill the pipe anew.

Thirty years ago it was, when I was a young man and had but
newly come to the ford. I was strong then, and the bunjaras had

no doubt when I said 'this ford is clear.' I have toiled all night up to my shoulder-blades in running water amid a hundred bullocks mad with fear, and have brought them across losing not a hoof. When all was done I fetched the shivering men, and they gave me for reward the pick of their cattle—the bell-bullock of the drove. So great was the honour in which I was held! But, today when the rain falls and the river rises, I creep into my hut and whimper like a dog. My strength is gone from me. I am an old man and the fire-carriage has made the ford desolate. They were wont to call me the Strong One of the Barhwi.

Behold my face, Sahib—it is the face of a monkey. And my arm—it is the arm of an old woman. I swear to you, Sahib, that a woman has loved this face and has rested in the hollow of this arm. Twenty years ago, Sahib. Believe me, this was true talk—twenty years ago.

Come to the door and look across. Can you see a thin fire very far away down the stream? That is the temple-fire, in the shrine of Hanuman, of the village of Pateera. North, under the big star, is the village itself, but it is hidden by a bend of the river. Is that far to swim, Sahib? Would you take off your clothes and adventure? Yet I swam to Pateera—not once but many times; and there are muggers in the river too.

Love knows no caste; else why should I, a Mussulman and the son of a Mussulman, have sought a Hindu woman—a widow of the Hindus—the sister of the headman of Pateera? But it was even so. They of the headman's household came on a pilgrimage to Muttra when She was but newly a bride. Silver tires were upon the wheels of the bullock-cart, and silken curtains hid the woman. Sahib, I made no haste in their conveyance, for the wind parted the curtains and I saw Her. When they returned from pilgrimage the boy that was Her husband had died, and

I saw Her again in the bullock-cart. By God, these Hindus are fools! What was it to me whether She was Hindu or Jain—scavenger, leper, or whole? I would have married Her and made Her a home by the ford. The Seventh of the Nine Bars says that a man may not marry one of the idolaters? Is that truth? Both Shiahs and Sunnis say that a Mussulman may not marry one of the idolaters? Is the Sahib a priest, then, that he knows so much? I will tell him something that he does not know. There is neither Shiah nor Sunni, forbidden nor idolater, in Love; and the Nine Bars are but nine little fagots that the flame of Love utterly burns away. In truth, I would have taken Her; but what could I do? The headman would have sent his men to break my head with staves. I am not—I was not—afraid of any five men; but against half a village who can prevail?

Therefore it was my custom, these things having been arranged between us twain, to go by night to the village of Pateera, and there we met among the crops; no man knowing aught of the matter. Behold, now! I was wont to cross here, skirting the jungle to the river bend where the railway bridge is, and thence across the elbow of land to Pateera. The light of the shrine was my guide when the nights were dark. That jungle near the river is very full of snakes—little karaits that sleep on the sand—and moreover, Her brothers would have slain me had they found me in the crops. But none knew—none knew save She and I; and the blown sand of the river-bed covered the track of my feet. In the hot months it was an easy thing to pass from the ford to Pateera, and in the first Rains, when the river rose slowly, it was an easy thing also. I set the strength of my body against the strength of the stream, and nightly I ate in my hut here and drank at Pateera yonder. She had said that one Hirnam Singh, a thief, had sought Her, and he was of a village up the river but on the same bank. All Sikhs are dogs, and they

have refused in their folly that good gift of God—tobacco. I was
ready to destroy Hirnam Singh that ever he had come nigh Her;
and the more because he had sworn to Her that She had a lover,
and that he would lie in wait and give the name to the headman
unless She went away with him. What curs are these Sikhs!

After that news, I swam always with a little sharp knife in my
belt, and evil would it have been for a man had he stayed me. I
knew not the face of Hirnam Singh, but I would have killed any
who came between me and Her.

Upon a night in the beginning of the Rains, I was minded to
go across to Pateera, albeit the river was angry. Now the nature
of the Barhwi is this, Sahib. In twenty breaths it comes down
from the Hills, a wall three feet high, and I have seen it, between
the lighting of a fire and the cooking of a chupatty, grow from a
runnel to a sister of the Jumna.

When I left this bank there was a shoal a half mile down,
and I made shift to fetch it and draw breath there ere going
forward; for I felt the hands of the river heavy upon my heels.
Yet what will a young man not do for Love's sake? There was
but little light from the stars, and midway to the shoal a branch
of the stinking deodar tree brushed my mouth as I swam. That
was a sign of heavy rain in the foot-hills and beyond, for the
deodar is a strong tree, not easily shaken from the hillsides. I
made haste, the river aiding me, but ere I touched the shoal,
the pulse of the stream beat, as it were, within me and around,
and, behold, the shoal was gone and I rode high on the crest
of a wave that ran from bank to bank. Has the Sahib ever been
cast into much water that fights and will not let a man use his
limbs? To me, my head upon the water, it seemed as though
there were naught but water to the world's end, and the river
drave me with its driftwood. A man is a very little thing in the
belly of a flood.

And *this* flood, though I knew it not, was the Great Flood about which men talk still. My liver was dissolved and I lay like a log upon my back in the fear of Death. There were living things in the water, crying and howling grievously—beasts of the forest and cattle, and once the voice of a man asking for help. But the rain came and lashed the water white, and I heard no more save the roar of the boulders below and the roar of the rain above. Thus I was whirled down-stream, wrestling for the breath in me. It is very hard to die when one is young. Can the Sahib, standing here, see the railway bridge? Look, there are the lights of the mail-train going to Peshawur! The bridge is now twenty feet above the river, but upon that night the water was roaring against the lattice-work and against the lattice came I feet first. But much driftwood was piled there and upon the piers, and I took no great hurt. Only the river pressed me as a strong man presses a weaker. Scarcely could I take hold of the lattice-work and crawl to the upper boom. Sahib, the water was foaming across the rails a foot deep! Judge therefore what manner of flood it must have been. I could not hear. I could not see. I could but lie on the boom and pant for breath.

After a while the rain ceased and there came out in the sky certain new washed stars, and by their light I saw that there was no end to the black water as far as the eye could travel, and the water had risen upon the rails. There were dead beasts in the driftwood on the piers, and others caught by the neck in the lattice-work, and others not yet drowned who strove to find a foothold on the lattice-work—buffaloes and kine, and wild pig, and deer one or two, and snakes and jackals past all counting. Their bodies were black upon the left side of the bridge, but the smaller of them were forced through the lattice-work and whirled down-stream.

Thereafter the stars died and the rain came down afresh and the river rose yet more, and I felt the bridge begin to stir under

me as a man stirs in his sleep ere he wakes. But I was not afraid,
Sahib. I swear to you that I was not afraid, though I had no
power in my limbs. I knew that I should not die till I had seen
Her once more. But I was very cold, and I felt that the bridge
must go.

There was a trembling in the water, such a trembling as goes
before the coming of a great wave, and the bridge lifted its flank
to the rush of that coming so that the right lattice dipped under
water and the left rose clear. On my beard, Sahib, I am speaking
God's truth! As a Mirzapore stone-boat careens to the wind, so
the Barhwi Bridge turned. Thus and in no other manner.

I slid from the boom into deep water, and behind me came
the wave of the wrath of the river. I heard its voice and the
scream of the middle part of the bridge as it moved from the
piers and sank, and I knew no more till I rose in the middle of
the great flood. I put forth my hand to swim, and lo! it fell upon
the knotted hair of the head of a man. He was dead, for no one
but I, the Strong One of Barhwi, could have lived in that race.
He had been dead full two days, for he rode high, wallowing,
and was an aid to me. I laughed then, knowing for a surety that
I should yet see Her and take no harm; and I twisted my fingers
in the hair of the man, for I was far spent, and together we went
down the stream—he the dead and I the living. Lacking that
help I should have sunk: the cold was in my marrow, and my
flesh was ribbed and sodden on my bones. But *he* had no fear
who had known the uttermost of the power of the river; and I
let him go where he chose. At last we came into the power of
a side-current that set to the right bank, and I strove with my
feet to draw with it. But the dead man swung heavily in the
whirl, and I feared that some branch had struck him and that
he would sink. The tops of the tamarisk brushed my knees, so I
knew we were come into flood-water above the crops, and, after

I let down my legs and felt bottom—the ridge of a field—and, after, the dead man stayed upon a knoll under a fig-tree, and I drew my body from the water rejoicing.

Does the Sahib know whither the backwash of the flood had borne me? To the knoll which is the eastern boundary-mark of the village of Pateera! No other place. I drew the dead man up on the grass for the service that he had done me, and also because I knew not whether I should need him again. Then I went, crying thrice like a jackal, to the appointed place which was near the byre of the headman's house. But my Love was already there, weeping. She feared that the flood had swept my hut at the Barhwi Ford. When I came softly through the ankle-deep water, She thought it was a ghost and would have fled, but I put my arms round Her, and—I was no ghost in those days, though I am an old man now.

Ho! Ho! Dried corn, in truth. Maize without juice. Ho! Ho!*

I told Her the story of the breaking of the Barhwi Bridge, and She said that I was greater than mortal man, for none may cross the Barhwi in full flood, and I had seen what never man had seen before. Hand in hand we went to the knoll where the dead lay, and I showed Her by what help I had made the ford. She looked also upon the body under the stars, for the latter end of the night was clear, and hid Her face in Her hands, crying, 'It is the body of Hirnam Singh!' I said, 'The swine is of more use dead than living, my Beloved,' and She said, 'Surely, for he has saved the dearest life in the world to my love. None the less, he cannot stay here, for that would bring shame upon me.' The body was not a gunshot from Her door.

---

*I grieve to say that the Warden of Barhwi Ford is responsible here for two very bad puns in the vernacular.—R. K.

Then said I, rolling the body with my hands, 'God hath judged between us, Hirnam Singh, that thy blood might not be upon my head. Now, whether I have done thee a wrong in keeping thee from the burning-ghat, do thou and the crows settle together.' So I cast him adrift into the flood-water, and he was drawn out to the open, ever wagging his thick black beard like a priest under the pulpit-board. And I saw no more of Hirnam Singh.

Before the breaking of the day we two parted, and I moved towards such of the jungle as was not flooded. With the full light I saw what I had done in the darkness, and the bones of my body were loosened in my flesh, for there ran two kos of raging water between the village of Pateera and the trees of the far bank, and, in the middle, the piers of the Barhwi Bridge showed like broken teeth in the jaw of an old man. Nor was there any life upon the waters—neither birds nor boats, but only an army of drowned things—bullocks and horses and men—and the river was redder than blood from the clay of the foot-hills. Never had I seen such a flood—never since that year have I seen the like—and, O Sahib, no man living had done what I had done. There was no return for me that day. Not for all the lands of the headman would I venture a second time without the shield of darkness that cloaks danger. I went a kos up the river to the house of a blacksmith, saying that the flood had swept me from my hut, and they gave me food. Seven days I stayed with the blacksmith, till a boat came and I returned to my house. There was no trace of wall, or roof, or floor—naught but a patch of slimy mud. Judge, therefore, Sahib, how far the river must have risen.

It was written that I should not die either in my house, or in the heart of the Barhwi, or under the wreck of the Barhwi Bridge, for God sent down Hirnam Singh two days dead, though I know not how the man died, to be my buoy and support. Hirnam Singh has been in Hell these twenty years, and the thought of that night must be the flower of his torment.

Listen, Sahib! The river has changed its voice. It is going to sleep before the dawn, to which there is yet one hour. With the light it will come down afresh. How do I know? Have I been here thirty years without knowing the voice of the river as a father knows the voice of his son? Every moment it is talking less angrily. I swear that there will be no danger for one hour or, perhaps, two. I cannot answer for the morning. Be quick, Sahib! I will call Ram Pershad, and he will not turn back this time. Is the paulin tightly corded upon all the baggage? Ohe, mahout with a mud head, the elephant for the Sahib, and tell them on the far side that there will be no crossing after daylight.

Money? Nay, Sahib. I am not of that kind. No, not even to give sweetmeats to the baby-folk. My house, look you, is empty, and I am an old man.

Dutt, Ram Pershad! Dutt! Dutt! Dutt! Good luck go with you, Sahib.

THROUGH THE FIRE

The Policeman rode through the Himalayan forest, under the moss-draped oaks, and his orderly trotted after him.

'It's an ugly business, Bhere Singh,' said the Policeman. 'Where are they?'

'It is a very ugly business,' said Bhere Singh; 'and as for THEM, they are, doubtless, now frying in a hotter fire than was ever made of spruce-branches.'

'Let us hope not,' said the Policeman, 'for, allowing for the difference between race and race, it's the story of Francesca da Rimini, Bhere Singh.'

Bhere Singh knew nothing about Francesca da Rimini, so he held his peace until they came to the charcoal-burners' clearing where the dying flames said *whit, whit, whit* as they fluttered and whispered over the white ashes. It must have been a great fire when at full height. Men had seen it at Donga Pa across the valley winking and blazing through the night, and said that the charcoal-burners of Kodru were getting drunk. But it was only Suket Singh, Sepoy of the Punjab Native Infantry, and Athira, a woman, burning—burning—burning.

This was how things befell; and the Policeman's Diary will bear me out.

Athira was the wife of Madu, who was a charcoal-burner, one-eyed and of a malignant disposition. A week after their marriage, he beat Athira with a heavy stick. A month later, Suket Singh, Sepoy, came that way to the cool hills on leave from his regiment, and electrified the villagers of Kodru with tales of service and glory under the Government, and the honour in which he, Suket Singh, was held by the Colonel Sahib Bahadur.

And Desdemona listened to Othello as Desdemonas have done all the world over, and, as she listened, she loved.

'I've a wife of my own,' said Suket Singh, 'though that is no matter when you come to think of it. I am also due to return to my regiment after a time, and I cannot be a deserter—I who intend to be Havildar.' There is no Himalayan version of 'I could not love thee, dear, as much, Loved I not Honour more;' but Suket Singh came near to making one.

'Never mind,' said Athira, 'stay with me, and, if Madu tries to beat me, you beat him.'

'Very good,' said Suket Singh; and he beat Madu severely, to the delight of all the charcoal-burners of Kodru.

'That is enough,' said Suket Singh, as he rolled Madu down the hillside. 'Now we shall have peace.' But Madu crawled up the grass slope again, and hovered round his hut with angry eyes.

'He'll kill me dead,' said Athira to Suket Singh. 'You must take me away.'

'There'll be a trouble in the Lines. My wife will pull out my beard; but never mind,' said Suket Singh, 'I will take you.'

There was loud trouble in the Lines, and Suket Singh's beard was pulled, and Suket Singh's wife went to live with her mother and took away the children. 'That's all right,' said Athira; and Suket Singh said, 'Yes, that's all right.'

So there was only Madu left in the hut that looks across the valley to Donga Pa; and, since the beginning of time, no one has had any sympathy for husbands so unfortunate as Madu.

He went to Juseen Daze, the wizard-man who keeps the Talking Monkey's Head.

'Get me back my wife,' said Madu.

'I can't,' said Juseen Daze, 'until you have made the Sutlej in the valley run up the Donga Pa.'

'No riddles,' said Madu, and he shook his hatchet above Juseen Daze's white head.

'Give all your money to the headmen of the village,' said Juseen Daze; 'and they will hold a communal Council, and the Council will send a message that your wife must come back.'

So Madu gave up all his worldly wealth, amounting to twenty-seven rupees, eight annas, three pice, and a silver chain, to the Council of Kodru. And it fell as Juseen Daze foretold.

They sent Athira's brother down into Suket Singh's regiment to call Athira home. Suket Singh kicked him once round the Lines, and then handed him over to the Havildar, who beat him with a belt.

'Come back,' yelled Athira's brother.

'Where to?' said Athira.

'To Madu,' said he.

'Never,' said she.

'Then Juseen Daze will send a curse, and you will wither away like a barked tree in the springtime,' said Athira's brother. Athira slept over these things.

Next morning she had rheumatism. 'I am beginning to wither away like a barked tree in the springtime,' she said. 'That is the curse of Juseen Daze.'

And she really began to wither away because her heart was dried up with fear, and those who believe in curses die from curses. Suket Singh, too, was afraid because he loved Athira better than his very life. Two months passed, and Athira's brother stood outside the regimental Lines again and yelped, 'Aha! You are withering away. Come back.'

'I will come back,' said Athira.

'Say rather that WE will come back,' said Suket Singh.

'Ai; but when?' said Athira's brother.

'Upon a day very early in the morning,' said Suket Singh;

and he tramped off to apply to the Colonel Sahib Bahadur for one week's leave.

'I am withering away like a barked tree in the spring,' moaned Athira.

'You will be better soon,' said Suket Singh; and he told her what was in his heart, and the two laughed together softly, for they loved each other. But Athira grew better from that hour.

They went away together, travelling third-class by train as the regulations provided, and then in a cart to the low hills, and on foot to the high ones. Athira sniffed the scent of the pines of her own hills, the wet Himalayan hills. 'It is good to be alive,' said Athira.

'Hah!' said Suket Singh. 'Where is the Kodru road and where is the Forest Ranger's house?'

~

'It cost forty rupees twelve years ago,' said the Forest Ranger, handing the gun.

'Here are twenty,' said Suket Singh, 'and you must give me the best bullets.'

'It is very good to be alive,' said Athira wistfully, sniffing the scent of the pine-mould; and they waited till the night had fallen upon Kodru and the Donga Pa. Madu had stacked the dry wood for the next day's charcoal-burning on the spur above his house. 'It is courteous in Madu to save us this trouble,' said Suket Singh as he stumbled on the pile, which was twelve foot square and four high. 'We must wait till the moon rises.'

When the moon rose, Athira knelt upon the pile. 'If it were only a Government Snider,' said Suket Singh ruefully, squinting down the wire-bound barrel of the Forest Ranger's gun.

'Be quick,' said Athira; and Suket Singh was quick; but Athira was quick no longer. Then he lit the pile at the four corners and climbed on to it, re-loading the gun.

The little flames began to peer up between the big logs atop of the brushwood. 'The Government should teach us to pull the triggers with our toes,' said Suket Singh grimly to the moon. That was the last public observation of Sepoy Suket Singh.

Upon a day, early in the morning, Madu came to the pyre and shrieked very grievously, and ran away to catch the Policeman who was on tour in the district.

'The base-born has ruined four rupees' worth of charcoal wood,' Madu gasped. 'He has also killed my wife, and he has left a letter which I cannot read, tied to a pine bough.'

In the stiff, formal hand taught in the regimental school, Sepoy Suket Singh had written—

'Let us be burned together, if anything remain over, for we have made the necessary prayers. We have also cursed Madu, and Malak the brother of Athira—both evil men. Send my service to the Colonel Sahib Bahadur.'

The Policeman looked long and curiously at the marriage bed of red and white ashes on which lay, dull black, the barrel of the Ranger's gun. He drove his spurred heel absently into a half-charred log, and the chattering sparks flew upwards. 'Most extraordinary people,' said the Policeman.

WHE-W, WHEW, OUIOU, said the little flames.

The Policeman entered the dry bones of the case, for the Punjab Government does not approve of romancing, in his Diary.

'But who will pay me those four rupees?' said Madu.

A SECOND-RATE WOMAN

Est fuga, volvitur rota,
On we drift: where looms the dim port?
One Two Three Four Five contribute their quota:
Something is gained if one caught but the import,
Show it us, Hugues of Saxe–Gotha.

—*Master Hugues of Saxe–Gotha* by Robert Browning

'Dressed! Don't tell me that woman ever dressed in her life. She stood in the middle of the room while her *ayah*—no, her husband—it *must* have been a man—threw her clothes at her. She then did her hair with her fingers, and rubbed her bonnet in the flue under the bed. I *know* she did, as well as if I had assisted at the orgy. Who is she?' said Mrs Hauksbee.

'Don't!' said Mrs Mallowe feebly. 'You make my head ache. I am miserable to-day. Stay me with *fondants*, comfort me with chocolates, for I am—Did you bring anything from Peliti's?'

'Questions to begin with. You shall have the sweets when you have answered them. Who and what is the creature? There were at least half-a-dozen men round her, and she appeared to be going to sleep in their midst.'

'Delville,' said Mrs Mallowe, '"Shady" Delville, to distinguish her from Mrs Jim of that ilk. She dances as untidily as she dresses, I believe, and her husband is somewhere in Madras. Go and call, if you are so interested.'

'What have I to do with Shigramitish women? She merely caught my attention for a minute, and I wondered at the attraction that a dowd has for a certain type of man. I expected to see her walk out of her clothes—until I looked at her eyes.'

'Hooks and eyes, surely,' drawled Mrs Mallowe.

'Don't be clever, Polly. You make my head ache. And round this hayrick stood a crowd of men—a positive crowd!'

'Perhaps *they* also expected—'

'Polly, don't be Rabelaisian!'

Mrs Mallowe curled herself up comfortably on the sofa, and turned her attention to the sweets. She and Mrs Hauksbee shared the same house at Simla; and these things befell two seasons after the matter of Otis Yeere, which has been already recorded.

Mrs Hauksbee stepped into the verandah and looked down upon the Mall, her forehead puckered with thought.

'Hah!' said Mrs Hauksbee shortly. 'Indeed!'

'What is it?' said Mrs Mallowe sleepily.

'That dowd and The Dancing Master—to whom I object.'

'Why to The Dancing Master? He is a middle-aged gentleman, of reprobate and romantic tendencies, and tries to be a friend of mine.'

'Then make up your mind to lose him. Dowds cling by nature, and I should imagine that this animal—how terrible her bonnet looks from above!—is specially clingsome.'

'She is welcome to The Dancing Master so far as I am concerned. I never could take an interest in a monotonous liar. The frustrated aim of his life is to persuade people that he is a bachelor.'

'O-oh! I think I've met that sort of man before. And isn't he?'

'No. He confided that to me a few days ago. Ugh! Some men ought to be killed.'

'What happened then?'

'He posed as the horror of horrors—a misunderstood man. Heaven knows the *femme incomprise* is sad enough and bad enough—but the other thing!'

'And so fat too! I should have laughed in his face. Men seldom confide in me. How is it they come to you?'

'For the sake of impressing me with their careers in the past. Protect me from men with confidences!'

'And yet you encourage them?'

'What can I do? They talk, I listen, and they vow that I am sympathetic. I know I always profess astonishment even when the plot is—of the most old possible.'

'Yes. Men are so unblushingly explicit if they are once allowed to talk, whereas women's confidences are full of reservations and fibs, except—'

'When they go mad and babble of the Unutterabilities after a week's acquaintance. Really, if you come to consider, we know a great deal more of men than of our own sex.'

'And the extraordinary thing is that men will never believe it. They say we are trying to hide something.'

'They are generally doing that on their own account. Alas! These chocolates pall upon me, and I haven't eaten more than a dozen. I think I shall go to sleep.'

'Then you'll get fat, dear. If you took more exercise and a more intelligent interest in your neighbours you would—'

'Be as much loved as Mrs Hauksbee. You're a darling in many ways, and I like you—you are not a woman's woman— but *why* do you trouble yourself about mere human beings?'

'Because in the absence of angels, who I am sure would be horribly dull, men and women are the most fascinating things in the whole wide world, lazy one. I am interested in The Dowd—I am interested in The Dancing Master—I am interested in the Hawley Boy—and I am interested in *you*.'

'Why couple me with the Hawley Boy? He is your property.'

'Yes, and in his own guileless speech, I'm making a good thing out of him. When he is slightly more reformed, and has passed his Higher Standard, or whatever the authorities think fit to exact from him, I shall select a pretty little girl, the Holt girl, I think, and'—here she waved her hands airily—'"whom Mrs Hauksbee hath joined together let no man put asunder." That's all.'

'And when you have yoked May Holt with the most notorious detrimental in Simla, and earned the undying hatred of Mamma Holt, what will you do with me, Dispenser of the Destinies of the Universe?'

Mrs Hauksbee dropped into a low chair in front of the fire, and, chin in hand, gazed long and steadfastly at Mrs Mallowe.

'I do not know,' she said, shaking her head, '*what* I shall do with you, dear. It's obviously impossible to marry you to some one else—your husband would object and the experiment might not be successful after all. I think I shall begin by preventing you from—what is it?—"sleeping on ale-house benches and snoring in the sun."'

'Don't! I don't like your quotations. They are so rude. Go to the Library and bring me new books.'

'While you sleep? *No!* If you don't come with me I shall spread your newest frock on my 'rickshaw-bow, and when any one asks me what I am doing, I shall say that I am going to Phelps's to get it let out. I shall take care that Mrs MacNamara sees me. Put your things on, there's a good girl.'

Mrs Mallowe groaned and obeyed, and the two went off to the Library, where they found Mrs Delville and the man who went by the nick-name of The Dancing Master. By that time Mrs Mallowe was awake and eloquent.

'That is the Creature!' said Mrs Hauksbee, with the air of one pointing out a slug in the road.

'No,' said Mrs Mallowe. 'The man is the Creature. Ugh! Good-evening, Mr Bent. I thought you were coming to tea this evening.'

'Surely it was for to-morrow, was it not?' answered The Dancing Master. 'I understood...I fancied...I'm so sorry... How very unfortunate!'

But Mrs Mallowe had passed on.

'For the practised equivocator you said he was,' murmured Mrs Hauksbee, 'he strikes *me* as a failure. Now wherefore should he have preferred a walk with The Dowd to tea with us? Elective affinities, I suppose—both grubby. Polly, I'd never forgive that woman as long as the world rolls.'

'I forgive every woman everything,' said Mrs Mallowe. 'He will be a sufficient punishment for her. What a common voice she has!'

Mrs Delville's voice was not pretty, her carriage was even less lovely, and her raiment was strikingly neglected. All these things Mrs Mallowe noticed over the top of a magazine.

'Now *what* is there in her?' said Mrs Hauksbee. 'Do you see what I meant about the clothes falling off? If I were a man I would perish sooner than be seen with that rag-bag. And yet, she has good eyes, but—Oh!'

'What is it?'

'She doesn't know how to use them! On my honour, she does not. Look! Oh look! Untidiness I can endure, but ignorance never! The woman's a fool.'

'Hsh! She'll hear you.'

'All the women in Simla are fools. She'll think I mean some one else. Now she's going out. What a thoroughly objectionable couple she and The Dancing Master make! Which reminds me. Do you suppose they'll ever dance together?'

'Wait and see. I don't envy her the conversation of The Dancing Master—loathly man! His wife ought to be up here before long?'

'Do you know anything about him?'

'Only what he told me. It may be all a fiction. He married a girl bred in the country, I think, and, being an honourable, chivalrous soul, told me that he repented his bargain and sent her to her mother as often as possible—a person who has lived in the Doon since the memory of man and goes to Mussoorie when other people go Home. The wife is with her at present. So he says.'

'Babies?'

'One only, but he talks of his wife in a revolting way. I hated him for it. *He* thought he was being epigrammatic and brilliant.'

'That is a vice peculiar to men. I dislike him because he is generally in the wake of some girl, disappointing the Eligibles. He will persecute May Holt no more, unless I am much mistaken.'

'No. I think Mrs Delville may occupy his attention for a while.'

'Do you suppose she knows that he is the head of a family?'

'Not from his lips. He swore me to eternal secrecy. Wherefore I tell you. Don't you know that type of man?'

'Not intimately, thank goodness! As a general rule, when a man begins to abuse his wife to me, I find that the Lord gives me wherewith to answer him according to his folly; and we part with a coolness between us. I laugh.'

'I'm different. I've no sense of humour.'

'Cultivate it, then. It has been my mainstay for more years than I care to think about. A well-educated sense of humour will save a woman when Religion, Training, and Home influences fail; and we may all need salvation sometimes.'

'Do you suppose that the Delville woman has humour?'

'Her dress betrays her. How can a Thing who wears her *supplément* under her left arm have any notion of the fitness of things—much less their folly? If she discards The Dancing

Master after having once seen him dance, I may respect her. Otherwise—'

'But are we not both assuming a great deal too much, dear? You saw the woman at Peliti's—half an hour later you saw her walking with The Dancing Master—an hour later you met her here at the Library.'

'Still with The Dancing Master, remember.'

'Still with The Dancing Master, I admit, but why on the strength of that should you imagine—'

'I imagine nothing. I have no imagination. I am only convinced that The Dancing Master is attracted to The Dowd because he is objectionable in every way and she in every other. If I know the man as you have described him, he holds his wife in slavery at present.'

'She is twenty years younger than he.'

'Poor wretch! And, in the end, after he has posed and swaggered and lied—he has a mouth under that ragged moustache simply made for lies—he will be rewarded according to his merits.'

'I wonder what those really are,' said Mrs Mallowe.

But Mrs Hauksbee, her face close to the shelf of the new books, was humming softly: *'What shall he have who killed the Deer?'* She was a lady of unfettered speech.

One month later she announced her intention of calling upon Mrs Delville. Both Mrs Hauksbee and Mrs Mallowe were in morning wrappers, and there was a great peace in the land.

'I should go as I was,' said Mrs Mallowe. 'It would be a delicate compliment to her style.'

Mrs Hauksbee studied herself in the glass.

'Assuming for a moment that she ever darkened these doors, I should put on this robe, after all the others, to show her what a morning-wrapper ought to be. It might enliven her. As it is,

I shall go in the dove-coloured—sweet emblem of youth and innocence—and shall put on my new gloves.'

'If you really are going, dirty tan would be too good; and you know that dove-colour spots with the rain.'

'I care not. I may make her envious. At least I shall try, though one cannot expect very much from a woman who puts a lace tucker into her habit.'

'Just Heavens! When did she do that?'

'Yesterday—riding with The Dancing Master. I met them at the back of Jakko, and the rain had made the lace lie down. To complete the effect, she was wearing an unclean terai with the elastic under her chin. I felt almost too well content to take the trouble to despise her.'

'The Hawley Boy was riding with you. What did he think?'

'Does a boy ever notice these things? Should I like him if he did? He stared in the rudest way, and just when I thought he had seen the elastic, he said, "There's something very taking about that face." I rebuked him on the spot. I don't approve of boys being taken by faces.'

'Other than your own. I shouldn't be in the least surprised if the Hawley Boy immediately went to call.'

'I forbade him. Let her be satisfied with The Dancing Master, and his wife when she comes up. I'm rather curious to see Mrs Bent and the Delville woman together.'

Mrs Hauksbee departed and, at the end of an hour, returned slightly flushed.

'There is no limit to the treachery of youth! I *ordered* the Hawley Boy, as he valued my patronage, not to call. The first person I stumble over—literally stumble over—in her poky, dark little drawing-room is, of course, the Hawley Boy. She kept us waiting ten minutes, and then emerged as though she had been tipped out of the dirty clothes-basket. You know my way, dear,

when I am at all put out. I was Superior, *crrrrushingly* Superior!
'Lifted my eyes to Heaven, and had heard of nothing—'dropped
my eyes on the carpet and—"really didn't know"—'played
with my cardcase and "supposed so." The Hawley Boy giggled
like a girl, and I had to freeze him with scowls between
the sentences.'

'And she?'

'She sat in a heap on the edge of a couch, and managed to
convey the impression that she was suffering from stomach-
ache, at the very least. It was all I could do not to ask after her
symptoms. When I rose, she grunted just like a buffalo in the
water—too lazy to move.'

'Are you certain?—'

'Am I blind, Polly? Laziness, sheer laziness, nothing else—
or her garments were only constructed for sitting down in. I
stayed for a quarter of an hour trying to penetrate the gloom,
to guess what her surroundings were like, while she stuck out
her tongue.'

'Lu—*cy!*'

'Well—I'll withdraw the tongue, though I'm sure if she
didn't do it when I was in the room, she did the minute I
was outside. At any rate, she lay in a lump and grunted. Ask
the Hawley Boy, dear. I believe the grunts were meant for
sentences, but she spoke so indistinctly that I can't swear to it.'

'You are incorrigible, simply.'

'I am *not!* Treat me civilly, give me peace with honour, don't
put the only available seat facing the window, and a child may
eat jam in my lap before Church. But I resent being grunted
at. Wouldn't you? Do you suppose that she communicates
her views on life and love to The Dancing Master in a set of
modulated "Grmphs"?'

'You attach too much importance to The Dancing Master.'

'He came as we went, and The Dowd grew almost cordial at the sight of him. He smiled greasily, and moved about that darkened dog-kennel in a suspiciously familiar way.'

'Don't be uncharitable. Any sin but that I'll forgive.'

'Listen to the voice of History. I am only describing what I saw. He entered, the heap on the sofa revived slightly, and the Hawley Boy and I came away together. *He* is disillusioned, but I felt it my duty to lecture him severely for going there. And that's all.'

'Now for Pity's sake leave the wretched creature and The Dancing Master alone. They never did you any harm.'

'No harm? To dress as an example and a stumbling-block for half Simla, and then to find this Person who is dressed by the hand of God—not that I wish to disparage *Him* for a moment, but you know the tikka dhurzie way He attires those lilies of the field—this Person draws the eyes of men—and some of them nice men? It's almost enough to make one discard clothing. I told the Hawley Boy so.'

'And what did that sweet youth do?'

'Turned shell-pink and looked across the far blue hills like a distressed cherub. *Am* I talking wildly, Polly? Let me say my say, and I shall be calm. Otherwise I may go abroad and disturb Simla with a few original reflections. Excepting always your own sweet self, there isn't a single woman in the land who understands me when I am—what's the word?'

'*Tête-fêlée*,' suggested Mrs Mallowe.

'Exactly! And now let us have tiffin. The demands of Society are exhausting, and as Mrs Delville says—' Here Mrs Hauksbee, to the horror of the khitmatgars, lapsed into a series of grunts, while Mrs Mallowe stared in lazy surprise.

'"God gie us a guid conceit of oorselves,"' said Mrs Hauksbee piously, returning to her natural speech. 'Now, in any other woman that would have been vulgar. I am consumed with curiosity to see Mrs Bent. I expect complications.'

'Woman of one idea,' said Mrs Mallowe shortly; 'all complications are as old as the hills! I have lived through or near all—*all*—All!'

'And yet do not understand that men and women never behave twice alike. I am old who was young—if ever I put my head in your lap, you dear, big sceptic, you will learn that my parting is gauze—but never, no *never*, have I lost my interest in men and women. Polly, I shall see this business out to the bitter end.'

'I am going to sleep,' said Mrs Mallowe calmly. 'I never interfere with men or women unless I am compelled,' and she retired with dignity to her own room.

Mrs Hauksbee's curiosity was not long left ungratified, for Mrs Bent came up to Simla a few days after the conversation faithfully reported above, and pervaded the Mall by her husband's side

'Behold!' said Mrs Hauksbee, thoughtfully rubbing her nose. 'That is the last link of the chain, if we omit the husband of the Delville, whoever he may be. Let me consider. The Bents and the Delvilles inhabit the same hotel; and the Delville is detested by the Waddy—do you know the Waddy?—who is almost as big a dowd. The Waddy also abominates the male Bent, for which, if her other sins do not weigh too heavily, she will eventually go to Heaven.'

'Don't be irreverent,' said Mrs Mallowe, 'I like Mrs Bent's face.'

'I am discussing the Waddy,' returned Mrs Hauksbee loftily. 'The Waddy will take the female Bent apart, after having borrowed—yes!—everything that she can, from hairpins to babies' bottles. Such, my dear, is life in a hotel. The Waddy will tell the female Bent facts and fictions about The Dancing Master and The Dowd.'

'Lucy, I should like you better if you were not always looking into people's back-bedrooms.'

'Anybody can look into their front drawingrooms; and remember whatever I do, and whatever I look, I never talk—as the Waddy will. Let us hope that The Dancing Master's greasy smile and manner of the pedagogue will soften the heart of that cow, his wife. If mouths speak truth, I should think that little Mrs Bent could get very angry on occasion.'

'But what reason has she for being angry?'

'What reason! The Dancing Master in himself is a reason. How does it go? "If in his life some trivial errors fall, Look in his face and you'll believe them all." I am prepared to credit *any* evil of The Dancing Master, because I hate him so. And The Dowd is so disgustingly badly dressed—'

'That she, too, is capable of every iniquity? I always prefer to believe the best of everybody. It saves so much trouble.'

'Very good. I prefer to believe the worst. It saves useless expenditure of sympathy. And you may be quite certain that the Waddy believes with me.'

Mrs Mallowe sighed and made no answer.

The conversation was holden after dinner while Mrs Hauksbee was dressing for a dance.

'I am too tired to go,' pleaded Mrs Mallowe, and Mrs Hauksbee left her in peace till two in the morning, when she was aware of emphatic knocking at her door.

'Don't be *very* angry, dear,' said Mrs Hauksbee. 'My idiot of an ayah has gone home, and, as I hope to sleep to-night, there isn't a soul in the place to unlace me.'

'Oh, this is too bad!' said Mrs Mallowe sulkily.

''Cant help it. I'm a lone, lorn grass-widow, dear, but I will *not* sleep in my stays. And such news too! Oh, *do* unlace me, there's a darling! The Dowd—The Dancing Master—I and the Hawley Boy—You know the North verandah?'

'How can I do anything if you spin round like this?' protested Mrs Mallowe, fumbling with the knot of the laces.

'Oh, I forget. I must tell my tale without the aid of your eyes. Do you know you've lovely eyes, dear? Well, to begin with, I took the Hawley Boy to a kala juggah.'

'Did he want much taking?'

'Lots! There was an arrangement of loose-boxes in kanats, and *she* was in the next one talking to *him*.'

'Which? How? Explain.'

'You know what I mean—The Dowd and The Dancing Master. We could hear every word, and we listened shamelessly—'specially the Hawley Boy. Polly, I quite love that woman!'

'This is interesting. There! Now turn round. What happened?'

'One moment. Ah—h! Blessed relief. I've been looking forward to taking them off for the last half-hour—which is ominous at my time of life. But, as I was saying, we listened and heard The Dowd drawl worse than ever. She drops her final g's like a barmaid or a blue-blooded Aide-de-Camp. "Look he-ere, you're gettin' too fond o' me," she said, and The Dancing Master owned it was so in language that nearly made me ill. The Dowd reflected for a while. Then we heard her say, "Look he-ere, Mister Bent, why are you such an aw-ful liar?" I nearly exploded while The Dancing Master denied the charge. It seems that he never told her he was a married man.'

'I said he wouldn't.'

'And she had taken this to heart, on personal grounds, I suppose. She drawled along for five minutes, reproaching him with his perfidy, and grew quite motherly. "Now you've got a nice little wife of your own—you have," she said. "She's ten times too good for a fat old man like you, and, look he-ere, you never told me a word about her, and I've been thinkin' about it a good deal, and I think you're a liar." Wasn't that delicious? The Dancing Master maundered and raved till the Hawley Boy suggested that he should burst in and beat him. His voice runs up into an impassioned squeak when he is afraid. The Dowd must be an extraordinary woman. She explained that had he been a bachelor she might not have objected to his devotion; but since he was a married man and the father of a very nice baby, she considered him a hypocrite, and this she repeated twice. She wound up her drawl with: "An' I'm tellin' you this because your wife is angry with me, an' I hate quarrellin' with any other woman, an' I like your wife. You know how you have behaved for the last six weeks. You shouldn't have done it, indeed you shouldn't. You're too old an' too fat." Can't you imagine how The Dancing Master would wince at that! "Now go away," she said. ''I don't want to tell you what I think of you, because I think you are not nice. I'll stay he-ere till the next dance begins." Did you think that the creature had so much in her?'

'I never studied her as closely as you did. It sounds unnatural. What happened?'

'The Dancing Master attempted blandishment, reproof, jocularity, and the style of the Lord High Warden, and I had almost to pinch the Hawley Boy to make him keep quiet. She grunted at the end of each sentence and, in the end, *he* went away swearing to himself, quite like a man in a novel. He looked more objectionable than ever. I laughed. I love that woman in—spite of her clothes. And now I'm going to bed. What do you think of it?'

'I shan't begin to think till the morning,' said Mrs Mallowe, yawning. 'Perhaps she spoke the truth. They *do* fly into it by accident sometimes.'

Mrs Hauksbee's account of her eavesdropping was an ornate one, but truthful in the main. For reasons best known to herself, Mrs 'Shady' Delville had turned upon Mr Bent and rent him limb from limb, casting him away limp and disconcerted ere she withdrew the light of her eyes from him permanently. Being a man of resource, and anything but pleased in that he had been called both old and fat, he gave Mrs Bent to understand that he had, during her absence in the Doon, been the victim of unceasing persecution at the hands of Mrs Delville, and he told the tale so often and with such eloquence that he ended in believing it, while his wife marvelled at the manners and customs of 'some women.' When the situation showed signs of languishing, Mrs Waddy was always on hand to wake the smouldering fires of suspicion in Mrs Bent's bosom and to contribute generally to the peace and comfort of the hotel. Mr Bent's life was not a happy one, for if Mrs Waddy's story were true, he was, argued his wife, untrustworthy to the last degree. If his own statement was true, his charms of manner and conversation were so great that he needed constant surveillance. And he received it, till he repented genuinely of his marriage and neglected his personal appearance. Mrs Delville alone in the hotel was unchanged. She removed her chair some six paces towards the head of the table, and occasionally in the twilight ventured on timid overtures of friendship to Mrs Bent, which were repulsed.

'She does it for my sake,' hinted the virtuous Bent.

'A dangerous and designing woman,' purred Mrs Waddy.

Worst of all, every other hotel in Simla was full!

~

'Polly, are you afraid of diphtheria?'

'Of nothing in the world except small-pox, Diphtheria kills, but it doesn't disfigure. Why do you ask?'

'Because the Bent baby has got it, and the whole hotel is upside down in consequence. The Waddy has "set her five young on the rail" and fled. The Dancing Master fears for his precious throat, and that miserable little woman, his wife, has no notion of what ought to be done. She wanted to put it into a mustard bath—for croup!'

'Where did you learn all this?'

'Just now, on the Mall. Dr Howlen told me. The manager of the hotel is abusing the Bents, and the Bents are abusing the manager. They *are* a feckless couple.'

'Well. What's on your mind?'

'This; and I know it's a grave thing to ask. Would you seriously object to my bringing the child over here, with its mother?'

'On the most strict understanding that we see nothing of the Dancing Master.'

'He will be only too glad to stay away. Polly, you're an angel. The woman really is at her wits' end.'

'And you know nothing about her, care less, and would hold her up to public scorn if it gave you a minute's amusement. Therefore you risk your life for the sake of her brat. No, Loo, I'm not the angel. I shall keep to my rooms and avoid her. But do as you please—only tell me why you do it.'

Mrs Hauksbee's eyes softened; she looked out of the window and back into Mrs Mallowe's face.

'I don't know,' said Mrs Hauksbee simply.

'You dear!'

'Polly!—and for aught you knew you might have taken my fringe off. Never do that again without warning. Now we'll get the rooms ready. I don't suppose I shall be allowed to circulate in society for a month.'

'And I also. Thank goodness I shall at last get all the sleep I want.'

Much to Mrs Bent's surprise she and the baby were brought over to the house almost before she knew where she was. Bent was devoutly and undisguisedly thankful, for he was afraid of the infection, and also hoped that a few weeks in the hotel alone with Mrs Delville might lead to explanations. Mrs Bent had thrown her jealousy to the winds in her fear for her child's life.

'We can give you good milk,' said Mrs Hauksbee to her, 'and our house is much nearer to the Doctor's than the hotel, and you won't feel as though you were living in a hostile camp. Where is the dear Mrs Waddy? She seemed to be a particular friend of yours.'

'They've all left me,' said Mrs Bent bitterly. 'Mrs Waddy went first. She said I ought to be ashamed of myself for introducing diseases there, and I am *sure* it wasn't my fault that little Dora—'

'How nice!' cooed Mrs Hauksbee. 'The Waddy is an infectious disease herself—"more quickly caught than the plague and the taker runs presently mad." I lived next door to her at the Elysium, three years ago. Now see, you won't give us the *least* trouble, and I've ornamented all the house with sheets soaked in carbolic. It smells comforting, doesn't it? Remember I'm always in call, and my *ayah's* at your service when yours goes to her meals, and—and—if you cry I'll never forgive you.'

Dora Bent occupied her mother's unprofitable attention through the day and the night. The Doctor called thrice in the twenty-four hours, and the house reeked with the smell of the Condy's Fluid, chlorine-water, and carbolic acid washes. Mrs Mallowe kept to her own rooms: she considered that she

had made sufficient concessions in the cause of humanity—
and Mrs Hauksbee was more esteemed by the Doctor as a help
in the sick-room than the half-distraught mother.

'I know nothing of illness,' said Mrs Hauksbee to the Doctor.
'Only tell me what to do, and I'll do it.'

'Keep that crazy woman from kissing the child, and let
her have as little to do with the nursing as you possibly can,'
said the Doctor; 'I'd turn her out of the sick-room, but that I
honestly believe she'd die of anxiety. She is less than no good,
and I depend on you and the ayahs, remember.'

Mrs Hauksbee accepted the responsibility, though it painted
olive hollows under her eyes and forced her to her oldest
dresses. Mrs Bent clung to her with more than childlike faith.

'I *know* you'll make Dora well, won't you?' she said at least
twenty times a day; and twenty times a day Mrs Hauksbee
answered valiantly, 'Of course I will.'

But Dora did not improve, and the Doctor seemed to be
always in the house.

'There's some danger of the thing taking a bad turn,' he
said; 'I'll come over between three and four in the morning
to-morrow.'

'Good gracious!' said Mrs Hauksbee. 'He never told me
what the turn would be! My education has been horribly
neglected; and I have only this foolish mother-woman to fall
back upon.'

The night wore through slowly, and Mrs Hauksbee dozed
in a chair by the fire. There was a dance at the Viceregal Lodge,
and she dreamed of it till she was aware of Mrs Bent's anxious
eyes staring into her own.

'Wake up! Wake up! Do something!' cried Mrs Bent
piteously. 'Dora's choking to death! Do you mean to let her
die?'

Mrs Hauksbee jumped to her feet and bent over the bed. The child was fighting for breath, while the mother wrung her hands despairingly.

'Oh, what can I do? What can you do? She won't stay still! I can't hold her. Why didn't the Doctor say this was coming?' screamed Mrs Bent. '*Won't* you help me? She's dying!'

'I—I've never seen a child die before!' stammered Mrs Hauksbee feebly, and then—let none blame her weakness after the strain of long watching—she broke down, and covered her face with her hands. The ayahs on the threshold snored peacefully.

There was a rattle of 'rickshaw wheels below, the clash of an opening door, a heavy step on the stairs, and Mrs Delville entered to find Mrs Bent screaming for the Doctor as she ran round the room. Mrs Hauksbee, her hands to her ears, and her face buried in the chintz of a chair, was quivering with pain at each cry from the bed, and murmuring, 'Thank God, I never bore a child! Oh! thank God, I never bore a child!'

Mrs Delville looked at the bed for an instant, took Mrs Bent by the shoulders, and said quietly, 'Get me some caustic. Be quick.'

The mother obeyed mechanically. Mrs Delville had thrown herself down by the side of the child and was opening its mouth.

'Oh, you're killing her!' cried Mrs Bent. 'Where's the Doctor? Leave her alone!'

Mrs Delville made no reply for a minute, but busied herself with the child.

'Now the caustic, and hold a lamp behind my shoulder. *Will* you do as you are told? The acid-bottle, if you don't know what I mean,' she said.

A second time Mrs Delville bent over the child. Mrs Hauksbee, her face still hidden, sobbed and shivered. One of the ayahs staggered sleepily into the room, yawning: 'Doctor Sahib come.'

Mrs Delville turned her head.

'You're only just in time,' she said. 'It was chokin' her when I came, an' I've burnt it.'

'There was no sign of the membrane getting to the air-passages after the last steaming. It was the general weakness I feared,' said the Doctor half to himself, and he whispered as he looked, 'You've done what I should have been afraid to do without consultation.'

'She was dyin',' said Mrs Delville, under her breath. 'Can you do anythin'? What a mercy it was I went to the dance!'

Mrs Hauksbee raised her head.

'Is it all over?' she gasped. 'I'm useless—I'm worse than useless! What are *you* doing here?'

She stared at Mrs Delville, and Mrs Bent, realising for the first time who was the Goddess from the Machine, stared also.

Then Mrs Delville made explanation, putting on a dirty long glove and smoothing a crumpled and ill-fitting ball-dress.

'I was at the dance, an' the Doctor was tellin' me about your baby bein' so ill. So I came away early, an' your door was open, an' I—I—lost my boy this way six months ago, an' I've been tryin' to forget it ever since, an' I—I—I am very sorry for intrudin' an' anythin' that has happened.'

Mrs Bent was putting out the Doctor's eye with a lamp as he stooped over Dora.

'Take it away,' said the Doctor. 'I think the child will do, thanks to you, Mrs Delville. *I* should have come too late, but, I assure you'—he was addressing himself to Mrs Delville—'I had not the faintest reason to expect this. The membrane must have grown like a mushroom. Will one of you help me, please?'

He had reason for the last sentence. Mrs Hauksbee had thrown herself into Mrs Delville's arms, where she was weeping bitterly, and Mrs Bent was unpicturesquely mixed up with both, while from the tangle came the sound of many sobs and much promiscuous kissing.

'Good gracious! I've spoilt all your beautiful roses!' said Mrs Hauksbee, lifting her head from the lump of crushed gum and calico atrocities on Mrs Delville's shoulder and hurrying to the Doctor.

Mrs Delville picked up her shawl, and slouched out of the room, mopping her eyes with the glove that she had not put on.

'I always said she was more than a woman,' sobbed Mrs Hauksbee hysterically, 'and *that* proves it!'

~

Six weeks later Mrs Bent and Dora had returned to the hotel. Mrs Hauksbee had come out of the Valley of Humiliation, had ceased to reproach herself for her collapse in an hour of need, and was even beginning to direct the affairs of the world as before.

'So nobody died, and everything went off as it should, and I kissed The Dowd, Polly. I feel *so* old. Does it show in my face?'

'Kisses don't as a rule, do they? Of course you know what the result of The Dowd's providential arrival has been.'

'They ought to build her a statue—only no sculptor dare copy those skirts.'

'Ah!' said Mrs Mallowe quietly. 'She has found another reward. The Dancing Master has been smirking through Simla, giving every one to understand that she came because of her undying love for him—for him—to save *his* child, and all Simla naturally believes this.'

'But Mrs Bent—'

'Mrs Bent believes it more than any one else. She won't speak to The Dowd now. *Isn't* The Dancing Master an angel?'

Mrs Hauksbee lifted up her voice and raged till bed-time. The doors of the two rooms stood open.

'Polly,' said a voice from the darkness, 'what did that American-heiress-globe-trotter girl say last season when she was tipped out of her 'rickshaw turning a corner? Some absurd adjective that made the man who picked her up explode.'

'"Paltry,"' said Mrs Mallowe. 'Through her nose—like this—"Ha-ow pahltry!"'

'Exactly,' said the voice. 'Ha-ow pahltry it all is!'

'Which?'

'Everything. Babies, Diphtheria, Mrs Bent and The Dancing Master, I whooping in a chair, and The Dowd dropping in from the clouds. I wonder what the motive was—*all* the motives.'

'Um!'

'What do *you* think?'

'Don't ask me. Go to sleep.'

A FRIEND'S FRIEND

Wherefore slew I the stranger? He brought me dishonour.
I saddled my mare Bijli. I set him upon her.
I gave him rice and goat's flesh. He bared me to laughter;
When he was gone from my tent, swift I followed after,
Taking a sword in my hand. The hot wine had filled him
Under the stars he mocked me. Therefore I killed him.

—'Hadramauti'

This tale must be told in the first person for many reasons. The man I desire to expose is Tranter of the Bombay side. I want Tranter black-balled at his Club, divorced from his wife, turned out of Service, and cast into prison, until I get an apology from him in writing. I wish to warn the world against Tranter of the Bombay side. You know the casual way in which men pass on acquaintances in India. It is a great convenience, because you can get rid of a man you don't like by writing a letter of introduction and putting him, with it, into the train. T. G.s [temporary gentlemen] are best treated thus. If you keep them moving, they have no time to say insulting and offensive things about 'Anglo-Indian Society.'

One day, late in the cold weather, I got a letter of preparation from Tranter of the Bombay side, advising me of the advent of a T. G., a man called Jevon; and saying, as usual, that any kindness shown to Jevon would be a kindness to Tranter. Every one knows the regular form of these communications. Two days later, Jevon turned up with his letter of introduction, and I did what I could for him. He was lint-haired, fresh-coloured, and very English. But he held no views about the Government

of India. Nor did he insist on shooting tigers on the Station
Mall, as some T. G.'s do. Nor did he call us 'colonists,' and
dine in a flannel-shirt and tweeds, under that delusion, as
other T. G.'s do. He was well behaved and very grateful for
the little I won for him—most grateful of all when I secured
him an invitation for the Afghan Ball, and introduced him to a
Mrs Deemes, a lady for whom I had a great respect and
admiration, who danced like the shadow of a leaf in a light
wind. I set great store by the friendship of Mrs Deemes; but,
had I known what was coming, I would have broken Jevon's
neck with a curtain-pole before getting him that invitation. But
I did not know, and he dined at the Club, I think, on the night
of the ball. I dined at home.

When I went to the dance, the first man I met asked me
whether I had seen Jevon. 'No,' said I. 'He's at the Club. Hasn't
he come?'—'Come!' said the man. 'Yes, he's very much come.
You'd better look at him.' I sought for Jevon. I found him sitting
on a bench and smiling to himself and a programme. Half a
look was enough for me. On that one night, of all others, he
had begun a long and thirsty evening, by taking too much! He
was breathing heavily through his nose, his eyes were rather
red, and he appeared very satisfied with all the earth. I put
up a little prayer that the waltzing would work off the wine,
and went about feeling uncomfortable. But I saw Jevon walk
up to Mrs Deemes for the first dance, and I knew that all the
waltzing on the card was not enough to keep Jevon's rebellious
legs steady. That couple went round six times. I counted.
Mrs Deemes dropped Jevon's arm and came across to me. I am
not going to repeat what Mrs Deemes said to me; because she
was very angry indeed. I am not going to write what I said to
Mrs Deemes, because I didn't say anything. I only wished that I
had killed Jevon first and been hanged for it. Mrs Deemes drew

her pencil through all the dances that I had booked with her, and went away, leaving me to remember that what I ought to have said—was that Mrs Deemes had asked to be introduced to Jevon because he danced well; and that I really had not carefully worked out a plot to insult her. But I realised that argument was no good, and that I had better try to stop Jevon from waltzing me into more trouble.

He, however, was gone, and every third dance I set off to hunt for him. This ruined what little pleasure I expected from the entertainment. Just before supper I caught him, at the buffet with his legs wide apart, talking to a very fat and indignant chaperone. 'If this person is a friend of yours, as I understand he is, I would recommend you to take him home,' said she. 'He is unfit for decent society.' Then I knew that goodness only knew what Jevon had been doing, and I tried to get him away. But Jevon wasn't going; not he. He knew what was good for him, he did; and he wasn't going to be dictated to by any loconial nigger-driver, he wasn't; and I was the friend who had formed his infant mind and brought him up to buy Benares brassware and fear God so I was; and we would have many more blazing good, drunks together, so we would; and all the she-camels in black silk in the world shouldn't make him withdraw his opinion that there was nothing better than Benedictine to give one an appetite. And then ... but he was my guest. I set him in a quiet corner of the supper-room, and went to find a wall-prop that I could trust.

There was a good and kindly Subaltern—may Heaven bless that Subaltern, and make him a Commander-in-Chief! who heard of my trouble. He was not dancing himself, and he owned a head like a five-year-old teak-baulks. He said that he would look after Jevon till the end of the ball. 'Don't suppose you much mind what I do with him?' said he. 'Mind!' said I.

'No! You can murder the beast if you like.' But the Subaltern did not murder him. He trotted off to the supper-room, and sat down by Jevon, drinking peg for peg with him. I saw the two fairly established, and went away, feeling more easy.

When 'The Roast Beef of Old England' sounded, I heard of Jevon's performances between the first dance and my meeting with him at the buffet. After Mrs Deemes had cast him off, it seems that he had found his way into the gallery, and offered to conduct the Band or to play any instrument in it just as the Bandmaster pleased. When the Bandmaster refused, Jevon said that he wasn't appreciated, and he yearned for sympathy. So he trundled downstairs and sat out four dances with four girls, and proposed to three of them. One of the girls was a married woman, by the way. Then he went into the whist-room, and fell face-down and wept on the hearth-rug in front of the fire, because he had fallen into a den of card-sharpers, and his Mamma had always warned him against bad company. He had done a lot of other things, too, and had taken about three quarts of mixed liquors. Besides speaking of me in the most scandalous fashion! All the women wanted him turned out, and all the men wanted him kicked. The worst of it was, that every one said it was my fault. Now, I put it to you, how on earth could I have known that this innocent, fluffy T. G. would break out in this disgusting manner? You see he had gone round the world nearly, and his vocabulary of abuse was cosmopolitan, though mainly Japanese which he had picked up in a low tea-house at Hakodate. It sounded like whistling.

While I was listening to first one man and then another telling me of Jevon's shameless behaviour and asking me for his blood, I wondered where he was. I was prepared to sacrifice him to Society on the spot. But Jevon was gone, and, far away in the corner of the supper-room, sat my dear, good Subaltern, a little flushed, eating salad. I went over and said, 'Where's Jevon?'—'In the cloakroom,' said the Subaltern. 'He'll keep till the women have gone. Don't you interfere with my prisoner.' I didn't want to interfere, but I peeped into the cloakroom, and found my guest put to bed on some rolled-up carpets, all comfy, his collar free, and a wet swab on his head. The rest of the evening I spent in timid attempts to explain things to Mrs Deemes and three or four other ladies, and trying to clear my character—for I am a respectable man—from the shameful slurs that my guest had cast upon it. Libel was no word for what he had said. When I wasn't trying to explain, I was running off to the cloakroom to see that Jevon wasn't dead of apoplexy. I didn't want him to die on my hands. He had eaten my salt.

At last that ghastly ball ended, though I was not in the least restored to Mrs Deemes' favour. When the ladies had gone, and some one was calling for songs at the second supper, that angelic Subaltern told the servants to bring in the Sahib who was in the cloakroom, and clear away one end of the supper-table. While this was being done, we formed ourselves into a Board of Punishment with the Doctor for President. Jevon came in on four men's shoulders, and was put down on the table like a corpse in a dissecting-room, while the Doctor lectured on the evils of intemperance and Jevon snored. Then we set to work. We corked the whole of his face. We filled his hair with meringue-cream till it looked like a white wig. To protect everything till it dried, a man in the Ordnance Department, who understood the work, luted a big blue-paper cap from a cracker, with meringue-cream, low down on Jevon's forehead. This was punishment, not play, remember. We took the gelatine of crackers, and stuck blue gelatine on his nose, and yellow gelatine on his chin, and green and red gelatine on his cheeks, pressing each dab down till it held as firm as goldbeaters' skin.

We put a ham-frill round his neck, and tied it in a bow in front. He nodded like a mandarin. We fixed gelatine on the back of his hands, and burnt-corked them inside, and put small cutlet frills round his wrists, and tied both wrists together with string. We waxed up the ends of his moustache with isinglass. He looked very martial. We turned him over, pinned up his coat-tails between his shoulders, and put a rosette of cutlet-frills there. We took up the red cloth from the ball-room to the supper-room, and wound him up in it. There where sixty feet of red cloth, six feet broad; and he rolled up into a big fat bundle, with only that amazing head sticking out. Lastly, we tied up the surplus of the cloth beyond his feet with cocoanut-fibre string as tightly as we knew how. We were so angry that we hardly laughed at all. Just as we finished, we heard the rumble of bullock-carts taking away some chairs and things that the General's wife had lent for the ball. So we hoisted Jevon, like a roll of carpets, into one of the carts, and the carts went away.

Now the most extraordinary part of this tale is that never again did I see or hear anything of Jevon, T. G. He vanished utterly. He was not delivered at the General's house with the carpets. He just went into the black darkness of the end of the night, and was swallowed up. Perhaps he died and was thrown into the river. But, alive or dead, I have often wondered how he got rid of the red cloth and the meringue-cream. I wonder still whether Mrs Deemes will ever take any notice of me again, and whether I shall live down the infamous stories that Jevon set afloat about my manners and customs between the first and the ninth waltz of the Afghan Ball. They stick closer than cream. Wherefore, I want Tranter of the Bombay side, dead or alive. But dead for preference.

BITTERS NEAT

The oldest trouble in the world comes from want of understanding. And it is entirely the fault of the woman. Somehow, she is built incapable of speaking the truth, even to herself. She only finds it out about four months later, when the man is dead, or has been transferred. Then she says she never was so happy in her life, and marries some one else, who again touched some woman's heart elsewhere, and did not know it, but was mixed up with another man's wife, who only used him to pique a third man. And so round again—all criss-cross.

Out here, where life goes quicker than at Home, things are more obviously tangled, and therefore more pitiful to look at. Men speak the truth as they understand it, and women as they think men would like to understand it; and then they all act lies which would deceive Solomon, and the result is a heartrending muddle that half a dozen open words would put straight. This particular muddle did not differ from any other muddle you may see, if you are not busy playing cross-purposes yourself, going on in a big Station any cold season. Its only merit was that it did not come all right in the end; as muddles are made to do in the third volume.

I've forgotten what the man was—he was an ordinary sort of man—a man you meet any day at the A.D.C.'s end of the table, and go away and forget about. His name was Surrey; but whether he was in the Army or the P.W.D., on the Commissariat, or the Police, or a factory, I don't remember. He wasn't a Civilian. He was just an ordinary man, of the light-coloured variety, with a fair moustache and with the average amount of pay that comes between twenty-seven and thirty-two—from six to nine hundred a month.

He didn't dance, and he did what little riding he wanted to do by himself, and was busy in office all day, and never bothered his head about women. No man ever dreamed he would. He was of the type that doesn't marry, just because it doesn't think about marriage. He was one of the plain cards, whose only use is to make up the pack, and furnish background to put the Court cards against.

Then there was a girl—ordinary girl, the dark-coloured variety—daughter of a man in the Army, who played a little, sang a little, talked a little, and furnished the background, exactly as Surrey did. She had been sent out here to get married if she could, because there were many sisters at home, and Colonels' allowances aren't elastic. She lived with an aunt. She was a Miss Tallaght, and men spelt her name 'Tart' on the programmes when they couldn't catch what the introducer said.

Surrey and she were thrown together in the same Station one cold weather; and the particular Devil who looks after muddles prompted Miss Tallaght to fall in love with Surrey. He had spoken to her perhaps twenty times—certainly not more—but she fell as unreasoningly in love with him as if she had been Elaine and he Lancelot.

She, of course, kept her own counsel; and, equally of course, her manner to Surrey, who never noticed manner or style or dress any more than he noticed a sunset, was icy, not to say repellent. The deadly dullness of Surrey struck her as a reserve of force, and she grew to believe he was wonderfully clever in some secret and mysterious sort of line. She did not know what line; but she believed, and that was enough. No one suspected anything of any kind, for the simple reason that no one took any deep interest in Miss Tallaght except her Aunt; who wanted to get the girl off her hands.

This went on for some months, till a man suddenly woke up to the fact that Miss Tallaght was the one woman in the world for him, and told her so. She jawabed him—without rhyme or reason; and that night there followed one of those awful bedroom conferences that men know nothing about. Miss Tallaght's Aunt, querulous, indignant and merciless, with her mouth full of hair-pins, and her hands full of false hair-plaits, set herself to find out by cross-examination what in the name of everything wise, prudent, religious and dutiful, Miss Tallaght meant by jawabing her suitor. The conference lasted for an hour and a half, with question on question, insult and reminders of poverty—appeals to Providence, then a fresh mouthful of hair-pins—then all the questions over again, beginning with:—'But what do you see to dislike in Mr __?' then, a vicious tug at what was left of the mane; then impressive warnings and more appeals to Heaven; and then the collapse of poor Miss Tallaght, a rumpled, crumpled, tear-stained arrangement in white on the couch at the foot of the bed, and, between sobs and gasps, the whole absurd little story of her love for Surrey.

Now, in all the forty-five years' experience of Miss Tallaght's Aunt, she had never heard of a girl throwing over a real genuine lover with an appointment, for a problematical, hypothetical lover to whom she had spoken merely in the course of the ordinary social visiting rounds. So Miss Tallaght's Aunt was struck dumb, and, merely praying that Heaven might direct Miss Tallaght into a better frame of mind, dismissed the ayah and went to bed; leaving Miss Tallaght to sob and moan herself to sleep.

Understand clearly, I don't for a moment defend Miss Tallaght. She was wrong—absurdly wrong—but attachments like hers must sprout by the law of averages, just to remind people that Love is as nakedly unreasoning as when Venus first gave him his kit and told him to run away and play.

Surrey must be held innocent—innocent as his own pony. Could he guess that, when Miss Tallaght was as curt and as unpleasing as she knew how, she would have risen up and followed him from Colombo to Dakar at a word? He didn't know anything, or care anything about Miss Tallaght. He had his work to do.

Miss Tallaght's Aunt might have respected her niece's secret. But she didn't. What we call 'talking rank scandal,' she called 'seeking advice'; and she sought advice, on the case of Miss Tallaght, from the Judge's wife 'in strict confidence, my dear,' who told the Commissioner's wife, 'of course you won't repeat it, my dear,' who told the Deputy Commissioner's wife, 'you understand it is to go no further, my dear,' who told the newest bride, who was so delighted at being in possession of a secret concerning real grown-up men and women, that she told any one and every one who called on her. So the tale went all over the Station, and from being no one in particular, Miss Tallaght came to take precedence of the last interesting squabble between the Judge's wife and the Civil Engineer's wife. Then began a really interesting system of persecution worked by women—soft and sympathetic and intangible, but calculated to drive a girl off her head. They were all so sorry for Miss Tallaght, and they cooed together and were exaggeratedly kind and sweet in their manner to her, as those who said: 'You may confide in us, my stricken deer!'

Miss Tallaght was a woman, and sensitive. It took her less than one evening at the Band Stand to find that her poor little, precious little secret, that had been wrenched from her on the rack, was known as widely as if it had been written on her hat. I don't know what she went through. Women don't speak of these things, and men ought not to guess; but it must have been some specially refined torture, for she told her Aunt she would go Home and die as a Governess sooner than stay in this hateful—hateful—place. Her Aunt said she was a rebellious girl, and sent her Home to her people after a couple of months; and said no one knew what the pains of a chaperone's life were.

Poor Miss Tallaght had one pleasure just at the last. Halfway down the line, she caught a glimpse of Surrey, who had gone down on duty, and was then in the up-train. And he took off his hat to her. She went Home, and if she is not dead by this time must be living still.

~

Months afterwards, there was a lively dinner at the Club for the Races. Surrey was mooning about as usual, and there was a good deal of idle talk flying every way. Finally, one man, who had taken more than was good for him, said, apropos of something about Surrey's reserved ways, 'Ah, you old fraud. It's all very well for you to pretend. I know a girl who was awf'ly mashed on you—once. Dead nuts she was on old Surrey. What had you been doing, eh?'

Surrey expected some sort of sell, and said with a laugh: 'Who was she?'

Before any one could kick the man, he plumped out with the name; and the Honorary Secretary tactfully upset the half of a big brew of shandy-gaff all over the table. After the mopping up, the men went out to the Lotteries.

But Surrey sat on, and, after ten minutes, said very humbly to the only other man in the deserted dining-room: 'On your honour, was there a word of truth in what the drunken fool said?'

Then the man who is writing this story, who had known of the thing from the beginning, and now felt all the hopelessness and tangle of it—the waste and the muddle—said, a good deal more energetically than he meant: 'Truth! O man, man, couldn't you see it?'

Surrey said nothing, but sat still, smoking and smoking and thinking, while the Lottery tent babbled outside, and the khitmutgars turned down the lamps.

To the best of my knowledge and belief that was the first thing Surrey ever knew about love. But his awakening did not seem to delight him. It must have been rather unpleasant, to judge by the look on his face. He looked like a man who had missed a train and had been half-stunned at the same time.

When the men came in from the Lotteries, Surrey went out. He wasn't in the mood for bones and 'horse' talk. He went to his tent, and the last thing he said, quite aloud to himself, was: 'I didn't see. I didn't see. If I had only known!'

Even if he had known I don't believe... But these things are kismet, and we only find out all about them just when any knowledge is too late.

AT TWENTY-TWO

'Narrow as the womb, deep as the Pit,
and dark as the heart of a man.'

—Sonthal miner's proverb

'A weaver went out to reap but stayed to unravel the corn-stalks.
Ha! Ha! Ha! Is there any sense in a weaver?'

Janki Meah glared at Kundoo, but, as Janki Meah was blind,
Kundoo was not impressed. He had come to argue with Janki
Meah, and, if chance favoured, to make love to the old man's
pretty young wife.

This was Kundoo's grievance, and he spoke in the name
of all the five men who, with Janki Meah, composed the gang
in Number Seven gallery of Twenty-Two. Janki Meah had
been blind for the thirty years during which he had served
the Jimahari Collieries with pick and crowbar. All through
those thirty years he had regularly, every morning before going
down, drawn from the overseer his allowance of lamp-oil—just
as if he had been an eyed miner. What Kundoo's gang resented,
as hundreds of gangs had resented before, was Janki Meah's
selfishness. He would not add the oil to the common stock of
his gang, but would save and sell it.

'I knew these workings before you were born,' Janki Meah
used to reply; 'I don't want the light to get my coal out by, and
I am not going to help you. The oil is mine, and I intend to
keep it.'

A strange man in many ways was Janki Meah, the white-
haired, hot-tempered, sightless weaver who had turned pitman.
All day long—except on Sundays and Mondays when he was

usually drunk—he worked in the Twenty-Two shaft of the Jimahari Colliery as cleverly as a man with all the senses. At evening he went up in the great steam-hauled cage to the pit-bank, and there called for his pony—a rusty, coal-dusty beast, nearly as old as Janki Meah. The pony would come to his side, and Janki Meah would clamber on to its back and be taken at once to the plot of land which he, like the other miners, received from the Jimahari Company. The pony knew that place, and when, after six years, the Company changed all the allotments to prevent the miners from acquiring proprietary rights, Janki Meah represented, with tears in his eyes, that were his holdings shifted, he would never be able to find his way to the new one. 'My horse only knows that place,' pleaded Janki Meah, and so he was allowed to keep his land.

On the strength of this concession and his accumulated oil-savings, Janki Meah took a second wife—a girl of the Jolaha main stock of the Meahs, and singularly beautiful. Janki Meah could not see her beauty; wherefore he took her on trust, and forbade her to go down the pit. He had not worked for thirty years in the dark without knowing that the pit was no place for pretty women. He loaded her with ornaments—not brass or pewter, but real silver ones—and she rewarded him by flirting outrageously with Kundoo of Number Seven gallery gang. Kundoo was really the gang-head, but Janki Meah insisted upon all the work being entered in his own name, and chose the men that he worked with. Custom—stronger even than the Jimahari Company—dictated that Janki, by right of his years, should manage these things, and should, also, work despite his blindness. In Indian mines where they cut into the solid coal with the pick and clear it out from floor to ceiling, he could come to no great harm. At Home, where they undercut the coal and bring it down in crashing avalanches from the roof, he would never have been allowed to set foot in a pit. He was not a popular man, because of his oil-savings; but all the gangs admitted that Janki knew all the khads, or workings, that had ever been sunk or worked since the Jimahari Company first started operations on the Tarachunda fields.

Pretty little Unda only knew that her old husband was a fool who could be managed. She took no interest in the collieries except in so far as they swallowed up Kundoo five days out of the seven, and covered him with coal-dust. Kundoo was a great workman, and did his best not to get drunk, because, when he had saved forty rupees, Unda was to steal everything that she could find in Janki's house and run with Kundoo to a land where there were no mines, and every one kept three fat bullocks and a milch-buffalo. While this scheme ripened it was his custom to drop in upon Janki and worry him about the oil savings. Unda sat in a corner and nodded approval. On the night when Kundoo had quoted that objectionable proverb about weavers, Janki grew angry.

'Listen, you pig,' said he, 'blind I am, and old I am, but, before ever you were born, I was grey among the coal. Even in the days when the Twenty-Two khad was unsunk and there were not two thousand men here, I was known to have all knowledge of the pits. What khad is there that I do not know, from the bottom of the shaft to the end of the last drive? Is it the Baromba khad, the oldest, or the Twenty-Two where Tibu's gallery runs up to Number Five?'

'Hear the old fool talk!' said Kundoo, nodding to Unda. 'No gallery of Twenty-Two will cut into Five before the end of the Rains. We have a month's solid coal before us. The Babuji says so.'

'Babuji! Pigji! Dogji! What do these fat slugs from Calcutta know? He draws and draws and draws, and talks and talks and talks, and his maps are all wrong. I, Janki, know that this is so. When a man has been shut up in the dark for thirty years, God gives him knowledge. The old gallery that Tibu's gang made is not six feet from Number Five.'

'Without doubt God gives the blind knowledge,' said Kundoo, with a look at Unda. 'Let it be as you say. I, for my part, do not know where lies the gallery of Tibu's gang, but I am not a withered monkey who needs oil to grease his joints with.'

Kundoo swung out of the hut laughing, and Unda giggled. Janki turned his sightless eyes toward his wife and swore. 'I have land, and I have sold a great deal of lamp-oil,' mused Janki; 'but I was a fool to marry this child.'

A week later the Rains set in with a vengeance, and the gangs paddled about in coal-slush at the pit-banks. Then the big mine-pumps were made ready, and the Manager of the Colliery ploughed through the wet toward the Tarachunda River swelling between its soppy banks. 'Lord send that this beastly beck doesn't misbehave,' said the Manager, piously, and he went to take counsel with his Assistant about the pumps.

But the Tarachunda misbehaved very much indeed. After a fall of three inches of rain in an hour it was obliged to do something. It topped its bank and joined the flood water that was hemmed between two low hills just where the embankment of the Colliery main line crossed. When a large part of a rain-fed river, and a few acres of flood-water, made a dead set for a nine-foot culvert, the culvert may spout its finest, but the water cannot all get out. The Manager pranced upon one leg with excitement, and his language was improper.

He had reason to swear, because he knew that one inch of water on land meant a pressure of one hundred tons to the acre; and here were about five feet of water forming, behind the railway embankment, over the shallower workings of Twenty-

Two. You must understand that, in a coal-mine, the coal nearest the surface is worked first from the central shaft. That is to say, the miners may clear out the stuff to within ten, twenty or thirty feet of the surface, and, when all is worked out, leave only a skin of earth upheld by some few pillars of coal. In a deep mine where they know that they have any amount of material at hand, men prefer to get all their mineral out at one shaft, rather than make a number of little holes to tap the comparatively unimportant surface-coal.

And the Manager watched the flood.

The culvert spouted a nine-foot gush; but the water still formed, and word was sent to clear the men out of Twenty-Two. The cages came up crammed and crammed again with the men nearest the pit-eye, as they call the place where you can see daylight from the bottom of the main shaft. All away and away up the long black galleries the flare-lamps were winking and dancing like so many fireflies, and the men and the women waited for the clanking, rattling, thundering cages to come down and fly up again. But the outworkings were very far off, and word could not be passed quickly, though the heads of the gangs and the Assistant shouted and swore and tramped and stumbled. The Manager kept one eye on the great troubled pool behind the embankment, and prayed that the culvert would give way and let the water through in time. With the other eye he watched the cages come up and saw the headmen counting the roll of the gangs. With all his heart and soul he swore at the winder who controlled the iron drum that wound up the wire rope on which hung the cages.

In a little time there was a down-draw in the water behind the embankment—a sucking whirlpool, all yellow and yeasty. The water had smashed through the skin of the earth and was pouring into the old shallow workings of Twenty-Two.

Deep down below, a rush of black water caught the last gang waiting for the cage, and as they clambered in, the whirl was about their waists. The cage reached the pit-bank, and the Manager called the roll. The gangs were all safe except Gang Janki, Gang Mogul, and Gang Rahim, eighteen men, with perhaps ten basket-women who loaded the coal into the little iron carriages that ran on the tramways of the main galleries. These gangs were in the out-workings, three-quarters of a mile away, on the extreme fringe of the mine. Once more the cage went down, but with only two English men in it, and dropped into a swirling, roaring current that had almost touched the roof of some of the lower side-galleries. One of the wooden balks with which they had propped the old workings shot past on the current, just missing the cage.

'If we don't want our ribs knocked out, we'd better go,' said the Manager. 'We can't even save the Company's props.'

The cage drew out of the water with a splash, and a few minutes later, it was officially reported that there were at least ten feet of water in the pit's eye. Now ten feet of water there meant that all other places in the mine were flooded, except such galleries as were more than ten feet above the level of the bottom of the shaft. The deep workings would be full, the main galleries would be full, but in the high workings reached by inclines from the main roads, there would be a certain amount of air cut off, so to speak, by the water and squeezed up by it. The little science-primers explain how water behaves when you pour it down test-tubes. The flooding of Twenty-Two was an illustration on a large scale.

~

'By the Holy Grove, what has happened to the air!' It was a Sonthal gangman of Gang Mogul in Number Nine gallery, and he was driving a six-foot way through the coal. Then there was a rush from the other galleries, and Gang Janki and Gang Rahim stumbled up with their basket-women.

'Water has come in the mine,' they said, 'and there is no way of getting out.'

'I went down,' said Janki—'down the slope of my gallery, and I felt the water.'

'There has been no water in the cutting in our time,' clamoured the women, 'Why cannot we go away?'

'Be silent!' said Janki, 'Long ago, when my father was here, water came to Ten—no, Eleven—cutting, and there was great trouble. Let us get away to where the air is better.'

The three gangs and the basket-women left Number Nine gallery and went further up Number Sixteen. At one turn of the road they could see the pitchy black water lapping on the coal. It had touched the roof of a gallery that they knew well—a gallery where they used to smoke their huqas and manage their flirtations. Seeing this, they called aloud upon their Gods, and the Meahs, who are thrice bastard Muhammadans, strove to recollect the name of the Prophet. They came to a great open square whence nearly all the coal had been extracted. It was the end of the out-workings, and the end of the mine.

Far away down the gallery a small pumping-engine, used for keeping dry a deep working and fed with steam from above, was throbbing faithfully. They heard it cease.

'They have cut off the steam,' said Kundoo, hopefully. 'They have given the order to use all the steam for the pit-bank pumps. They will clear out the water.'

'If the water has reached the smoking-gallery,' said Janki, 'all the Company's pumps can do nothing for three days.'

'It is very hot,' moaned Jasoda, the Meah basket-woman. 'There is a very bad air here because of the lamps.'

'Put them out,' said Janki; 'why do you want lamps?' The lamps were put out and the company sat still in the utter dark. Somebody rose quietly and began walking over the coals. It was Janki, who was touching the walls with his hands. 'Where is the ledge?' he murmured to himself.

'Sit, sit!' said Kundoo. 'If we die, we die. The air is very bad.'

But Janki still stumbled and crept and tapped with his pick upon the walls. The women rose to their feet.

'Stay all where you are. Without the lamps you cannot see, and I—I am always seeing,' said Janki. Then he paused, and called out: 'Oh, you who have been in the cutting more than ten years, what is the name of this open place? I am an old man and I have forgotten.'

'Bullia's Room,' answered the Sonthal, who had complained of the vileness of the air.

'Again,' said Janki.

'Bullia's Room.'

'Then I have found it,' said Janki. 'The name only had slipped my memory. Tibu's gang's gallery is here.'

'A lie,' said Kundoo. 'There have been no galleries in this place since my day.'

'Three paces was the depth of the ledge,' muttered Janki, without heeding—'and—oh, my poor bones!—I have found it! It is here, up this ledge, Come all you, one by one, to the place of my voice, and I will count you,'

There was a rush in the dark, and Janki felt the first man's face hit his knees as the Sonthal scrambled up the ledge.

'Who?' cried Janki.

'I, Sunua Manji.'

'Sit you down,' said Janki, 'Who next?'

One by one the women and the men crawled up the ledge which ran along one side of 'Bullia's Room.' Degraded

Muhammadan, pig-eating Musahr and wild Sonthal, Janki ran his hand over them all.

'Now follow after,' said he, 'catching hold of my heel, and the women catching the men's clothes.' He did not ask whether the men had brought their picks with them. A miner, black or white, does not drop his pick. One by one, Janki leading, they crept into the old gallery—a six-foot way with a scant four feet from hill to roof.

'The air is better here,' said Jasoda. They could hear her heart beating in thick, sick bumps.

'Slowly, slowly,' said Janki. 'I am an old man, and I forget many things. This is Tibu's gallery, but where are the four bricks where they used to put their huqa fire on when the Sahibs never saw? Slowly, slowly, O you people behind.'

They heard his hands disturbing the small coal on the floor of the gallery and then a dull sound. 'This is one unbaked brick, and this is another and another. Kundoo is a young man—let him come forward. Put a knee upon this brick and strike here. When Tibu's gang were at dinner on the last day before the good coal ended, they heard the men of Five on the other side, and Five worked their gallery two Sundays later—or it may have been one. Strike there, Kundoo, but give me room to go back.'

Kundoo, doubting, drove the pick, but the first soft crush of the coal was a call to him. He was fighting for his life and for Unda—pretty little Unda with rings on all her toes—for Unda and the forty rupees. The women sang the Song of the Pick—the terrible, slow, swinging melody with the muttered chorus that repeats the sliding of the loosened coal, and, to each cadence, Kundoo smote in the black dark. When he could do no more, Sunua Manji took the pick, and struck for his life and his wife, and his village beyond the blue hills over the

Tarachunda River. An hour the men worked, and then the women cleared away the coal.

'It is farther than I thought,' said Janki. 'The air is very bad; but strike, Kundoo, strike hard,'

For the fifth time Kundoo took up the pick as the Sonthal crawled back. The song had scarcely recommenced when it was broken by a yell from Kundoo that echoed down the gallery: 'Par hua! Par hua! We are through, we are through!' The imprisoned air in the mine shot through the opening, and the women at the far end of the gallery heard the water rush through the pillars of 'Bullia's Room' and roar against the ledge. Having fulfilled the law under which it worked, it rose no farther. The women screamed and pressed forward, 'The water has come—we shall be killed! Let us go.'

Kundoo crawled through the gap and found himself in a propped gallery by the simple process of hitting his head against a beam.

'Do I know the pits or do I not?' chuckled Janki. 'This is the Number Five; go you out slowly, giving me your names. Ho! Rahim, count your gang! Now let us go forward, each catching hold of the other as before.'

They formed a line in the darkness and Janki led them—for a pit-man in a strange pit is only one degree less liable to err than an ordinary mortal underground for the first time. At last they saw a flare-lamp, and Gangs Janki, Mogul, and Rahim of Twenty-Two stumbled dazed into the glare of the draught-furnace at the bottom of Five; Janki feeling his way and the rest behind.

'Water has come into Twenty-Two. God knows where are the others. I have brought these men from Tibu's gallery in our cutting; making connection through the north side of the gallery. Take us to the cage,' said Janki Meah.

~

At the pit-bank of Twenty-Two, some thousand people clamoured and wept and shouted. One hundred men—one thousand men—had been drowned in the cutting. They would all go to their homes to-morrow. Where were their men? Little Unda, her cloth drenched with the rain, stood at the pit-mouth calling down the shaft for Kundoo. They had swung the cages clear of the mouth, and her only answer was the murmur of the flood in the pit's eye two hundred and sixty feet below.

'Look after that woman! She'll chuck herself down the shaft in a minute,' shouted the Manager.

But he need not have troubled; Unda was afraid of Death. She wanted Kundoo. The Assistant was watching the flood and seeing how far he could wade into it. There was a lull in the water, and the whirlpool had slackened. The mine was full, and the people at the pit-bank howled.

'My faith, we shall be lucky if we have five hundred hands on the place to-morrow!' said the Manager. 'There's some chance yet of running a temporary dam across that water. Shove in anything—tubs and bullock-carts if you haven't enough bricks. Make them work now if they never worked before. Hi! you gangers, make them work.'

Little by little the crowd was broken into detachments, and pushed toward the water with promises of overtime. The dam-making began, and when it was fairly under way, the Manager thought that the hour had come for the pumps. There was no fresh inrush into the mine. The tall, red, iron-clamped pump-beam rose and fell, and the pumps snored and guttered and shrieked as the first water poured out of the pipe.

'We must run her all to-night,' said the Manager, wearily, 'but there's no hope for the poor devils down below. Look here, Gur Sahai, if you are proud of your engines, show me what they can do now.'

Gur Sahai grinned and nodded, with his right hand upon the lever and an oil-can in his left. He could do no more than he was doing, but he could keep that up till the dawn. Were the Company's pumps to be beaten by the vagaries of that troublesome Tarachunda River? Never, never! And the pumps sobbed and panted: 'Never, never!' The Manager sat in the shelter of the pit-bank roofing, trying to dry himself by the pump-boiler fire, and, in the dreary dusk, he saw the crowds on the dam scatter and fly.

'That's the end,' he groaned. ''Twill take us six weeks to persuade 'em that we haven't tried to drown their mates on purpose. Oh, for a decent, rational Geordie!'

But the flight had no panic in it. Men had run over from Five with astounding news, and the foremen could not hold their gangs together. Presently, surrounded by a clamourous crew, Gangs Rahim, Mogul, and Janki, and ten basket-women, walked up to report themselves, and pretty little Unda stole away to Janki's hut to prepare his evening meal.

'Alone I found the way,' explained Janki Meah, 'and now will the Company give me pension?'

The simple pit-folk shouted and leaped and went back to the dam, reassured in their old belief that, whatever happened, so great was the power of the Company whose salt they ate, none of them could be killed. But Gur Sahai only bared his white teeth and kept his hand upon the lever and proved his pumps to the uttermost.

~

'I say,' said the Assistant to the Manager, a week later, 'do you recollect *Germinal*?'

'Yes. 'Queer thing, I thought of it in the cage when that balk went by. Why?'

'Oh, this business seems to be *Germinal* upside down. Janki was in my veranda all this morning, telling me that Kundoo had eloped with his wife—Unda or Anda, I think her name was.'

'Hillo! And those were the cattle that you risked your life to clear out of Twenty-Two!'

'No—I was thinking of the Company's props, not the Company's men.'

'Sounds better to say so now; but I don't believe you, old fellow.'